Praise for

Tales from The Edge Volume One

The blurb was exciting, the cover enticing, and I'm sure this is the kind of story many will like...I recommend this one to people looking for an easy going, sweet BDSM story about injured people getting a second chance at life and love. ~ *Sid Love*

This was a really good story that I enjoyed, a lot. The writing was fast paced and clean, the characters were a good mix of strong and dominant, and submissive and cheeky, with the storyline being a little predictable but in a good way. I look forward to reading more from this author.
~ *Rainbow Book Reviews*

I loved the relationship between Olly and Joe, though. There was definitely some rough play between the two, but the genuine affection they had for each other balanced it out. These are my favorite type of BDSM books, where the Dom is a sexy muscled man in leather, and the sub is an angel-faced waif. It may not be original, but it works.
~ *Mrs Condit Reads Reviews*

They are fun, entertaining, and steamy diversions for an afternoon, though, so don't hesitate to pick one of them up when you're in the mood for some power play and sexy older men. ~ *Joyfully Jay*

Living on the Edge is Yummy! This quick read is loaded with great characters, sizzling M/M sex, and engaging twists... The gay erotic encounters are hot and explicit. The BDSM aspect is wickedly naughty...most certainly worth the read.

~ *The Jeep Diva*

Totally Bound Publishing books by L.M. Somerton:

The Portrait
Black Dog
Stroke Rate
Mountain Rescue

TALES FROM THE EDGE
EDGE
Volume One

Reaching the Edge

Living on the Edge

L.M. SOMERTON

Tales from The Edge Volume One
ISBN # 978-1-78184-654-4
©Copyright L.M. Somerton 2013
Cover Art by Posh Gosh ©Copyright 2013
Interior text design by Claire Siemaszkiewicz
Totally Bound Publishing

Published in 2013 by Totally Bound Publishing, Newland House, The Point, Weaver Road, Lincoln, LN6 3QN, United Kingdom.

REACHING THE EDGE

Dedication

To facing fears.

Chapter One

"Alyson, I realise that I'm a clinical psychologist, but my specialism, as you well know, is criminal psychology. What on earth makes you think I can help this boy?"

"He's not a boy, Joe, he's a young man. He's been through the kind of trauma that would turn most of us into gibbering wrecks, and survived, against all the odds. But I can't get him to trust anyone enough that they can help him. He's so closed down that he's barely functioning."

"What exactly does that mean?"

"He looks after himself on a basic level. He eats. He keeps clean. He does housework. But he hasn't been able to return to work and he has horrific nightmares. I don't think he's slept properly in months."

"What aren't you telling me? There has to be something..."

"Just read his file. I'll buy you dinner." The slightly wheedling tone grated on Joe's nerves and he found himself agreeing just to get the annoying woman off the phone.

"Fine. Send it over and I'll take a look, but that's it, Alyson. I'm not promising anything."

He could feel her triumph reverberating through the handset as he replaced the phone in its cradle. He'd known Alyson Bell for several years. She was well respected and, despite the fact that he didn't like her all that much, he knew she was good at her job. She had referred patients to him in the past when the skills of her colleagues at the private clinic where she worked had been exhausted. He had no illusions about being the call of last resort. It was that very thing that intrigued him—the challenge of trying to help people whom everyone else had given up on.

It was Friday evening and he was looking forward to the first free weekend he'd had in nearly two months. He picked up the phone again and dialled his business partner and best friend.

"Heath. How's it going?"

He smiled as he listened to Heath relay information about the week's courses at The Edge, the corporate training company they ran together. He divided his time between his growing private practice and what was turning into a very successful business venture.

"I'll be up next week as planned. Enjoy the weekend off." Joe tried not to sound too jealous.

Heath chuckled knowingly. "You don't sound very sincere, my friend. What will you be getting up to?"

Joe was still trying to decide what to do with his own free time. "Not sure. Think I might put in an appearance at The Underground tonight."

He fiddled with a pen on the desk, then dropped it as Heath made a couple of very detailed suggestions as to what a night at The Underground might offer.

"It's been so long since I played, I think I may have forgotten how to use one of those!"

A snort of disbelief sounded down the line, followed by a few caustic comments.

"I'm just going for a quiet drink and maybe a little innocent voyeurism. It won't do the business any harm if I put in an appearance, anyway."

He held the phone away from his ear slightly and waited for the laughter to subside.

"Fine. Have your fun. I know that 'just watching' has never been my thing, but I'm fed up of all those doe-eyed submissives who just want to play for a night, then go back to their safe little worlds. I'm pushing thirty, Heath. I want something more and he has to be out there somewhere."

He tilted his chair back and smiled at the kinder words that followed.

"All right, all right! Twenty-eight isn't thirty! Yes, I will have a good time. Yes, I will be careful and no, I will not be fucking telling you about it in the morning. Goodnight, Heath."

He began to tidy his office and prepare to leave, letting his mind wander back to the first time he and Heath had met. The Underground was an exclusive — and expensive — private club catering to London's gay BDSM scene. Joe had been lounging against the main bar, craving a nice, soft merlot, whilst nursing a glass of something involving mango and apple that the barman had convinced him to try. He entirely understood the club's 'no alcohol' policy but sometimes it was a pain in the taste buds.

Heath had drawn every eye in the place as he had strolled across the room, black leather clinging to long legs and a gorgeous arse, his body draped in a filmy silver-grey shirt. There'd been a few disappointed sighs as it had become obvious that this was not a new, tender submissive but a confident, young

Dominant who would provide dangerous competition for all of them.

He'd ordered water with a twist of lime, glanced at Joe's fruity concoction with a smirk and introduced himself. "Heath Anders. I need someone to teach me and I'm told you're the best."

It had gone from there, and Joe had enjoyed every moment of showing his willing student what it meant to be submissive, and how to be the best possible Dominant. Friendship had led to partnership and the development of The Edge into something more than just a corporate training company. The Underground had provided them with a number of excellent clients and he was proud of the fact that they were making an active contribution to making their world safer and more respectful of others' needs.

Joe pulled on his dark cashmere overcoat, turned off the lights and strolled into the cold London night. It wasn't far to the small, secluded mews where he lived when he wasn't working at The Edge. The house was worth a fortune, left to him by his doting grandmother upon her death seven years earlier. It was one of those pretty London streets that would never be seen by visitors to the city, tucked away from any major thoroughfare. The hum of London traffic was deadened almost to silence. The small row contained only five houses, each with a large walled garden to the rear, and Joe's was the farthest down the cul-de-sac. He turned the key in the shiny brass lock and entered his own personal oasis.

He knew if he didn't get himself ready and leave again straight away, he would settle into an armchair with a book and a glass of wine, and end up staying there all night. He was nothing if not self-disciplined. He showered, shaved and ran his fingers through his short blond hair. Dressing was a little harder. He couldn't pull off leather in the way that Heath could, but he needed something that wasn't too boring or conservative. He opted for narrow black trousers and a dark green silk shirt. The studded leather band around his wrist and the buckled boots were concessions to looking the part. He threw his coat on again, locked the door and headed back out into the night.

The Underground was housed in two underground levels below an innocuous-looking building on a Westminster backstreet. A surprising number of its members had connections to the government, which made its location convenient. For Joe it was a gentle stroll of less than half a mile. Initial entry was gained via an electronic keypad, though Joe knew that the two dark-suited men leaning against the wall opposite were doing a deliberately poor job of looking inconspicuous because they were the club's security detail. He acknowledged their presence with a small smile and received big grins in return.

He tapped his six-digit code into the pad and pushed the door open. In front of him was a set of lift doors and a single button. There was nowhere else to go. The lift, mercifully free of piped music, descended smoothly and ejected him into another world. Deep burgundy carpeting cushioned his steps as he approached a mahogany desk staffed by a pretty redhead with a scattering of freckles across his neat little nose. The young man looked up and Joe noted that the green eyes widened. He gave a reassuring smile.

"Good evening, Christian. It's nice to see you."

"You too, Sir." Christian recovered his composure very quickly. "Is there anything I may assist you with this evening?"

Joe removed his coat and handed it over. "Perhaps you could let Carey know I'm here and ask him if he would like to join me for dinner?"

"Certainly, Sir. Would you like to wait in the lounge?"

Joe nodded, and a door to his left clicked open as Christian pressed a release button beneath his desk.

The lounge could easily have passed for an ordinary gentlemen's club. Subtle lighting warmed scattered groups of leather armchairs. Small side tables held chilled bottles of water and glasses loaded with ice. There were several men already seated—a few pairs and small groups, and one or two individuals sat alone. Joe picked an empty pair of chairs in an alcove and sat down in one of them. Openly curious glances were sent his way and he acknowledged those people he knew with nods.

Within seconds he felt a quiet presence at his elbow. He turned and looked appreciatively at the waiter standing quietly next to him. The boy was slim, blond and had his eyes cast appropriately down. He was dressed in nothing but a black leather kilt that skimmed his arse, and Joe knew that underneath he would be wearing a skimpy net thong. It was the required dress of all the subs that served on the staff at The Underground. The boys were uniformly pretty, very well paid and not required to do anything they didn't want to. Joe knew from personal experience that most of them wanted to do whatever he ordered them to do.

The blond knelt gracefully at his feet, poured him a glass of sparkling water and handed it to him with a shy smile.

"Thank you, Alistair."

"My pleasure, Sir. Is there anything else I can do for you this evening?"

Joe ruffled his hair. "Not tonight. I'm meeting Mr Hoffman."

"If you change your mind later, Sir, I'd be very happy to be at your service."

Joe detected a certain amount of mischief in the smile that accompanied that statement. He'd played with Alistair several times and, despite his waiflike appearance, the boy adored a good paddling.

"I'll certainly keep that in mind, Alistair." He turned as someone squeezed his shoulder firmly. "Carey! It's been a while. Sorry about showing up unannounced." He stood and shook his friend's hand. "You're looking well."

Carey Hoffman grinned with a perfect set of even white teeth. The smile reached twinkling, warm brown eyes and dimpled his tanned cheeks. Short, dark hair lightly streaked with silver swept across an unwrinkled forehead, and his strong chin was dusted with stubble.

"Joe, my friend. You know I'm always delighted to see you. Dinner's on me." He took the other seat and gave Alistair a stern look. "Menus, boy. You'll attend our table tonight."

Joe noted the flush of pleasure on Alistair's pale cheeks as he scurried away, and gave his old friend a knowing look. "When are you going to give that boy what he wants? He adores you."

"He's a brat and he needs to learn some patience."

"He knew you were watching when he came on to me, didn't he? He wanted to make you jealous."

Carey winked. "Why do you think he was sent over here in the first place?"

Joe chuckled. "I've missed you, Carey."

Joe thoroughly enjoyed the next couple of hours, catching up with his friend over an excellent meal. Alistair served the food and kept their drinks refreshed, and was rewarded by an occasional pat to his leather-covered arse. Finally they settled back in the lounge over coffee. Joe breathed in the rich aroma and sighed happily. Carey looked at him quizzically. "So... Are you just here for the pleasure of my company, or are you interested in playing tonight?"

"That depends on who's in. It seems quite busy and I wouldn't want to deprive any of your more regular customers."

Carey's cup clinked against its saucer. "I know you, Joe. You're bored. You need someone new. Someone different."

Joe shrugged. "Do you have someone in mind, then? You know my taste."

"Perhaps." Carey pursed his lips and frowned. "There's a new boy who showed up a few weeks ago looking for a job that gave him free membership. I've been keeping him away from the members so far—he seems a bit too vulnerable. There's something he's not telling me. He's had some training, that much I can tell, so he's not a complete innocent."

"It's not like you to hold back, Carey." Joe's curiosity was definitely piqued.

"I know. It was Alistair, actually, who said the boy was sad about something he'd lost. I must be getting soft in my old age! Anyway, he's been earning his keep in the kitchens, but now you're here..." Carey gestured to Alistair, who was hovering close by. "Fetch the new boy. Get him prepared and dressed first. Mr Dexter is going to take a look at him."

Alistair beamed at Joe then at Carey before hurrying away. Forty-five minutes and another pot of coffee later, he was back. Another blond stood at his side, dressed identically, his gaze firmly fixed to the floor. Carey stood and shook Joe's hand. "Just come and find me if it doesn't work out, Joe."

Joe nodded, totally distracted by the young man now kneeling in front of him. A pair of the biggest, bluest eyes he'd ever seen looked up shyly from beneath tumbling curls. Joe's lips curved into a slow, hungry smile. He hardly heard Carey's departing comment to Alistair. "I think our work here is done."

Chapter Two

Joe realised that everyone still in the lounge was either openly watching him, or watching but pretending not to. He took a deep breath and tried to find some focus.

"Come with me."

He didn't look to see if he was being followed, just strode confidently towards the stairs to the sub-basement level. Everything was deeply carpeted, muting the sound of movement. It was eerily quiet. At the bottom of the stairs another keypad gave him access to a long corridor with a series of numbered doors on either side. Each door had a small light above it. Some were red, but the majority were green.

Joe had used several of the rooms in the past. Each had a theme and there was enough variety to suit all tastes. He was hoping that one particular room would have a green light above the door. He took measured strides, not hurrying, not dawdling. He could sense the quiet presence behind him, but didn't look back.

Joe smiled inwardly when he saw the room he wanted was vacant. He punched in his code and opened the door, noting with satisfaction that nothing had changed. Everything about the room was soft, warm and unthreatening. There were two big, soft sofas piled with cushions in a range of tactile fabrics. Thick rugs covered the carpeted floor, and the walls were adorned with tapestries in muted colours. Everything was gold and cream and earthy shades of brown. The focal point was a large wood-burner that was already ablaze. There was an oak cupboard in one corner of the room and a low table with a kettle and the makings of various hot drinks.

He gestured to the rug in front of the fire.

"Stand there."

The young man stood where he'd been told to and curled his toes into the soft rug. He looked confused and more than a bit bewildered. His enormous blue eyes followed Joe's every movement.

"What's your name?" Joe kept his voice low and gentle. The boy was doing a good job of hiding his fear, but not good enough that Joe hadn't caught on to the fact that he was absolutely terrified.

"People call me Angel."

"Well, Angel, that will do for now." Joe smiled at him in what he hoped was a reassuring way. "Put your hands behind your back, please." He waited for Angel to obey the order, then took his time walking in a circle around him. Angel was slim, his body smooth and firm. The short leather kilt he wore sat low on his hips and emphasised the gentle curve of his arse. Joe judged that he must be around five feet ten. Apart from his spectacular eyes, his hair was his most remarkable feature—a tangle of unruly, loose golden curls that cascaded onto his neck and around his face. No wonder his nickname was Angel.

Joe knew that he must look intimidating and tried to move slowly. He reached out and tackled the buckle that held Angel's kilt closed. Angel didn't move, but there was obvious tension in his stance.

"It's all right, I'm not going to hurt you."

With the buckle undone, Joe allowed the scanty strip of leather to slip to the floor. The tiny net thong that held Angel's dick was doing a very poor job of containing his burgeoning erection. Joe allowed himself one more circuit, drinking in the sight of a perfect arse, before he headed across to the cupboard and pulled out a big, fluffy robe.

He wanted to test Angel's willingness to be naked in front of him, so he ordered him to remove the thong. There was no hesitation, but as Angel clasped his hands behind his back again Joe could detect the trembling he was trying to control. Angel's cock bounced just a little, then settled into position, jutting firmly from his body. His chest was completely smooth and hairless, his cock and balls in perfect proportion to his body, nesting in delicate golden curls.

"Beautiful." Joe handed over the robe with some regret. "Put this on, Angel, and take a seat."

Angel looked at the robe in his hands as if it were a totally unfamiliar object. "I don't understand, Sir."

"It was a simple instruction. Do as you're told."

The firmness in Joe's voice did the trick. Angel looked almost relieved at the tone of command. He slipped the robe on and wrapped it around himself, then took a seat on the sofa as far away from Joe as he could get, tucking his bare feet beneath him in an attempt to make himself as small as possible.

"Relax, Angel. You haven't done anything wrong."

Big blue eyes glistened with tears. "Do I displease you, Sir?" His voice shook.

Joe gave a small smile. "Quite the opposite, I can assure you."

"Then why…?"

"Why have I brought you here, and not to a playroom full of whips and chains? Why don't I have you naked on your knees? Or why am I not fucking you senseless?"

"All three, Sir?" Angel sounded as though he didn't believe his own courage in asking that question.

"What have you heard about me, Angel?" Joe waited patiently for a reply.

"That you are the strictest Dom at The Underground. That you don't tolerate disobedience. That your punishments are harsh but fair."

"I can't dispute any of those things. What else?"

"Alistair told me that you are patient and kind. One of the best Doms he's ever met."

"And what do you think makes a good Dominant, Angel?" Joe took a seat on the other sofa, leant back into the cushions and stretched out his legs.

Angel ran a hand through his tangled mop. "Someone who respects his partner, gives clear orders, makes his expectations known. Someone who doesn't…who doesn't…" His voice caught and he seemed to choke back a sob.

"Doesn't what?"

"Someone who doesn't give up on you when you fail."

He sounded inestimably sad, and Joe felt his heart break just a little bit.

"So is that why you're here, Angel? Because your last Master gave up on you?"

Joe received a silent nod in response. He got up and walked over to the kettle. While Angel sat and hugged his knees, Joe made two mugs of hot chocolate and took them back to the sofa. He handed one over and took his own back to his seat. He sipped his drink and tried to forget that Angel was naked beneath the robe. He preferred his submissives bare and ready for his pleasure, but for a while he was happy to let Angel hide himself away.

"Do you want me to leave?" Angel's question was hesitant, his voice full of resignation.

Joe put down his mug. "Come here."

Angel unfolded himself and edged across the rug. He stopped between Joe's knees and looked down, chewing his lower lip anxiously.

"Turn around."

Joe pulled Angel down onto his lap and wrapped his arms around him. A small squeak came from his prisoner, but the stiff body he embraced gradually relaxed.

"I have two requirements, neither of which involves you going anywhere." Joe swivelled Angel's legs around so that he was stretched out along the sofa, then pulled the boy's head back against his chest. "Honesty and obedience. I expect you to be honest with me at all times. That means telling me when you want me to stop, telling me what you like and what you don't like. Not liking something may not stop me from doing it, however. I demand obedience. Disobey me deliberately and I will punish you." He placed subtle emphasis on the word 'will'.

Angel was quiet but calm. He seemed to be thinking.

"I haven't told you my real name, Sir."

"That's your choice, not dishonesty."

Angel's body tensed slightly.

"Did you keep something from your last Master, Angel?" Joe kept his voice soothing—there was no hint of accusation in his tone.

"Had to. He didn't understand."

Joe didn't push the point. Angel would tell him what he wanted to, in his own time. For now, all he wanted to do was build the boy's trust and investigate a few responses.

"Finish your drink. I'm going to use the bathroom. The door will be unlocked."

He lifted Angel off his lap and onto the sofa easily. Outside the door, he waited for a couple of minutes to see if the boy would bolt. When nothing happened he walked a short distance to the bathroom, washed his face and stared hard into the mirror. What did Angel see when he looked at him? Joe knew that he was considered handsome. He wasn't vain—it was just a fact of life. He didn't obsess over the way he looked, but he was a little concerned that he might seem cold and intimidating to someone as young as Angel. He did have a habit of schooling his features into an emotionless blank. It helped in his job to appear completely calm and neutral and it had rubbed off in his private life. Experienced subs seemed to like the hardness but Joe was concerned that Angel was far more sensitive and vulnerable than the boys he usually played with.

He rubbed a hand through his short blond hair and softened his expression from icy to mildly frosty. There was a definite twinkle of amusement in his blue eyes—eyes that looked faded compared to Angel's startling bright blue ones. He shook his head wryly— Angel was everything he looked for in a partner, and he was already feeling intensely possessive and protective.

He finished up and headed back to the room, half wondering if Angel would be gone. He hid his relief well when he opened the door to find him placing their empty mugs on the side table. He took his seat on the sofa and waited to see whether Angel would join him again. To his delight, a slender body was soon squirming in his lap, getting comfortable. Soft golden curls tickled his neck as Angel nuzzled closer, and Joe felt his dick harden in response. Joe wrapped an arm around Angel's waist and held him tightly. He positioned his other arm higher up, which allowed him to slip his hand inside the folds of the fluffy robe that concealed Angel's body. For a moment he just rested his open palm against a warm, smooth chest, enjoying the slow rise and fall.

Gradually he moved his hand until he found the small rise of a nipple. He waited again, giving Angel the chance to protest or pull away. Feeling more secure in his exploration, he rubbed slowly, delighted at the instant response. The little nub peaked and hardened instantly under the pads of his fingertips. He moved again and found its twin, already hard for him. He rolled it carefully between his thumb and forefinger before flicking it hard. That got him a whimper and more nuzzling. Joe took that as a signal that more would be welcome and began to twist and pinch, getting a little rougher each time he moved from one hot bud to the other. He was still holding Angel firmly in place and the boy made no attempt to get free as Joe slid his hand down to stroke his flat belly in slow circles, gradually working his way lower.

Angel wriggled just a little, and his robe parted to reveal pale, smooth skin covered by Joe's large hand. He shifted round on the sofa and parted his legs wider in blatant invitation. Joe smiled. Perhaps the boy wasn't as shy as he'd thought. He nudged the fleecy cloth aside, exposing him completely. Angel pressed against him. His smooth cock bobbed temptingly, a wet gleam coming from the tip, but Joe resisted the urge to touch. He looked at the contrast between his own tanned hand, the fingers splayed across Angel's stomach, and Angel's creamy, perfect skin.

A whimper brought him out of his thoughts.

"Do you want me to touch you, Angel?"

Angel trembled and reached for his cock, only to have his hand slapped away.

"No. Your release is for me to control." Joe kissed his neck teasingly. "I asked you a question."

"Yes, Sir! Yes! Please…"

Angel gasped as Joe edged his hand a little lower but then stopped. Even to Joe, his chuckle sounded a little evil. "No. Submissive angels need to learn serenity and patience. Let's see just how angelic you can be."

He pushed the robe away from Angel's shoulders and began to stroke his skin. Arms, chest, thighs… He moved his hand in gentle circles until it settled in the crease of Angel's thigh. The boy was quivering with need, dripping and slick. The only sound was of his rapid, uneven breathing.

Joe gave a feral smile that Angel couldn't see and tightened his arm around Angel's waist. He touched his lips to his velvet earlobe and whispered, "Beg, pretty Angel. I want to hear you beg."

Chapter Three

Angel arched his back, thrusting his cock forward. If he could just get his thoughts in order he might have time to be embarrassed, but all he could process were the words being whispered in his ear. Joe's strong arm was pinning him in place but he didn't feel trapped— he just felt safe. Joe was stroking his thigh, using his thumb to graze the crease at his groin. It was the most exquisite torture. He had never been more desperate to come.

"Please! Please…"

Joe cupped his aching balls. The sounds coming from Angel's throat were unfamiliar and uncontrolled. He was going to come regardless of whether Joe touched his dick or not. Then Joe squeezed his sac lightly.

"Aagh! Fuck!" He spurted semen in an impressive arc, bucking his hips and riding the spasms for what seemed like a lifetime. Red spots danced before his eyes and his ears buzzed. Utterly spent, he collapsed back against Joe's hard body, sticky white drops decorating his abdomen.

When Joe slid from under him, he felt bereft and panic blossomed. He'd come without permission. He'd come before his Master. He'd behaved like a wanton slut and now Joe would leave him in disgust. He sat up and started to pull the fluffy robe back onto his shoulders, determined to cover the evidence of his failure.

"What do you think you are doing?" Joe loomed menacingly over him. "I didn't say you could cover up."

Angel froze, his hands shaking. He couldn't meet Joe's eyes. Then there was soft, wet warmth on his stomach. Joe was cleaning him up with a washcloth, looking after him. He couldn't stop the fat tear that rolled from his eye and splashed onto his chest.

"Hey, now. No crying." Joe wiped Angel's face. "You can dress if you want to."

"That's not why... I mean, do you want me to, Sir?"

"No. I want you naked in my arms, but I'm not going to force you to do anything you don't want to."

Angel smiled and threw himself into Joe's arms. It felt so good to be held. Joe was so strong, but very gentle. Even though he'd only known this amazing man for a short time, Angel felt safer than he ever had before. Joe was completely in control, so self-assured, but he wasn't arrogant or demanding. His orders were precise and there was no anger or frustration in his voice. Angel wanted nothing more than to do exactly as Joe commanded.

They ended up back on the sofa—Joe stretched out with Angel lying almost on top of him. Angel snuggled beneath his chin and dared to press a small kiss to Joe's neck. Joe's hold on him tightened, before he caressed and cupped the curve of Angel's arse. The sensation of Joe's large hand on his skin sent a glow through Angel's body, and he could feel his dick spark back into life.

He wondered what it would feel like if that hand were spanking him instead of stroking. That thought made him squirm and hardened his dick a little more. It crossed his mind that Joe was still fully dressed while he was completely naked. Joe had also had no release while Angel had enjoyed one of the most spectacular orgasms ever. But he knew that Joe would tell him if he wanted his mouth or his arse — he didn't need to worry. Decisions were Joe's job.

"How old are you, Angel?"

Joe was stroking his arse with one hand and petting his hair with the other. It was distracting, but Angel managed to find his voice.

"Twenty-two, Sir."

"Do you have a job? Other than working here, of course."

Angel tried not to flinch. "I'm a nurse, Sir. I trained straight from school."

"So why did you look for work here at The Underground?"

Angel could feel his skin reddening. "I needed to find a new Master, Sir. The Underground has the best reputation, but I couldn't afford the membership."

"So you're looking for something long term, not just for play?"

Joe's hand stilled on his arse and Angel debated whether or not to lie. He didn't want to put Joe off by coming across as needy or demanding.

The truth slipped from his lips. "Yes, Sir."

Joe pushed his finger between Angel's arse cheeks. "That's good. If you want to be with me, Angel, I won't allow you to work here. Parading around in front of other men in that uniform is not acceptable."

Angel couldn't speak. Did that mean that Joe wanted him?

"I will support your membership, but you will not come here unaccompanied."

"No, Sir. I mean, yes, Sir." Angel groaned—he was sounding like an idiot. "That net thong chafes something evil anyway." He jerked as Joe's finger circled his hole.

"I thought you looked rather good in it. I was going to ask Carey for a few spares."

Angel groaned again and buried his head into Joe's chest, which was vibrating with laughter.

There was a firm pat to his arse. "But for now, Angel, it's time to leave. It's very late and, as much as I would love to bend you over this sofa and fuck you senseless, you need time to think about what you want to do next. In the clear light of day you may see things differently."

Angel sighed. He was disappointed but happy. Joe was everything that Alistair had said he would be, and no good Dominant would move too quickly into a long-term arrangement. Joe's thighs shifted under him, so Angel climbed off the sofa and knelt on the rug in front of the wood-burner, luxuriating in the feel of the warmth on his back. Joe stood in front of him and looked down. Fuck, the man was handsome, if a little scary.

"I'll have your clothes sent down. Do you have a ride home?"

He nodded. "Yes, Sir. I..."

"You can speak freely, Angel."

"When can I see you again, Sir?" The words blurted out even though Angel knew that it would be Joe's decision.

"Here. Tomorrow at nine. I'll meet you outside."

Angel beamed and his stiff cock jerked happily.

"Oh, and no touching yourself in the meantime." Joe turned towards the door. "I'll see you tomorrow, Angel."

The door clicked closed behind him, and Angel sat back on his heels and looked down at his erection with some consternation. "Wonderful. What the hell am I going to do with you now? Why can't you behave yourself?"

He giggled and grabbed the fluffy robe to pull around himself. He felt strange and a little giddy. Slowly, he realised that he was happy. It was strange to feel so light and carefree after so long. Perhaps he was finally getting over everything that had happened.

He curled into the corner of the sofa and let himself dream about Joe. He could almost feel strong arms around him and gentle hands on his body. A tiny knot of anxiety began to form in the pit of his stomach. What if Joe didn't like him? Alistair had assured him that he was Joe's type, but Joe was so perfect. Why would Joe ever want someone like him? Still, he had at least one more chance to make a good impression. His last Master had trained him well, if nothing else. Things had been good between them for a while, though Angel wasn't naïve enough to think that the man had ever loved him.

There was a knock at the door, and Alistair came in with a big grin on his face and a pile of clothes in his arms.

"Hey, you! How did it go? Did you like Mr Dexter?"

His bubbly enthusiasm was infectious. Angel gave him a shy smile. "He's amazing."

"I can't believe he brought you to this room! I thought he'd have you strapped to a cross or chained to the ceiling. Did he fuck you?"

Angel blushed furiously. "Alistair!"

"Come on, Angel, spill it! I set you two up – I'm entitled to the juicy details."

"No. He didn't. Happy now?"

"He spoke to Carey before he left. You definitely made an impression. He's banned you from wearing the staff uniform." He twirled around, letting the short leather kilt he was wearing swing upwards to reveal his arse.

"What else did he say?" Angel pulled on his jeans and a T-shirt.

"Don't know. Couldn't hear – they sent me down here. I'll ask Carey later."

"I need to go home and get some sleep. Will you be here tomorrow night?"

"Of course. It may look like I play around, but Carey keeps me on a pretty short leash."

"You love him?"

Alistair nodded. "I do. Never thought it would happen."

"Maybe one day I'll have that too." Angel gave Alistair a hug. "Thanks for suggesting that Joe might like me. I'll try not to let you down."

"Just be you. How could he fail to fall for you?"

That made Angel think. Perhaps he could be himself with Joe. He nodded to himself. *Yes.* Tomorrow he would give Joe his real name.

Chapter Four

Joe woke late on Saturday morning and luxuriated in the knowledge that, for once, he didn't have to get up. He plumped one of his goose-feather pillows and closed his eyes. A smile tweaked his lips as he thought about the previous evening and how deliciously responsive Angel had been. That boy had been born to be submissive, though Joe suspected that once Angel was more relaxed and trust between them more deeply established, he was going to be quite a handful. Those beautiful blue eyes had held more than a hint of mischief, and Joe couldn't wait to free the imp behind the angel.

He had already formed a picture in his mind as to how he would handle Angel that night, and which of The Underground's themed rooms would suit his purpose. Later he would call Carey and make the arrangements. For now, his only plans were to spend far too long soaking in the tub, followed by a shopping trip to find a suitable outfit for the evening. It had been an age since he had treated himself to new clothes, and he wanted to wear something that Angel would respond to.

He swung his legs out of bed and pulled an old sweater on—it was a bit chilly to wander around in nothing more than the boxers he'd slept in. He padded down to the kitchen and made himself a mug of tea before retreating back under his duvet with the newspaper. Just as he was settling down with the books section, the phone rang. He balanced the receiver beneath his chin and grunted a greeting.

"Heath. You'd better have a bloody good reason for disturbing my morning before I've even swallowed a mouthful of tea."

"I hear you made a new friend."

Joe could clearly detect the smirk in Heath's voice.

"I can't believe Carey rang you. I'm going to kill him."

"Carey says the two of you are made for each other." His friend sounded curious now.

Joe shifted the phone into a more comfortable position. "One night, Heath, that's all it was. It's a little too soon to be planning a wedding, don't you think?"

He took a sip of tea and winced. *Too hot.*

"So what happened? How did he take to a spanking? You did spank him, didn't you?" Heath was laying it on thick.

"The only person in need of a spanking is you, and I'd be happy to oblige. A few pretty stripes across that Dominant arse of yours might remind you to show your mentor some respect."

He chuckled as a few choice expletives came back at him.

"You should spend less time gossiping with Carey. Did he mention Alistair? The two of them are exclusive now — it's about time he collared that boy."

"Stop trying to deflect me, Joe." Heath was sulking.

Joe grinned. "I am not trying to change the subject. Go and run some laps. You've got far too much energy this morning."

After a few more exchanges of light-hearted banter, he replaced the receiver and got back to his tea.

* * * *

It had been a good day, though it had seemed to pass very slowly. Joe itched to get back to the club and make sure that his memories of Angel were not too rose-tinted. The boy couldn't possibly have been *that* pretty, could he?

Carey had been very accommodating. He'd reserved a table for dinner and booked the playroom Joe wanted for later. He'd even managed to resist asking too many questions, and Joe suspected that Heath might have called Carey back and warned him to back off. Joe was an intensely private person and he didn't like talking about himself. Heath was the only exception to that rule, but they had a unique relationship based on absolute trust.

Joe was just about to start getting ready when the doorbell rang. A motorcycle courier was just yanking off his helmet as Joe opened the door, revealing a wild mop of carrot-coloured hair.

"Sign here, please." The boy's cheeky grin was infectious.

Joe scribbled his signature and took the slim packet curiously. It wasn't until he saw the hospital stamp that he realised it must contain the patient's records that Alyson Bell had promised to send him. Work could wait. He locked the unopened envelope into his desk and went back to dressing.

Instead of a formal jacket he'd chosen a black, brushed-velvet waistcoat that accentuated his shape, with military-style buttons done up over a sheer, black silk shirt. He folded the wide cuffs back so that it looked a little less reserved and tied a slim leather plait around his wrist. His Dolce and Gabbana jeans were dark grey rather than black, and sat comfortably on his hips. If he lifted his arms, a narrow strip of toned midriff came into view. He stuck to a pair of comfortable, buckled ankle boots and his usual overcoat.

He'd shaved carefully to leave a fine layer of stubble, and had rubbed a small dollop of gel into his blond hair, making it look artfully untidy. That would have to do. With any luck Angel would have better things to think about than what his new Master looked like.

Joe paused and gave himself a mental slap. He was already thinking of himself as the boy's Master, and that was far too presumptuous at this stage. That would be Angel's choice, not his. He sighed. If only people realised that all the power in his world belonged with the submissives.

He made one final check that the house was in order before he left. If there was even a slim chance that he might be bringing Angel home with him, he wanted his place to feel safe and comfortable. There was no more reason to wait, so he locked up and headed down the quiet street towards the bustle of the main road.

The walk felt good. Stretching his legs and letting the sharp wind blow away mental cobwebs was refreshing. When he rounded the corner into the narrow street that housed the entrance to The Underground, he felt rejuvenated and eager. Angel was already there, leaning back against a wall, one knee bent. The nonchalant pose didn't fool Joe, who immediately spotted nervous fingers drumming against the bricks and teeth worrying at a sweetly swollen lower lip.

At his approach, Angel looked up from beneath his blond curls and immediately blushed. He stood up, away from the wall, and clasped his hands behind his back. Joe looked him up and down, taking in the neat striped shirt over navy blue chinos and polished shoes. He caught himself wondering what kind of underwear the boy was wearing, if any. He shook his head. He was already losing focus, drawn into lust by tousled curls and blue eyes.

"Good evening, Angel. I appreciate your punctuality."

"Hello, Sir."

"You can call me Joe. We're not in a scene yet."

"Yes, Sir."

Was that a hint of devilment in his tone? Joe suspected it was. He didn't push the point. If Angel felt more comfortable using a formal address, then so be it.

They went through the formalities of gaining entry to the club and made their way through to the dining room. It was very busy, and the noise level was quite high. Alistair appeared next to them and silently led the way to a table tucked into a private alcove. Joe ignored the stares that followed their passage and took his seat at the table. Alistair handed him a menu.

"Will your boy be joining you, Mr Dexter, or should I fetch a cushion?"

Joe looked at the flush on Angel's pretty cheekbones. He wasn't sure whether the boy would relish the opportunity to kneel at his feet, or whether he would find the idea humiliating.

"Angel will join me at the table, Alistair. Thank you."

Angel gave a small sigh of relief as he took a seat at the table. Joe gave him a hard look.

"I'm not your Master, Angel, and even if I was, I would not humiliate you. We will agree firm boundaries between us. You must tell me if there is anything you won't do."

"It's Oliver Glenn, Sir. My name. Olly's fine as well. Sorry. I just wanted there to be no secrets between us from the start. Of course I would kneel for you if it gave you pleasure. It's just... All these people are watching and I didn't think you wanted other men looking at me." He took a deep breath and froze, as if his own courage had frightened him.

Joe glanced around. Olly was right. There were far too many people looking in their direction. He scowled. "If I wasn't so bloody hungry I'd skip dinner. Still, I imagine they'll get bored soon enough when all we do is eat and talk."

"I hope that's not all we're going to do."

Joe quirked an eyebrow at Olly's whispered comment and hardened his gaze.

"Sorry, Sir."

Olly was trying not to grin and wasn't making a very good job of it. Joe sighed and twirled his butter knife between his long fingers. Olly's inner brat was beginning to show.

The food they'd ordered was delicious and Joe was pleased to note that Olly had a good appetite. Alistair's service was attentive, and it only took a couple of icy glares to stop the looks being exchanged between him and his friend. Joe resolved to have a word with Carey as Alistair wiggled his arse as he took away their plates. That boy needed calming before he got out of control.

He and Olly talked about anything and everything. He learnt that Olly loved white water canoeing and could play the piano passably well. He had a younger brother who still lived at home, and loving parents who knew he was gay but were kept in ignorant bliss about his lifestyle. Olly talked enthusiastically about nursing, but didn't elaborate on why he wasn't currently working at the hospital.

Joe was curious to know more about his previous Master, but every time he tried to slide a subtle question into their conversation, Olly clammed up and his eyes darkened.

Joe talked about The Edge and the small island that the business was based on. Olly reacted excitedly to descriptions of the sheltered beaches and woods, and asked lots of questions about the people who lived and worked there. Joe found himself sharing more information about his life than he ever had before, but every new piece of information brought a shine to Olly's pretty eyes and that made every word worth the trouble.

It was a little after ten when they headed for the stairs. Joe paused as Carey beckoned him over.

"Go on downstairs, Oliver. Wait for me outside room six."

Olly disappeared with a nod and Joe walked over to where Carey was waiting, a serious expression on his face.

"I thought you should know, someone's been asking after Angel."

"His name's Oliver," Joe said a little distractedly. "Who?"

"Mark Vickery."

"That psychopath? What does he want with Oliver?"

"He hasn't told you then?" Carey folded his arms across his chest. "Vickery was his last Master."

"Fuck!" Joe didn't swear often, but the occasion warranted it. He knew Mark Vickery by reputation. He was a talented surgeon with an ego the size of a small planet. He played hard and expected perfection from the subs he played with. That explained a lot about Olly's reticence to talk about his past.

"What did you tell him, Carey?"

"Nothing, of course. But he won't give up. If he has it in his head that Angel—sorry, Oliver—still belongs to him, he will do everything in his power to get his property back."

"Hasn't he found himself a new toy to abuse?"

"Oh, he's been through a few boys, apparently. None of them want to stay with him and I'm not surprised. He's a bit too fond of the whip."

"Okay. Thanks, Carey. Don't mention this to Oliver."

"I won't. Try to enjoy your evening. I may be making a fuss about nothing."

Joe headed down to the lower corridor, every protective gene in his body in overdrive. Olly was sat cross-legged on the floor outside his chosen room, humming to himself, blond curls falling into his eyes. Joe couldn't help but smile as the sub spotted him and scrambled to his feet. Joe made no comment but opened the door and led Olly inside, keen to see his reaction. He wasn't disappointed. Olly's eyes widened in astonishment and his soft, pink lips parted in a gasp.

Joe clicked the door closed and looked around. All the walls and the ceiling were covered in mirrors. The floor was a glossy, black rubber that also reflected the light and was nicely cushioned for sensitive knees. There was a small, black leather couch positioned slightly away from one wall, and a polished metal rail that stretched across the room at waist height, disappearing seamlessly into the mirrored surfaces. He knew that there were concealed cupboards behind one wall that contained all kinds of toys, but he didn't want to reveal his intentions too soon.

He pointed to the floor and Oliver sank obediently to his knees.

"Do you trust me?" Joe went to stand behind him, knowing that he could be seen in the mirrors.

"Yes, Sir." There was no hesitation.

"I picked this room because there is nowhere to hide. Every reaction, every emotion will be laid bare. Are you ready for that?"

Olly nodded his blond head tentatively.

"Tonight is about me getting to know your body, and you understanding that it is mine, to do with as I please. If you don't want that, you're free to leave." Joe thought he detected a slight shiver of anticipation run through Olly's body. "If you stay, you are mine for the night." He met Olly's eyes in the mirror and watched the boy's features reflect need, desire and fear. Joe wondered which emotion would win the battle.

"Yours, Sir."

Joe walked slowly to the sofa, sat down, then made himself comfortable, stretching one arm along its back.

"Stand up."

Olly gracefully got to his feet and looked at him attentively.

"Strip."

Shoes and socks went first, followed by the stripy shirt. Olly unbuttoned it so slowly that the act of removing it became deeply erotic. Joe schooled his expression into a cool mask and ignored the swollen ache of his cock. It took Olly a full minute to unbutton his trousers and slide down the zip. Joe wanted to snap at him to go faster, but he managed to maintain his composure and said nothing. A small smile ghosted across Olly's lips as if he knew the effect he was having on the man sitting so silently in front of him. Black fabric slipped down his slim thighs and pooled around his ankles. He bent slowly and picked up the garment, folding it and placing it carefully with his discarded shirt.

Joe swallowed hard to stop himself drooling. Olly's G-string was pure white and microscopic. He could see in the mirror that the T-strap at the back wasn't fabric, but a silver chain.

"You may keep that on for now. Move your legs apart and put your hands behind your head."

He waited for Olly to comply and enjoyed the view. The position displayed the boy's firm body to perfection, his arousal concealed yet accentuated by the scrap of cloth covering him. Joe smiled inside. Olly was turned on by his own vulnerability. Perfect.

Joe got up and, for a moment, just stood and looked at the young man in front of him. He couldn't believe how lucky he felt to have Olly's trust. It gave him a warm glow inside, and he was determined not to do anything to scare him. He went to the wall behind the sofa and pressed gently on one of the mirrored panels. A concealed door swung open to reveal shelves holding a range of restraints and toys. After a moment's deliberation, he selected wrist and ankle cuffs in black leather lined with velvet. They were heavy enough to be effective but soft enough not to mark Olly's skin.

Just buckling the cuffs around Olly's slim wrists and ankles was enough to bring Joe to the edge. Olly watched his every move and worried at his swollen lower lip with even, white teeth, but otherwise he kept completely still. Once the restraints were in place, Joe stood back and admired the picture he had created. He ran his hand over Olly's arse before cupping him gently. He pulled the flimsy fabric of the white thong down until it was positioned beneath Olly's balls. That had the effect of propping up his erection and displaying him very prettily.

Olly moaned and whimpered as Joe deliberately brushed the end of his cock with the backs of his fingers. Joe chuckled and fetched a short length of chain from the cupboard, linking one end to the D-ring on the inside of one wrist cuff. He passed the chain around the metal rail that crossed the room, then fastened the other end so that Olly's wrists were held in front of him. He could now move sideways, but not forwards or back.

"On your knees."

Olly did as he'd been bidden, ending up on his knees with his hands held at shoulder height. His image—bound, helpless and painfully aroused—was everywhere. There was no escape from it.

Joe was about to sit down again but changed his mind. He selected a long spreader bar from the cupboard and fixed it to Olly's ankle cuffs, spreading him wide.

"Better." He settled back and relaxed.

Olly pouted and shifted uncomfortably. His sinking down had the effect of spreading his arse and making his cock jut higher—an effect that pleased Joe enormously.

"How does it make you feel, Oliver? Being so exposed and vulnerable."

Joe kept his eyes on Olly's face with some effort.

"Nervous, Sir."

"Frightened?"

"No. Just… I want to know what you are going to do next."

"But you don't need to know. Your job is to do only as I tell you."

Olly flicked his pink tongue across his lips, and his brow creased. "I just want to please you, Sir."

"And you do, Oliver. You please me greatly. I could sit and look at your beautiful body for hours."

Olly shook his head, sending his curls bouncing. "Please don't do that, Sir."

"Why not?" Joe's grin was feral. "You can speak freely."

"Because I need you, Sir. I need you inside me so badly it hurts, and if you're only going to sit and look at me, I'm going to explode." Olly dropped his head and looked up from beneath golden lashes. "It won't be pretty, Sir."

"Well." Joe had to fight not to smile. "We can't have that."

Chapter Five

Olly needed something—anything—to happen. Something that would distract him from the multiple images of himself reflected around the room. He tried to focus on Joe, staring into his pale blue eyes. The man was incredibly handsome, the planes of his face chiselled, a hint of golden stubble shadowing his chin. Olly wondered what it would feel like grazing his sensitive skin.

The short chain linking his wrists around the metal rail clinked. It hadn't escaped his notice that the cuffs weren't locked. He could get away any time he wanted to. Not that he did—he'd always loved being bound for another man's pleasure until...until that day. The day his life had shattered into a million shards of pain. The day he had become worthless garbage to the man he'd thought had loved him. The day he hadn't been able to get away.

Joe wasn't Mark. He was different. Olly repeated the words over and over in his head. Joe was kind and patient. Joe wouldn't make him do anything he didn't want to. The lump of ice in the pit of his stomach thawed a little. He hadn't been lying when he'd said he wanted to please Joe—he did. He just wasn't sure if he could.

So far, so good. He hadn't freaked out when Joe had restrained him and that was a huge step. It had been six months since he had allowed himself to be this vulnerable. His body had none of the issues that his mind struggled with. His cock was hard and twitchy. His arse felt empty. He longed for Joe's touch and the feeling of strong arms wrapping him up in safety and love. Joe hadn't even got cross when he'd been cheeky, though a punishment would probably be lurking around the next corner. He certainly deserved one.

His cock bounced against the thong stretched beneath it and Olly squirmed, wiggling his arse in an attempt to get more comfortable. The fabric was rubbing just behind his balls and it was driving him crazy.

Lost in his own hazy world of lust and fear, Olly only just heard Joe's command to stand. He got shakily to his feet and held the metal rail to give himself some much-needed stability. Joe unclipped the clasp at the back of his thong before pulling it away. The slim silver chain dragged through his cleft and he whimpered pitifully.

"Serves you right for wearing something so provocative." Joe's voice was full of humour.

"I like chains."

Oops. That had slipped out accidentally.

"Did I say that aloud?" Olly felt himself go hot all over.

"Mmm. You did." Joe encircled him with his arms from behind. "It's something we have in common."

Olly whimpered as Joe's exploring fingers reached his nipples and pinched them both at the same time.

"These would look pretty clamped and chained."

Joe rubbed small circles round and round, occasionally flicking the hard raised nubs until Olly wanted to scream. Every touch sensitised the flesh more and sent lines of fire to his swollen cock. Joe trailed one finger in a line to his groin. "Perhaps another chain to a nice metal ring here?" With the pad of his fingertip, he circled the root of Olly's cock just once, so lightly that it was barely a touch at all. "Would you like that, Oliver? To be decorated in chains for me?"

Olly yanked hard on his wrist cuffs. He was desperate to touch himself, but the chain was far too short. Joe remained behind him, pressed close to his back, stroking everywhere but the place Olly really needed him to touch.

"Look in the mirrors, Olly. How does it make you feel, knowing that I can do anything I want to you? Touch you anywhere and everywhere."

On the last word, Joe stepped back and grasped Olly around the waist. With his legs forced apart by the spreader bar, Olly couldn't even attempt to get away as Joe stroked his hips with tantalising tenderness.

"Look at your cock, swollen and dripping. Your arse—so perfectly tempting. What do you want, Olly? Would you like me to bend you over the rail and fuck you?"

Olly couldn't manage anything more than a squeak as Joe moved to cup his arse, then stroked each cheek gently. Then Joe was gone and Olly had to grip the rail to maintain his balance and stay upright. He watched with wide eyes as Joe went to the cupboard and came back with a pump bottle of glistening lube.

"Hold this." Joe pushed the bottle into his shaking hands. "Pump some onto my fingers."

Olly could barely do as he'd been asked, but eventually managed to release a shiny puddle into the palm of Joe's hand. Then he was being bent over the rail. The bottle fell to the floor as Joe wrapped his slick hand around Olly's cock and spread the silky lubrication over his shaft and around his balls.

"Please... Sir!"

Joe picked up the bottle and slicked his fingers again. He placed it carefully on the floor, then pushed Olly against the rail, holding him there with one arm. Olly squirmed and panted as lube smeared his arse, then Joe dragged his cool finger down the line between Olly's cheeks to probe gently at the tight bud of his entrance. He gripped the rail like a lifeline. His body demanded more, craving sensation and pleasure. His mind, however, screamed with alarm.

Joe gripped his swollen shaft and began to jack him slowly before moving to cup his aching balls and roll them gently. He was still rubbing Olly's pucker, not breaching him, just stroking and smoothing. Olly could feel his muscles tensing and started to panic. His body rebelled, thrusting hard into Joe's hand, demanding release, but his mind flashed back to another time, another man with a different face.

"No... No!" Tears flooded his face as he came with a desperate shudder into Joe's hand. Then he was being held close and tightly, his hair stroked, his neck kissed gently.

"It's all right, Olly. I'm not going to..."

In just a few seconds Joe had swiftly unbuckled the cuffs from his ankles and wrists, then Olly found himself gathered into a warm embrace. Somewhere inside him, a wall broke down and he sobbed into

Joe's chest. He couldn't look at him and the sobs came anew as he realised that he had just destroyed any chance he'd ever had of being with this wonderful, beautiful man.

"It's all right, sweetheart, let it go."

Soothing words calmed him. Gentle hands held him close and safe. Gradually the tremors that racked his body diminished and the tears dried.

"I'm so sorry."

"Look at me, Oliver."

Tentatively, Olly looked up into eyes that held only warmth and care.

"You have nothing to be sorry about. Nothing. You are beautiful. Responsive, obedient and hot as hell. You could tempt the devil himself. You're just not ready to take the final step with me yet, and that's fine. We have all the time in the world."

"We do?" Olly allowed himself to hope.

"Yes, we do." Joe's voice was firm but kind. "All the time you need."

Olly clung to him like a limpet, utterly relieved at Joe's patience. Joe chuckled softly. "Why don't you put some clothes on? I'd like to take you home with me tonight, and nobody gets to see your cute little rear but me."

"You want me to come home with you?" Olly looked up, shocked and delighted.

"I don't want you to be alone tonight. Let me take care of you, okay? I have a spare room you can use."

Olly grabbed his clothes and pulled them on hurriedly. He could hardly believe that a man like Joe would have any interest in an emotional wreck like him. He couldn't wait to see him in his home environment, away from the club. He felt very guilty that once again he had got off while Joe hadn't so much as lowered his zipper. It was hardly fair. He chewed on his lip anxiously.

"Stop worrying, Olly. That's my job."

He swallowed hard, wondering if Joe could read his mind. Good Dominants looked after their submissives. Always. Joe was perfect. He made Olly feel warm inside, and he'd been cold for so long he'd forgotten what it felt like to be cared for.

He followed Joe upstairs to the outer door, and waited while he collected his coat. Outside it was dark, the pavements gleaming from a recent shower, and there was a distinct chill in the air. He shivered, wishing he had thought to bring a fleece.

Joe frowned at him, then wrapped his overcoat around Olly's shoulders. The coat was too long, but it was warm and smelt of Joe. Olly snuggled into it with a happy sigh as Joe put a protective arm around his shoulders. He didn't question whether Joe was cold. His Master wanted him to be warm and that was what mattered. His Master. That thought felt so good. Perhaps if he kept it in his mind, it would become the truth.

As they strolled down the street and turned the corner, a car edged from a side turning, its engine almost silent. Olly glimpsed the movement from the corner of his eye but dismissed it. Only Joe deserved his attention.

Olly became oblivious to everything but the weight of Joe's arm. They strolled along in silence, but it didn't feel uncomfortable. Every now and again, Olly glanced up to check that Joe didn't look angry or annoyed, but all he saw was determination. It wasn't a long walk to Joe's house. Their footsteps echoed in the quiet of the mews, which was bathed in the amber glow of old-fashioned streetlights.

Olly felt a little nervous as he waited for Joe to unlock his front door. The obvious wealth of his surroundings was a little intimidating. Mark Vickery was rich too, but his house was all about ostentation. Joe's place was smart but inviting. Olly relaxed the moment he stepped into the hall and felt no fear when the heavy door clicked shut behind him.

He returned Joe's coat and looked around curiously. The walls in the hall were painted a deep burgundy, and there was a subtly patterned runner on the stairs, fixed in place by gleaming brass stair rods. On the walls was a series of black and white photographs, and as Olly looked at them he realised that they weren't abstract, as he had first thought, but pictures of parts of the body. The male body, to be more accurate. The one closest to him was a side view of a lightly stubbled jaw and the curve of a neck in shadow. The next was a close-up of well-defined abdominal muscles. His gaze travelled up the stairs as he admired image after image, all beautifully captured on camera.

"Are they all of the same man?"

"Yes. Do you like them?"

Olly felt Joe's hand on the small of his back. There was no pressure, but he knew he was supposed to move up the stairs.

"They're beautiful. So is the model."

Joe chuckled. "It's kind of you to say so. I'm flattered."

Olly nearly fell down the stairs. "The pictures are of you?"

"They are. Now let's get you to bed. It's late."

Olly really wanted to take a closer look at all of the pictures, but that would have to wait. There were two doors on the landing, both standing slightly ajar.

Joe pushed open the door to the left and leaned in to turn on the light. "This is the guest room. It has its own bathroom and there are towels and toiletries you can use—just help yourself. I'm over here." He stood in the other doorway. "Goodnight, Oliver. Sleep well."

He turned away and Olly whimpered. Did he dare ask?

"Please, Sir. May I sleep in your room?" He didn't presume to ask for a place in Joe's bed. The floor would be fine. He just wanted to feel safe and wanted.

Joe didn't say a word. He just pushed his bedroom door open wider and waited for Olly to join him.

Joe guided Olly to the ensuite bathroom and left him alone. Olly stripped and climbed into the shower cubicle, admiring the shiny fittings and pristine tiles. The water was plentiful and hot, and the spray nice and hard. Olly washed quickly and dried himself off with a deep red towel. He didn't really want to put his clothes back on, but he was nervous about walking out into Joe's bedroom in just a towel. He shrugged. Joe had seen it all before, so what did it matter?

He peeked around the door and couldn't stop the gasp that slipped from his lips. Joe was silhouetted against the window as he drew the curtains. He was barefoot and shirtless, the outline of broad shoulders tapering to a narrow waist stark against the soft light outside. Olly held his breath as Joe turned towards him. He was so graceful, every movement a study in controlled elegance.

There was a scattering of golden hair across his chest, but it didn't hide his well-defined chest and distinct abdominal muscles. Olly had to fight not to lick his lips. He suddenly realised that he was staring and that Joe was looking directly at him, an amused glint in his cool blue eyes. Olly ducked his head and peeked up from beneath his lashes. He just couldn't stop looking.

"Do you intend to wear that towel to bed, Oliver?"

He looked down in confusion. *Towel. What towel? Oh! That towel.*

"No, Sir." He trotted back into the bathroom and folded the offending object neatly over the side of the bath before returning to the bedroom, hands crossed demurely over his cock.

"Hands behind your back."

Olly obeyed, wishing that his cock would behave itself. The moment he had caught sight of Joe's semi-clothed body, the bloody thing had risen in immediate and ardent appreciation.

"Hide yourself from me again and I'll spank you so hard you won't want to sit down for a week."

Olly moaned as his cock got even harder at that thought. Joe hadn't raised his voice. He didn't even sound cross. He was just stating a very simple fact, and Olly was left in no doubt that it was the truth.

Joe stripped off his trousers, revealing a hip-skimming pair of black briefs, before climbing into bed. Olly's heart beat a little faster. He waited for an order because that was the easiest thing to do.

When Joe patted the bed next to him, Olly let out a breath he hadn't realised he'd been holding and clambered up next to him. His head sank into a soft pillow and he sighed happily as Joe pulled the downy duvet over him. Forgetting that he should never touch without being asked, he snuggled into Joe's side and rested his head on the bigger man's chest. When Joe pulled him even closer, Olly purred with satisfaction. His cock was stiff, demanding attention, so he instinctively went to grasp it.

"Touch that and I'll have you in chastity for a month." Joe's whispered words were accompanied by a light kiss to the top of Olly's head. "Now go to sleep."

Chapter Six

Joe had always liked the rain. As a child, he had loved to watch the shiny droplets chasing each other down his bedroom windowpane. As an adult, he found the gentle thrumming sound soothing. It was even better when he didn't have to go out in it, and as it was Sunday, he was secure in knowing that a day in front of a warm fire awaited him.

He turned and looked down at the young man sleeping soundly in his bed. Olly's blond curls decorated the pillow and fell in unruly tangles across his eyes. He looked so peaceful, and Joe didn't have the heart to wake him. He had the feeling that undisturbed nights were a rare occurrence for his young guest.

He must be absolutely exhausted.

Joe managed to extract himself from Olly's limbs, shower and dress without waking him. He stretched and pulled on an old, charcoal-grey T-shirt over his ancient jeans. He then gathered up Olly's discarded clothes and slipped from the room. He padded downstairs and threw everything in the washing machine before turning on the coffee maker. He rescued the weighty slab that was his Sunday newspaper from the doormat and returned to the kitchen to the tantalising aroma of his favourite blend. He extracted his preferred sections from the paper and spread them on the breakfast bar ready to read.

At some point, halfway through an article on the latest film releases, it crossed Joe's mind that Olly would wake up and have nothing to wear. That put a smile on his face. He fully intended that the boy should spend the day naked anyway, apart from a nice supple collar and some cuffs, perhaps. The paper suddenly wasn't all that interesting. He allowed his mind to drift. The day offered the perfect opportunity to discover exactly how submissive Olly was—he just needed to make sure the boy was open to a little testing.

He was halfway through his second cup of coffee and starting to wonder about breakfast when the kitchen door opened slowly and a blond head appeared. Olly brought a whole new meaning to the phrase 'artfully tousled', and Joe had to press his lips together to stop himself from smiling. When the rest of Olly's slender body sidled round the door, he had to dig his fingers into his thigh to stop himself from swearing. Olly was wearing one of Joe's cotton work shirts. Light blue, it brought out the colour of his huge eyes, but that wasn't what drew Joe's attention. Olly wasn't wearing anything else and he had only done up a couple of buttons. The shirt-tail just reached the bottom of his arse, but every time he moved Joe caught a tantalising glimpse of curving muscle. At the front, Olly's sweet, eager dick was trying to poke its way free.

Olly had rolled the sleeves up loosely so that they sat just above his wrists. He looked absolutely adorable. Joe found it hard to resist gathering him up in a hug and kissing him all over.

"Sorry, Joe—I mean, Sir—I mean... Just sorry. I woke up and my clothes were gone and I didn't know what to do, so I found this on the back of a chair and borrowed it, and I hope you don't mind, Sir. I'll wash it and return it, I promise, and where are my clothes?"

"My God, Olly! Listening to you is like listening to a reading of *Ulysses*. Stream of consciousness in motion. Take a breath."

"Sorry. When I'm nervous I talk. And when I'm happy. I can't help it."

"So are you nervous or happy?"

"Both?" Olly seemed to be looking for some kind of confirmation.

Joe rolled his eyes. "I was going to offer you coffee, but I don't think that's a good idea. Ever. I'll get you a glass of milk." He gestured to one of the tall stools against the counter. "Take a seat."

Olly clambered onto the stool and tried, unsuccessfully, to cover his lap with the ends of the shirt. Joe poured a glass of milk and put it down next to him, then he pushed the pieces of fabric away from Olly's lap, leaving him exposed below the waist.

"Do you remember what I told you last night, Oliver?"

Olly fidgeted on the stool. "You said if I tried to hide myself, you would spank me."

"I did. I'm glad you were listening."

Olly wriggled some more. "So will you, Sir?"

"Will I what?"

"Spank me, Sir?"

"You'll learn, Oliver, that I always do what I say I will."

"Oh."

Joe deliberately didn't take the conversation any further. Olly didn't need to know when, where or how he would receive his punishment.

"It's almost lunchtime, so I suggest we have brunch and discuss the rest of our day. Of course, that's unless you would prefer to leave?"

Olly shook his head silently.

"Good. Do you like pancakes?"

"I love them! But wouldn't you like me to cook for you, Sir?"

"If I wanted you to do anything, Olly, I would ask you. I'm not looking for a slave or a housekeeper. I'm looking for a partner. Being submissive doesn't make you any less intelligent, nor does it mean that you have to do menial chores, and as it happens I like to cook."

Olly ducked his head. "You're so different, Joe... I don't know what I should do."

Joe patted his shoulder. "You're doing just fine. Perhaps it would help if you told me a little about Mark? You don't have to if you don't want to, but if I understand how it was between you two I can explain what I like to do differently." He didn't push, just gathered the ingredients he needed, measured them out and began beating the flour and milk together in a large jug.

For a while there was silence. The scent of cooking filtered into the air as Joe cooked pancakes and layered them onto a warm plate that he transferred to and from the oven. When all his batter was gone, he chopped strawberries and retrieved maple syrup from the larder. Olly looked deep in thought, and when he started talking it was unexpected. It was as if he had made a decision in his mind and pressed the 'go' button to speak.

"I was twenty when I met Mark. I'd just qualified as an RN and was working in the casualty department as a triage nurse. He came down for a surgical consultation on one of his patients and after that I kept bumping into him. In the canteen, in the locker room. He always seemed to be around, but it never crossed my mind that it was by design until he asked me out. He took me to a club called Steel that weekend."

Joe raised an eyebrow. Steel was a pretty hard-core venue for those into the S & M scene. It would have been quite a shock to someone as inexperienced as Olly.

"You can imagine that I was a bit shocked—but intrigued as well. Mark was very open about his kinks. He told me that I was the most obvious submissive he had ever come across and that he wanted to train me. It freaked me out a bit. I avoided him as much as I could for a few weeks but he always seemed to know where I was. I did a bit of research into the lifestyle and I realised that it did appeal to me. I like rules. I like to be told what to do. I'd already experimented with light bondage...so I agreed to another date."

Olly sipped his milk and fidgeted on the stool. Joe served the food then handed him a fork, watching with an amused smile as Olly poured liberal amounts of syrup over everything on his plate.

"It went from there, I suppose. At first we'd just meet for the odd night out, then weekends. Mark liked to be called Master. Our relationship was all about me servicing him, and that meant chores and spending a lot of time on my knees. With hindsight it's easy to see how one-sided our relationship was. I had a safe word and he respected that, but he didn't consult me about anything else. Don't get me wrong, he's handsome and charming, but he got progressively more controlling and physically harsher as the months went on."

Olly chewed on a mouthful of pancake and strawberry. "Oh, God! These are amazing!"

Joe sat next to him. "Thank you. Though I think I might have to limit your access to sugar as well as caffeine."

Olly pouted and Joe couldn't resist leaning forward to nip at his plump lower lip. Olly tasted as sweet as he looked. He opened willingly to Joe's questing tongue, and for a while food took second place to a passionate kiss.

When Joe sat back he could see the glint of tears in Olly's eyes.

"Mark never kissed me. He didn't like to cuddle and I never spent the whole night in his bed. He had a cage in his bedroom…"

Joe tried to keep the anger from his face. Olly was such a tactile person, so responsive to touch. It would have been incredibly cruel to deny him that contact.

"Why did you stay with him?"

Olly sighed. "I don't know. I thought about leaving so many times. Then he arranged for me to move to a new job—he thought I met too many people in casualty and he didn't like that. He arranged for me to move to the psychiatric hospital attached to the prison."

"Interesting work."

"Yes. It was. I missed the bustle of triage, but the experience of a new area was good for a while. Then something happened…something bad."

Joe stopped eating and slipped an arm around Olly's shaking shoulders. "Take your time, Olly. I'm not going anywhere."

"Mark did!" Olly's face was streaked with tears. "Afterwards he abandoned me. He couldn't wait for me to be me again. He wanted everything to go back to the way it was, as if nothing had ever happened. But I couldn't! I couldn't, Joe…"

Joe wrapped his arms around Olly's slender frame as tightly as he dared and held him until the shuddering sobs subsided. He murmured nonsense words of comfort, knowing the soothing sounds would make as much sense as real words until Olly calmed down.

"It's okay. I'm sorry. Not because I wanted you to talk to me, but because whatever happened to you was clearly deeply traumatic. Mark Vickery is a prize idiot for letting you go, sweetheart."

"I felt so lost without a Master, without someone to give me what I need. So I went to The Underground and spoke to Mr Hoffman. He must have realised I wasn't really ready to play again. He let me work in the kitchens and kept me away from the members."

"Carey has always been a good judge of people, Olly, and I'm very glad he kept you hidden away. He saved you just for me."

That set Olly's tears rolling again, but despite the emotion Joe could feel the boy's dick hardening against him. Olly's slim body felt so good in his arms, and he began to stroke the lines of Olly's back and arms. It didn't matter that Olly still hadn't told him the whole story—he knew that would come with time. In that moment, Joe just wanted to reassure Olly that his heart wasn't as cold as Mark Vickery's.

Pancakes forgotten, it took him seconds to flick open the two buttons on Olly's shirt and slide it from his shoulders. Having Olly naked within the protection of his arms felt so right. He pulled him close and slid a hand down to cup his arse. Olly pressed against him as if he couldn't get near enough. He was sending all the right signals, so Joe took a chance and rubbed a finger over his entrance.

Olly whimpered and wriggled, pushing back against his touch. Joe turned him around and pushed him against the counter. He grabbed the olive oil he'd been cooking with and used it to slick his fingers before pressing one firmly into Olly's hole.

"Bend over and spread your legs wider." He nudged at Olly's ankles with a bare foot until he was satisfied. "I want you to choose a safe word. Say it and I stop." He twisted his finger, stretching Olly's channel until he was satisfied that he could take another one, then plunged a second finger deep inside him. Olly gasped and thrust back hard. Joe smiled at his enthusiasm and used his other hand to pinch Olly's vulnerable nipple.

"Fuck!" Olly squirmed and panted hard, "Sir! It's kind of hard to focus on words when you do that!" Joe scissored his fingers. "Oh! Pancake, my word is pancake... Red is too boring." When Joe withdrew his fingers to get more oil, Olly whimpered in complaint and got a sharp smack on the arse in return.

"Patience, Oliver. You get what I choose to give and no more." Joe spanked him again before giving in and plunging three fingers into velvet heat. He pinched the other nipple hard and felt for the knot of nerves inside Olly that would heighten his pleasure. Finding what he sought, he scissored his fingers and grinned as Olly screamed. Slowly he began to fuck Olly with his fingers, gradually gathering speed before reaching with his other hand to encircle the boy's rigid dick. After a couple of short, sharp tugs, Olly spilled onto the kitchen tiles with an ecstatic moan. He turned and melted into Joe's arms before tilting his head back expectantly. Joe obliged and kissed him hard.

Olly beamed and wriggled free, dropping to his knees and looking up hopefully.

"Are you sure, Olly? You don't have to." Joe could hardly believe his own restraint. This beautiful young man was naked, on his knees in front of him, and still he was holding back. Thankfully, Olly decided to take the initiative. He fumbled at Joe's fly until the zipper slid down and he was able to push Joe's jeans to the floor. He kicked them away and turned around so that Joe could take his turn using the kitchen counter for support. Olly pulled off Joe's underwear as if he were unwrapping a birthday present, his eyes bright with anticipation.

"Oh! Oh, wow!"

Joe barely had time to register the words before Olly wrapped his soft lips around the tip of his cock and lapped at the drops of pre-cum gathered there with a warm tongue. Joe wound his fingers into Olly's hair but didn't tug, letting Olly decide how deep to take him. Then there were heat and suction and the light grazing of teeth. Olly let him slide free before ducking to mouth his balls and suckle them gently.

"I'm not going to last, Olly…"

He tried desperately to hold back as Olly went back to sucking his cock as if it was the most wonderful treat he'd ever been given, but when he plunged down on him, lodging Joe's cock in his throat, there was nothing he could do. He came hard, spurting repeatedly into Olly's welcoming mouth. When he sagged back against the counter, Olly delicately licked him clean.

"You have the most beautiful cock, Sir." Olly peeked up at him shyly. Joe pulled Olly into a hug.

"And you have an incredible mouth."

After a few minutes he picked Olly up and sat him back on the stool before rescuing his abandoned jeans. He pulled them on, not bothering to retrieve his underwear. Olly reached for his shirt but Joe pushed it out of his reach.

"No. I want you naked for the rest of the day."

Olly's cheeks pinked but he didn't refuse. He cocked his head to one side and produced a beguiling smile.

"What do you want, imp?" Joe ruffled his curls indulgently.

"Well, Sir, I need to build up my energy again, don't I? Especially if you intend to punish me later."

Joe attempted to look stern. "That's true."

"Well…would you cook some more pancakes then?" Olly fluttered his lashes shamelessly and Joe rolled his eyes. "That is, if you didn't use all the oil, Sir."

Chapter Seven

Joe looked at his handiwork and smiled. The steel cock ring nestling at the base of Olly's dick was heavy enough that there would be no forgetting its presence, and it locked with a nice solid click.

"Comfortable?"

Olly scowled back at him. "It doesn't hurt, Sir. I wouldn't exactly call it comfortable, though."

Joe shrugged. "It stays. It looks good on you."

He admired the play of firelight on Olly's skin and the flicker of gold in his curls. He really was a very beautiful young man. Joe had positioned him with his back to the open fire, legs slightly apart, hands cuffed behind him. They had moved to the small sitting room after Olly had overdosed on pancakes and seemed unable to stop talking. When he had begun to twirl in circles on the swivel stool he was perched on, Joe had decided that action was needed before the brat landed in a heap on the floor.

The sitting room was just across the hall from the kitchen. It contained two armchairs, a leather footstool, a low coffee table and several tall bookcases, all of which were overflowing. There was no central ceiling light—the room was lit by three small lamps positioned so as to allow enough light to read in comfort. There was no TV, just a sound system that was playing something soft and classical. It was Joe's favourite room, a place he came to relax and let the stresses of his job seep away.

He picked a book at random from a shelf and settled into one of the armchairs. He placed a cushion on the floor at his feet and pointed to it. Olly walked across and sank gracefully to his knees.

"I want you to be silent. Take the time to think about what it is you really want. No fidgeting and no talking unless it's to say your safe word. Understand?"

Olly nodded, though Joe could see he wasn't impressed with the orders. That had been his intention. Submission wasn't something that could be switched on and off. If Olly truly was as submissive as Joe suspected, he would do as he was told, though keeping still and quiet were probably his least favourite activities.

* * * *

Nearly an hour later, Joe was cursing his own lack of foresight. He'd only been reading for fifteen minutes when Olly's head had come to rest gently on his thigh. Innocent blue eyes had pleaded silently, and Joe had allowed him to remain where he was. Of course, the proximity of Olly's head to his groin and the fluttering of golden lashes had hardened his cock to the point of pain. He'd read the same page about fifteen times now and still had no idea what was going on.

He lasted an hour by sheer force of will, then tangled his fingers into Olly's curls and tugged. At first, Olly just nuzzled closer. It took a couple of sharp pulls before he lifted his head and Joe was met with a bewildered expression.

"You can move now, Olly."

"Do I have to, Sir?"

"Yes. You do. I don't want to hurt your shoulder muscles and you've been in cuffs for a while now. I need to take them off."

Obligingly, Olly shuffled around on his knees so that Joe could release his hands.

"Stand up and stretch."

Joe chuckled as Olly rolled his shoulders, then wiggled his hips. He shook his head at the antics — anyone would think Olly had been stuck unmoving for days, not an hour.

"May I use the bathroom, Sir?"

"Of course. When you get back I'm going to administer your punishment, so don't be long." Joe glanced at the clock and noted the time. It would be interesting to see just how long Olly took to return now that he knew what was in store.

Joe shifted the coffee table to one side and moved the round leather footstool into the centre of the rug in front of the fire. From the top shelf of a bookcase he retrieved a collection of implements and laid them out neatly on the table. There was a slim cane, a leather paddle and a crop with a red leather handle. His personal preference would be to have Olly across his knees and to use his bare hand to spank him, but that was very intimate. Olly would have the choice, so that he could keep more of a distance between them if he wanted to. Joe had a feeling that accepting punishment at all was going to be a huge step for Olly to take, but it was important that the boy understood that everything he had heard about Joe as a Dominant was true.

Joe threw another log onto the fire and levered it into place with a long brass poker. He turned around just as Olly came back into the room, and for a moment couldn't understand the look of horror on the boy's face. Then he realised that the poker was still in his hand and must look extremely threatening from Olly's perspective.

"It's okay, Olly. The poker is for the fire, not you. I won't ever mark you permanently."

Olly visibly relaxed and looked more than a little embarrassed, though there was still some tension in his stance.

Joe sat in one of the armchairs and gestured to the floor. Olly sank to his knees in front of him and looked up nervously.

"Tell me why you are to be punished, Oliver."

"I tried to cover myself after you specifically told me not to, Sir."

"That's right. It's important that you understand that my orders are to be obeyed, not ignored." Joe paused. "You remember your safe word?"

"Yes, Sir."

"Very well. You have earned six strokes for disobedience. You may choose how they are delivered."

He pointed to the table and Olly swivelled around on his knees. He looked at the items laid out, then turned back to Joe. "Are these my only choices, Sir?"

Joe frowned. "Did you have something else in mind?"

There was a light pink flush on Olly's cheeks and his cock stood stiffly to attention. Joe realised that the anticipation of punishment, of pain, was something that his angelic boy found arousing.

"Your hand, Sir." Olly whispered the words as if he hardly dared to hope that his wish would be granted.

Joe hesitated for a moment, but his misgivings were swept away by the mute appeal on Olly's face.

"Very well. Prepare yourself."

Instead of moving to lie across the footstool, Olly immediately placed himself across Joe's knees, wriggling until he found a comfortable position. Joe sighed and relinquished control of the situation to the submissive squirming in his lap. He placed one hand at the small of Olly's back so that he was balanced and had no chance of falling, then brought his other hand down hard, without warning. A rosy glow suffused one side of Olly's arse, and Joe stroked the warm skin gently. He knew he shouldn't ask until the punishment was complete, but he couldn't stop himself. "Okay?"

"Mmm. More please, Sir."

Olly sounded as if he were being rewarded, not disciplined. Joe shook his head and brought his hand down again and again. After six strokes he stopped and began to knead the reddened curves in front of him. Olly's skin was so smooth, Joe felt as if he could keep him there all night. Instead, he tilted him up and lifted him around to sit on his lap. Olly leaned against his bare chest.

"Thank you, Sir."

Joe could see that the boy was painfully hard, and if not for the cock ring would probably have come untouched.

"Why do I get the feeling that you just got exactly what you wanted?"

Olly snuggled closer. "I don't know what you mean, Sir."

Joe snorted his exasperation. "Brat. I can see I will have to think up ways to punish you that you don't enjoy quite so much."

"Whatever you say, Sir."

"And what if I say you may not come for the next week?"

That got some attention. "A week! But that would be very cruel, Sir!"

"A week, to prove to me that you can practise restraint."

Olly's lower lip trembled, so Joe kissed it into stillness.

"But where will you be, Sir? Do you not want me...?"

"Hush, Olly. I'm not sending you away. I have appointments all day tomorrow and then I have to return to Yorkshire to work for the rest of the week. I will be back next weekend."

Olly shuffled onto the floor, pulled his knees up and hugged them. He looked thoughtful. "You expect me to do as you say even when you're not here?"

"I do." Joe smiled as he saw realisation dawn in Olly's eyes.

"That would make you my Master, Sir."

"Yes, Oliver. It would. If you'll have me?"

All kinds of emotions shot through Joe's body as he waited for Olly's response. Hope warred with the fear of rejection. He worried that he had moved too quickly, that Olly would be scared away, but he didn't want to leave Olly alone without some kind of understanding between them. What he really wanted to do was wrap a nice, obvious collar around the boy's neck and announce his claim to the world, but it was far too soon for that.

"I'd like that, Sir."

Joe had almost missed the words he'd longed to hear, Olly had spoken them so quietly. He knelt on the floor next him and gathered him into a warm hug.

"Thank you, Olly. Thank you for trusting me."

After a few moments, he released the boy and stood up.

"Stand up, Olly. Display yourself for me."

Olly clambered to his feet and stood still with his hands clasped behind his back. He seemed more calm and settled than he had since Joe had met him.

Joe stroked the boy's rigid cock gently. "This is mine now. And so is this." He moved his hand to cup Olly's arse. "Is that clear?"

"Yes, Sir."

Joe reluctantly unlocked the metal ring at the base of Olly's twitching cock. "I'll miss you this week."

"For a Dominant you are very soppy, Sir." Olly's lips twitched, then he hissed as a sharp slap seared his arse. "I'll miss you too!"

"If you think you can behave yourself between here and the kitchen, you may fetch your clothes from the drier."

Olly scurried away and Joe smiled at his own reflection in the mirror over the fire. The warmth he felt had nothing to do with the flickering flames, and even the frosty blue of his eyes seemed to have softened.

* * * *

When he showed Olly out half an hour later, he felt a pang of regret. Olly was wearing one of his jumpers and looked adorably swamped in its folds. It was just starting to get dark as they shared a chaste kiss on the doorstep.

"You have my private number, Olly. Don't be afraid to use it. Be good."

"Yes, Sir." Olly smiled shyly over his shoulder as he walked away and Joe had to resist the urge to pull him back and lock him away somewhere safe. He watched until Olly turned the corner, then frowned as a dark saloon passed the end of the road, far too slowly. He turned to go back into the house, then changed his mind and strolled to the end of the street. He looked both ways but there was no sign of either Olly or the car. He had no reason to worry, but still a small knot of anxiety sat in the pit of his stomach as he returned to the house and pulled the door closed.

Chapter Eight

"I hate Monday mornings," Joe muttered to himself as he took a seat at his desk. The building he shared with two colleagues and one secretary-cum-receptionist was still quiet. He was first in, as was usually the case, which meant he could set the coffee maker up just the way he liked it and make sure that no one stole his favourite mug.

He was spending more and more of his time taking classes at The Edge, and he knew that sooner or later he would have to make a decision about continuing to practise in London at all. It was no longer that appealing, and as the business he and his best friend had worked so hard to establish flourished, he found himself missing the country air.

He'd soon sorted the pile of mail on his desk into neat stacks. He scanned his email, read the case notes of the two clients he was seeing that morning and reviewed some requests for consultation work. When all the day-to-day stuff had been dealt with, he unlocked his briefcase and pulled out the envelope from Alyson Bell. Inside was a slim manila folder containing just two sheets of paper covered in close type. One listed patient details and medical history, the other a report on the case.

All the warmth drained from Joe's body, and he suspected that any colour in his face had gone with it. He lowered his mug to the desk with a shaking hand, scattering a few drops of coffee onto the wooden surface. He was used to seeing photographs of crime victims, even dead bodies, but when the person in the image was someone he knew, his capacity for stoical calm dissipated into thin air.

The boy in the photograph had unruly blond curls and startling blue eyes. Even beneath the cuts and bruises, it was apparent that he was beautiful, almost feminine in appearance.

"Olly... Oh, no."

Joe knew that he should close the file without reading it, ring Alyson and decline the case. He knew it, but couldn't do it. Slowly and with growing fury, he began to read.

It took less than five minutes to absorb the details of a shattered life. Joe stood slowly, walked calmly from his office to the small men's room and vomited into the lavatory. He flushed, washed his hands and face in cold water, dried off with a paper towel and returned to his chair.

"Okay. Now that's out of your system, fucking concentrate, Joe." Giving himself a talking to was therapeutic. He read the file again and this time he was able to consider each detail clinically.

Olly had initially been referred to Dr Bell for treatment after displaying symptoms of post-traumatic stress following an incident at work. 'Incident' didn't even begin to describe what Olly had gone through in Joe's mind, but he was accustomed to the detached terminology used in medical reports. He had responded well to treatment initially but then had regressed dramatically when his personal circumstances had changed. Joe sighed and rubbed a hand through his short hair — that must have been the point at which Mark had abandoned him.

He fired up his computer and began to search for media stories on the root cause of Olly's problems. He found plenty of material and realised that he did remember a little of what had happened. It had been at a time when a series of riots had swept through overcrowded prisons. There had been protests, fires, whole buildings vandalised. The violence had escalated as the problem had spread, culminating at the prison where Olly had been working in the hospital wing.

There had been a lot of speculation about what had happened to ignite the trouble at a prison that, compared to most, was modern and well run. A fire in the kitchens had initiated an evacuation, during which several inmates had taken advantage of the situation and attacked their guards. What had started as an escape attempt had escalated into a full-scale riot, and, though the worst of the trouble had been swiftly quelled, a small contingent had barricaded themselves into the hospital wing.

Olly had been one of several staff members trapped. What hadn't been reported in the newspapers was that he had been separated from his colleagues and taken to another room by two violent offenders. He had then been subjected to a horrifying catalogue of sexual abuse over a twelve-hour period.

When armed police had eventually forced their way inside, Olly had been the last to be rescued. They had found him locked into a straitjacket, naked and beaten, huddled in the corner of a small room.

Joe couldn't stop the tears from welling in his eyes. "My poor love..." He knew, right at that moment, that he did love Oliver. He'd fallen fast and hard, and now icy fingers were squeezing his heart.

Despite the hideous ordeal he had experienced, Olly had responded well to the therapy that had followed. He'd shown remarkable strength—something that Alyson Bell had noted several times. She had attributed his relapse completely to the breakdown of his relationship with 'a controlling and dominant partner'.

Alyson's summary stated that she felt no more recovery would be possible until the subject found the protective relationship he clearly needed.

Joe picked up the phone and called Dr Bell.

"Alyson, it's Joe Dexter."

"I was expecting your call. You've read the file."

"Yes."

"I know you can't take the case."

"You do?" Joe, for once, felt as if he were groping around in the dark and Alyson had stolen the light bulb.

"Carey Hoffman is a friend of mine."

Well, he hadn't seen that one coming. "You set me up? The two of you...?"

"Arranged for you to meet Oliver. Yes."

"I'm going to kill him. And then you."

"Of course you are." Sarcasm dripped from every syllable.

"Of all the unprofessional, unethical..."

Alyson interrupted before he could vent any further. "I already know how well the two of you have connected, Joe. I'm sorry we were so devious, but

Oliver needed a Master, not more therapy — and that's not something I could blatantly recommend to the clinic board, now, was it? I went to Carey because he's an old friend and I knew he was into the lifestyle. If I had known that you were too, I might have come to you directly, but this way at least you met under circumstances that weren't staged. Carey said you are the best. I think Oliver is worth that, don't you?"

Joe started to speak, then stuttered to a halt. He took a couple of deep, calming breaths, then started again, "Did Olly know this was a set-up?"

"No, of course he didn't. He doesn't know you've seen his file either."

Joe realised that his fingers were drumming an urgent rhythm on the edge of his desk, and forced them into stillness.

"Are you absolutely sure that Oliver doesn't need more therapy?"

"That is my professional opinion, yes. He still has some healing to do but he's a very strong young man. What he needs is the security of a committed relationship and a partner who will give him what he needs without judging him."

Joe sighed. "I'm not seeing him again until Friday evening."

"That's fine. You must treat your relationship as though we never had this conversation. Take things slowly and he'll respond." Alyson paused, then spoke a little hesitantly. "How do you feel about him, Joe? Do you think that the two of you have a long-term future?"

Joe wanted to retort that it was none of her fucking business, but he could detect the genuine concern and caring tone in her voice, so he resisted the urge to snap. "I've only known him a few days, Alyson, but yes. Much as I hate to admit it, Olly is exactly what I've been looking for."

They spent a few minutes discussing some of the finer details of Olly's past treatment, then Joe hung up. He stared at the file on his desk for a long time, trying to decide how high on his pissed-off scale he was currently reaching. Not quite high enough to go after Carey with an axe — though that idea had some appeal — but not low enough that he could ignore his need to break something. He opted to call a friend and make an appointment for a kickboxing session. It was his favourite sport and something that he was dangerously proficient at.

* * * *

He managed to maintain a professional calm during his client consultations, cleared a huge stack of paperwork with ruthless efficiency and spent his lunch break delivering bruises to his willing, if somewhat overwhelmed, sparring partner. At the end of the day he made a quick trip home to change, locked up the house then headed for the station to catch the train.

The journey north involved a mainline train, then a short journey on a rickety old branch line that had miraculously escaped closure. Joe normally spent most of the journey reading, but that night he rested his head against his seat in the empty first-class carriage and allowed his mind to drift. The rhythm of the train lulled him into a semi-dream state, not quite asleep but not fully aware of his surroundings.

His thoughts were dominated by images of Olly. His coy, but mischievous looks when he relaxed. The swollen lower lip that he habitually chewed on. His enormous eyes that truly were the windows to his soul. And what a tormented soul it was. Joe couldn't believe the strength hidden in that slender frame. To have survived such trauma and still be able to smile was a miracle in itself, but then having to cope with being left alone... Joe was sure that he wouldn't have come out of it as well.

Relationships between Dominants and submissives were often quite carefully controlled, even contracted. He was very aware of the responsibility of his position and just how vulnerable a partner could be. He'd been lucky. The few serious relationships he'd been involved in had finished amicably and he'd always made sure that ex-partners were looked after until they'd either found their feet alone or established a new relationship. Olly had been callously abandoned by a man who had no compassion and no respect for the courage it took to offer submission to another.

It made Joe feel warm inside that Olly wanted to belong to him. It was also quite scary. Dominating another man came naturally to Joe—it turned him on in ways that more vanilla relationships would never do—but he would never want that at the expense of someone else. He was only interested in relationships that were mutually pleasurable.

When the train finally shuddered to a stop at the tiny halt at the end of the line, Joe collected his bag from the overhead rack and wondered if there would be a taxi waiting. Getting to the island that housed The Edge was always a bit of a lottery.

He clambered out of the train and waited patiently as a woman in front of him on the platform righted the suitcase she had kicked over. She was all fumbling fingers and red-faced confusion. Joe helped her out, then looked around to see what had got her so flustered. He rolled his eyes when he saw the lean, six-feet-five-inch frame of his best friend Heath lounging against the waiting room wall. Heath was all steely eyes and rugged good looks. His short, dark hair framed a chiselled jaw covered with a couple of days' worth of dark stubble.

Joe pulled his attention back to the woman in front of him, who was now looking between him and Heath with a distinctly interested expression. Joe caught the wicked glint in Heath's eyes as he strolled across to them, so he wasn't too surprised when his friend cupped the side of his face with a strong hand and kissed him. Hard.

His fellow passenger sighed in disappointment, picked up her case and walked away. Joe stood with his hands on his hips and glared at his friend. "You just ruined her fantasies for the next few weeks."

Heath smirked. "How do you know? She'll probably be dreaming about the two of us tonight."

Joe shouldered his bag and grunted, "I should take you over my knee for your cheek."

"Once was enough, thank you very much. But if you feel the need… I'd be happy to hone my skills on you?"

"In your dreams, sunshine." Joe made a move towards the exit. "But thanks for coming to pick me up. I appreciate it."

"We've just got time to get a drink in before last orders if you speed your arse up a bit."

"Oh, you are so asking for it. You can buy, then."

They bundled into Heath's waiting transport—the company's four by four—and headed for their local pub, The Highwayman's Arms. The bar was quiet, only a couple of locals propping up the bar and chatting with the landlord.

"Heath, Joe — what can I get you boys tonight?"

"The usual please, Frank. Quiet tonight?" Joe nodded to the other two customers, whom he also knew.

"Was busy earlier. Here you go." Frank pushed two foaming pints of beer across the bar and took Joe's money. Heath had settled his long legs beneath a corner table near the open fire so Joe picked up their drinks and joined him.

The two men took their first sips in appreciative silence then Heath gave Joe a calculating look. "You've fallen for him, haven't you? Your Angel?"

Joe scowled behind his pint. "His name's Oliver, and how the fuck would you know?"

"Body language. Everything about you screams luuurve." The word rolled off his tongue alongside a chuckle.

Joe gave him the finger and took another swig of his beer.

"Come on. Spill it. This one must be special to turn you into a pile of goo."

Joe quirked an eyebrow. "Goo?"

"Definitely. Stop trying to avoid the subject."

"You're not going to let this go, are you?" Joe sighed as Heath shook his dark head slowly. "Fine. He's beautiful. Sensitive. Responsive. Perfect."

"And presumably endearingly submissive if he's fallen for you?"

"Like I said, perfect. But he's been badly hurt in the past so I'm taking it slow."

"Is that why you haven't brought him back with you? I would have thought you'd want him where you could keep a close eye on him."

Joe smiled. "You know what it's like. Every instinct screaming to keep him safe and protected. Of course I would have preferred to bring him back here, but it was too soon."

Heath leant forward and clinked their glasses together. "Well, congratulations. I look forward to meeting the man who has already managed to wrap you round his little finger."

Joe was about to issue a sarcastic retort when his phone rang.

"Yes? Carey? I'm glad you called, I've been plotting ways to kill you slowly." There was a pause as Joe listened to his friend with growing horror.

"Understood. I'll be back first thing tomorrow. I'll meet you at the club."

He rang off and registered the concern on his friend's face.

"Carey says that Olly's previous Master showed up at The Underground tonight and is already boasting about how he has taken him back." Joe felt as if he might throw up at any moment.

"Who…?"

"Mark Vickery."

"Fuck. Was Oliver at the club with him?"

"No. Carey asked where he was and all Vickery would say was that he was being punished."

Joe was trembling now with a mixture of fear and fury. Heath took control.

"There's nothing you can do now. We'll go back to the island, make cover arrangements for tomorrow and the rest of the week if necessary, then I'll drive you back to London in the morning. If we leave at six we can be there by nine."

Joe pushed his chair back and stood up abruptly. "If that fucker has hurt one hair on Olly's head, I'll detach his balls with blunt pliers."

Heath's grin was feral. "Well, I know just where we can find a pair. Let's go."

Chapter Nine

Olly scrubbed his face with his hands, trying to rid himself of the dried salt that streaked his cheeks. Crying wasn't going to do him any good and he was sick of being a victim.

"You're such a fucking wuss, Olly. The only reason you're in this mess is because you're an idiot."

Talking to himself helped to break the silence, something that he didn't do well with. He liked music, chatter, life—not this muffled, dead world he now found himself in. He looked around and sighed. It was obvious from his surroundings that Mark had been planning all this for some time. During the months he had lived with Mark, the attic had been just like everyone else's, full of old suitcases, discarded rolls of wallpaper, dusty Christmas decorations and other assorted junk. Now it was a prison cell.

The eaves had been boarded up and he could see wisps of thick insulation poking through every crack and crevice. The floor was also boarded and covered in old, patterned carpet. The Velux window had been painted black and barred. Access was still through a hatch in the hall ceiling below, but rather than the retractable ladder that had been there previously, it was now reached by a proper set of wooden stairs. A heavy bolt secured the hatch—he'd spotted that when Mark had pushed him roughly up the stairs the night before.

The single large room in the roof had been modified to include a shower, sink and toilet at one end, screened off by what looked like a chipboard partition. Other than that, there was just the double bed that Olly now sat on. When he'd first been left alone he had wondered how on earth Mark had managed to get the bed through the loft hatch. Examination had shown that the bed frame was a kit of metal parts welded together. There were no screws or bolts to be loosened so that he could make himself a weapon. The mattress looked and smelt new.

What the hell had been going on in Mark's head that he would go to these lengths? Olly presumed that he had passed the work off as a normal loft conversion. In London, the window bars wouldn't be considered unusual as a security measure. There would have been no reason for anyone to report anything suspicious and he probably would have used workmen from out of the area anyway.

Olly had no way of knowing what the time was, but he guessed that around twenty-four hours had passed since he'd been put in the attic. Light came from a single fluorescent tube set in the apex of the roof, and it was on some kind of timer system because there was no switch that he could see. There had been one period of darkness so far and, if his sense of time was good, another was probably coming soon.

The room was comfortably warm though there was no visible source of heat. Still, the temperature was something to be grateful for because he had no clothes. There wasn't even a towel that he could wrap around himself. He shuddered at the memory of Mark roughly stripping him, and the slaps that had come when he'd tried to resist. It had been hopeless, of course. Mark was much bigger and stronger than he was. He also seemed to be fuelled by barely repressed fury. Olly touched his cut lip and winced as the fresh wound opened again.

He swallowed a sob and turned his attention to the metal belt around his waist. He had already examined every inch, desperate to find a weakness that he could exploit, but it seemed impregnable. The polished steel was half an inch thick, fitted close to his skin, and was held closed by a heavy padlock. A welded D ring connected to the long length of chain that allowed him to roam around the room. It was attached to the bed frame and just long enough that he could use the toilet but if, by some miracle, he managed to open the loft hatch, it would prevent him from getting any farther.

Olly punched the mattress in frustration. Joe was going to be so pissed off. Minutes after accepting Joe as his Master, Olly had climbed into a car with another man, and now look at him. Naked, chained to a bed and completely at the mercy of his apparently psychotic ex. Joe's handsome face filled his head. How he loved the stern look that dissolved so easily into indulgent affection. Joe was everything that Mark would never be. He was strict but kind, firm but loving. Every submissive bone in Olly's body ached to please him.

He shivered with desire as thoughts of Joe took him briefly away from the horror of his situation. Against all the odds, his cock began to swell. Tentatively he wrapped his fingers around his length and stroked gently.

"No! Stop it!" Olly dropped his dick as if he had been burnt. "Joe said no, so stop getting excited. Jesus!"

He half wished that Mark had tied his hands, because then it wouldn't be possible for him to disobey his Master. He moaned to himself, then the lights clicked off, leaving him in darkness.

"Great. Just fucking great."

He curled up on the mattress and closed his eyes, trying to ignore the throbbing heat between his legs. He replaced Joe's face in his mind with Mark's and focused on the light that had glinted on the scalpel in his hand. That did the trick. Reliving the threats, the terror that Mark would hurt Joe, had the same effect as a freezing cold shower.

Olly wrapped his arms around his body and pretended he was held in Joe's secure embrace. He'd been so happy. He'd left Joe's house suffused in a warm glow, feeling safer and more content than he had since his ordeal at the prison. He'd smelt Joe on the jumper he had borrowed—mixed spice, like freshly baked cakes. He had been happy with his thoughts and the world in general as he'd strolled along the street to the bus stop. He had already been looking forward to Friday when he would see Joe again, and had known his dreams that night would be coloured with thoughts of what they might do together.

He'd only gradually become aware of the car crawling slowly alongside him. When a window had whirred down he'd automatically leaned towards it, assuming the driver was looking for directions. Mark

Vickery had been the last person he'd expected, or wanted, to see. Their exchange replayed in his head.

"Mark? What are you doing here?"

"That's 'Sir' to you, Oliver. Get in the car."

"No! I don't belong to you anymore. You dumped me, remember?"

"Show some respect and get in the fucking car."

Olly had started to back away from the window. There had been a wild, uncontrolled look about his former Master that had scared him. Mark had parked the car and got out, propelling him back into a shop doorway. He had tried to push him away, but the glint of silver had stopped him in his tracks.

"You'll come with me, Oliver, or I'll bury this in Joe Dexter's heart."

The scalpel had touched Olly's neck, and even that light brush had raised a line of fiery pain.

"How do you know about Joe?"

"He's not what you need, boy."

"You didn't want me, Mark! You dumped me like so much garbage."

"You've had time to recover from your little mishap. You'll be more willing now. I'm looking forward to pounding that sweet little arse of yours."

The words had been whispered viciously into Olly's ear as a hand had twisted into his hair, holding him in place. "Of course, you'll need warming up first. How long has it been since you felt the kiss of leather on your skin?"

Olly had struggled, but none of the passers-by had so much as glanced in his direction. Mark's big frame had concealed him from view and anyone looking would have assumed the tall man had been getting up close and personal with his wife or girlfriend.

"Keep still, you little fucker. You can save the struggling for later. I enjoy a bit of resistance. Now, you and I are going to walk to the car like we are the best of friends. I know where Dexter lives and where he works. Do as you're told and he won't get hurt."

Terrified that Mark would do as he threatened, Olly had climbed into the car and sat there helplessly as Mark had driven away. What else could he have done? Mark seemed to have reached a new level of insanity, and there was no way that Olly would risk Joe being hurt. He hadn't resisted when they'd reached Mark's house and Mark had pulled him inside.

He had stripped Olly right there in the hallway.

"These clothes stink of Dexter. Get them off."

When Olly had hesitated, Mark had shoved him down on the stairs then ripped off his shoes and socks, launching them at the front door like missiles. Olly had tried to crawl away from him up the stairs, but had been dragged back, gaining some bruises in the process. His trousers and underwear had been unceremoniously yanked down and tossed aside. The neck of Joe's jumper had torn as Mark had ripped it off, and his shirt had lost a few buttons.

Naked and terrified, Olly had tried to protect himself, only to have his arm brutally twisted behind his back. Mark had thrust him up the stairs, then up again into the attic. Olly had barely had time to realise what Mark had been doing before the metal belt had been locked around his waist. That was when Mark had hit him with a violent backhander across the face.

"That's for jumping into bed with another man, you little slut. It's going to be fun teaching you a lesson, because you deserve to be punished for running away from me, Oliver. Don't you?"

Vickery hadn't even waited for a reply. He'd left Olly cowering on the floor, pulled the hatch door closed behind him and had disappeared. Olly hadn't seen him since.

Olly whimpered and curled into a tighter ball. He could feel the press of metal around his waist and it was impossible to sleep. He was hungry and scared, dreading the thought of what Mark might do to him.

The room was so well soundproofed that he hadn't heard Mark climbing the stairs. It was the rattle of the bolt withdrawing on the hatch that gave him away. Light flooded the room and Olly scuttled to the back of the bed, drawing his knees up defensively.

Mark shut the hatch firmly and smiled at him.

"Did you miss me, boy?"

Olly caught sight of the whip coiled in his hand and shuddered.

"Let me go, Mark. I won't tell anyone, I promise."

"I've been out tonight telling everyone at the club how you've seen the error of your ways and come back to me. I have no intention of letting you go."

"Why are you doing this? You didn't want me... What's changed?"

Olly started to feel desperate. If Mark was telling a plausible story in public, no one would look for him. Joe would assume he'd changed his mind. A tear rolled unchecked down his face.

Mark stood menacingly at the end of the bed, letting the whip uncoil and drape against his thigh.

"I spent a lot of time and money turning you into what I wanted. Did you really think I'd let all that effort go to waste?"

"I don't understand..."

"Things went a little wrong at the prison — they took their roles a little too seriously. It was never supposed to go so far."

Mark was pacing up and down, snapping the whip against the floor. Olly winced at the sound but concentrated on what Mark was saying, what he was admitting.

"You mean you were involved in what happened to me?"

"The riot was an unfortunate coincidence. They were supposed to take you, frighten you a bit and then I was going to ride to the rescue in true hero style. You would have been so grateful you'd have done anything."

Olly felt sick.

"You paid those thugs?"

Mark nodded. "It was a good plan. But then the riot blew up and they took advantage of the situation."

"Took advantage! Have you any idea what they did to me?"

Mark smiled coldly. "Oh, yes. I know every detail. But you weren't strong enough, were you? You wouldn't let me touch you after it happened. What fucking use were you then?"

"You son of a bitch!" Olly's fear was swallowed up by his fury. When Mark grabbed him by the arms, he fought back with all his strength but, though he managed to land a couple of satisfying blows, Mark was just too big. A glancing strike to the side of his head blanked his vision and Mark threw him onto the bed, then used his belt to strap his hands to the metal rail at its head.

When the whip lashed his back for the first time, Olly screamed. By the tenth stroke he could no longer make any sound. The pain was all-consuming. When he was done, Mark came to sit next to him on the bed and began to stroke and squeeze his arse.

"It's late and I need my beauty sleep, so you stay here and think about what a bad boy you've been. I'll see you in the morning."

Olly barely registered the sounds of Mark leaving. His back was on fire, his wrists ached where Mark had left them tied and his skin crawled where the man's hands had been on him. He couldn't believe how naïve he'd been to think that Mark had ever felt anything for him. Now, knowing what he had done, he felt nothing but raw hatred. He was absolutely certain of one thing, though — he would never give Mark Vickery the satisfaction of seeing him beaten. No matter what the bastard did to him, he would not give up.

Chapter Ten

When Olly drifted out of a sleep fractured by nightmares, he wished he could have remained oblivious a little while longer. He was still lying on his front, but his arms were free and that could only mean one thing. The pressure of a hand on his arse confirmed it. *Mark.*

He twisted his head round with a groan to see Mark leering down at him from where he was sitting on the edge of the bed.

"Good morning, Oliver. I hope you are feeling a little more contrite this morning?"

"Fuck off."

"You never were a morning person, were you? You've got fifteen minutes to use the bathroom before I go to work, so get up."

"Why can't I use it after you've gone?"

"Because I'm not stupid enough to leave you with anything that you could hurt yourself with, and that includes towels and razors. Get the fuck up when I tell you to."

Mark yanked on the chain attached to Olly's belt, forcing him to move and discover that his back was agonisingly painful. Olly bit back the curse that rose to his lips and limped across to the shower.

The spray was weak and tepid but it felt good to get clean, even if he had to do everything while Mark watched. At least he'd had the decency to turn away while he'd relieved himself. Olly's hands shook a little as he shaved without a mirror. His lip and one side of his face were tender to the touch, and he could imagine what the bruises must look like. Mark gave him a toothbrush and paste, then, as soon as he was finished, took everything back and dumped it all in a plastic bag.

"Go and get back on the bed, face down."

Olly glared at him but did as he'd been told.

"I want you ready for me when I get back tonight."

Olly squirmed as Mark pressed down on the small of his back, agitating some of the welts left by the whip.

"Open your legs wider — it will hurt less."

Out of the corner of his eye, Olly could see Mark lubing a metal plug. The bullet-shaped piece of metal looked huge, and was attached to a rubber tube that ended in a flat metal disc.

"Relax."

Olly gasped as Mark pushed the cold, slick metal against his entrance. Relaxing was not an option and it hurt. The thing was bloody massive.

"I chose this specifically because it's impossible for you to push it out. You'll be beautifully stretched for me by this evening."

Olly panted as his body adjusted to the invader.

"And just to make sure that you don't get off without me or try to take the plug out..." Mark locked

Olly's bruised wrists into leather cuffs and attached them by short chains to D-rings on the sides of his belt, ensuring that he could reach neither the base of the plug nor his cock.

"You can't leave me like this, you bastard!" Olly rolled awkwardly onto his back to see Mark disappearing through the loft hatch.

"I can do whatever the hell I like with you, boy. You belong to me."

The hatch slammed shut on Mark's disdainful laugh, cutting the sound off. For a few moments Olly fought the cuffs, but it was no use. He slowed his breathing and tried to calm down. The plug was pressing against his prostate with every movement he made, and his cock had hardened to the point of pain. He screamed his frustration into the silence and kicked his heels into the mattress. The tantrum didn't help, so he levered himself into a sitting position on the edge of the bed and began to re-examine the room for anything he might be able to use to pick the padlocks on the wrist cuffs.

He circled the bed and, to his surprise, found a tray on the floor. There were two cartons of juice—both with the straws already inserted—a plate of chopped fruit and another that was piled with small cubes of cheese and ham. Olly's stomach growled. The food wasn't much but it was better than nothing, even if he did have to get down on his hands and knees and eat it like an animal.

Pride didn't even come a close second to hunger. He ate half the food on both plates and drank one of the juice drinks. He was still hungry but had no idea how long it would be before he got anything else, and saving some of the food at least gave him something to look forward to.

He resumed his search of the room, desperately hoping that a stray nail or screw might have been dropped into a crack or crevice at the edge of the carpet. By the time he had crawled the entire circumference of the attic, his knees ached and his back was giving him sharp reminders of the punishment it had taken. Despairing and exhausted, he collapsed back onto the bed and allowed his eyes to close. A few minutes of rest wouldn't hurt. For a while, thoughts whirled around his head, but eventually fatigue defeated his anxiety and fear and he drifted off to sleep.

* * * *

"This place could be straight out of a scene from *Stepford Wives*."

Heath's comment brought the ghost of a smile to Joe's lips. They were parked a couple of hundred yards away from Mark Vickery's Victorian detached house, which sat on a tree-lined street of similar buildings. Most had high walls to protect their privacy and cast-iron gates in front of their drives. Mark's place was no exception. Two enormous oak trees that predated the house by a couple of centuries blocked any sight of the front door or ground-floor windows. Through the branches it was possible to catch glimpses of the roof, chimney pots and the glint of glass.

"If you ask me it's more disturbia than suburbia," Carey's low tones grunted from the rear seat.

Joe shifted impatiently in his seat. "He's been gone half an hour. How about we indulge in a little breaking and entering?"

"Patience. I've got Alistair watching the hospital. He's going to call when Doctor Psycho gets to work."

Joe drummed his fingers on the dashboard until Heath laid a hand across them. "He'll be okay, Joe."

"He's been through too much. I want him back with me. I want him safe." Joe's voice broke a little, shattering the illusion of calm that he was trying to maintain.

Carey's mobile rang. "It's Alistair." He listened for a few seconds, then rang off. "Vickery's there and he's scheduled for surgery for most of the day. Unless he cuts off his own fingers there's not much chance he'll be back."

Joe was already halfway out of the car. Fortunately it was a quiet street and nobody but a passing tabby saw them cross the street and slip through the gates. Joe took the direct approach and hammered on the front door before stabbing at the bell a few times. He peered through the letterbox but there was no sign of life.

"If he's in there, he can't come to the door. Check the windows, Heath. I'll head around the back."

There was a large alarm box on a side wall with a blue light beneath it that blinked at regular intervals, but on closer inspection Joe could see that it was a fake. There were no wires leading from it at all.

"Cheap bastard," he muttered under his breath, though he was grateful. Carey was good with electronics, but the less time they had to spend disabling security devices, the better. The back door was firmly locked and there was no glass that he could break. He cursed and moved on, meeting Heath at the corner of the house.

"I've found a window with a rotten frame. It should be easy to prise open."

Heath showed him where it was. It was fairly small but Joe reckoned he might be able to squeeze through. Heath used the long screwdriver he had with him to lever the frame, and the wood splintered easily.

It took a bit of wriggling before Joe could fit his broad shoulders through the small gap. He cursed as his shirtsleeve tore and a jagged splinter penetrated his flesh. He collapsed into what proved to be a larder, scattering tins of food around him as he went.

"Fuck!" He pulled the shard of wood from his arm and mopped carelessly at the blood that trickled from the small wound. "Heath—I'll let you in the back door."

He negotiated his way out of the larder and into the adjoining kitchen. The key was in the door and he grinned. It was beginning to feel like luck was on their side. Soon the three of them stood in the kitchen.

"Be methodical. Search every room and every cupboard. Meet back here in five minutes."

They split up and began to search. Heath headed upstairs, Joe took the ground floor and Carey offered to go and check any outbuildings. He was the first back, clutching a bundle of torn clothes that he showed to Joe. "Are these Olly's?"

Joe stroked the wool of his own jumper and nodded grimly. "Yes. He has to be here somewhere."

There was an excited shout from above them. "There's a locked hatch up here. Did we bring bolt cutters?"

Joe shot up the stairs with Carey in hot pursuit. He stared up at the hatch. "That lock's excessive for an attic. Have you tried banging?"

Heath nodded. "Yes, but the sound is very muffled as if there's some kind of soundproofing up there."

"No bolt cutters, but we do have this." Carey held out a small hacksaw. "I'll go and check out the tool shed for anything better."

Joe found that his hands were shaking too much to use the saw effectively, so he left that job to Heath and sat miserably on the bottom of the attic steps.

"It's going through, Joe. It won't take long."

Joe knew that Heath was trying to be reassuring, but every second it took to get Olly back was a second too long. He hated feeling this out of control. The sound of the hacksaw cutting into the metal padlock was grating on his nerves and he really, really wanted to hit something.

Carey thundered back up the stairs, a triumphant look on his face. "I think Mr Vickery has been doing some metalwork recently. I found this!"

He was holding a plasma torch and a welder's mask. Heath grinned. "Hand them over."

"Try not to set the house on fire, okay?" Joe was a bit disconcerted at Heath's enthusiasm for power tools.

"Do you want your boyfriend back or not?" Heath raised a dark eyebrow.

Joe growled. Heath winked and fired up the torch. Seconds later, he was pulling metal pieces apart and shoving the loft hatch up. Heath disappeared into the loft and for a few seconds Joe couldn't move. He was frozen to the bottom step, his mind a blank. *What if...?*

Heath's yell brought him back to reality. "He's here, Joe, he's fine. Get up here."

Joe scrambled up the steps and into the harshly lit loft space. Olly was cowering back against the end of the bed, looking absolutely terrified. Joe took in the metal belt around Olly's waist and the chains at his wrists and screamed inside. He kept his voice as calm as he could manage.

"Olly, it's me, Joe. Everything's going to be okay."

He walked across to the bed and folded Olly into his arms. "I love you, sweetheart. You're safe now."

Olly's slight form trembled in his hold and he felt the warm wetness of tears soaking into his shirt where Olly's face was pressed against him. Joe just held him tightly as Heath paced around them, looking at the chains that held Olly to the bed.

"I'll use the torch to cut the chain. The hacksaw will take care of the cuffs. The belt will have to wait until we're away from here. I can't use the torch that close to his body."

"Do it." Joe stroked Olly's tangled hair and kept him still as Heath used the torch to free him. Heath used a pair of pliers to twist the links apart that attached the cuffs to the belt, and Olly was able to fling his arms around Joe's body.

"You shouldn't have come, Joe, he'll hurt you." Olly's words were laced with panic.

"Hush, now. Vickery's a coward, through and through. Don't worry—we have a plan to deal with him. Just worry about yourself for now. Let's get you dressed."

Heath passed over the pile of clothes that Carey had rescued from the shed and Joe detached himself carefully from Olly's hold.

"Fuck, Joe! Have you seen his back?" Heath's voice was dark with anger.

Joe turned Olly around and saw the welts that covered his back for the first time. His voice was brittle. "Vickery will pay for this, but now's not the time. Let's get Olly away from here. I want him safe. Then we can deal with this sadistic bastard."

Chapter Eleven

Olly sank beneath the scented water and held his breath for a few seconds. He wanted every square inch of his body to be steamed and scrubbed clean. The memory of Vickery's hands on his body made him feel dirty. He surfaced, brushed strands of wet hair away from his eyes and relaxed against the end of the tub with a sigh.

"That sounded sad." Joe twirled a finger into the water from his seat on the end of the tub.

"Will I ever be free of him, Joe?"

"You already are." Joe sounded absolutely certain and that made Olly's world a little bit better.

"But..."

"But nothing. I'm your Master now. It's my job to keep you safe. Vickery will never lay a finger on you again."

Olly knew that Joe's words should make him feel completely secure. It wasn't his place to worry about things. Though it was a huge relief to be free and to know that Joe didn't blame him for being taken, there was still the niggling fear that Vickery would make good on his threats. When Olly closed his eyes, he could still see the evil gleam of the scalpel in his hand.

"He said he'd hurt you if I didn't go with him. He forced me into the car and he was too strong. I tried to fight but I couldn't get away." He knew there was a note of panic in his voice.

"It wasn't your fault, Olly. None of it." Joe sounded tense and angry, but Olly knew that it wasn't directed at him. "The man has a serious problem and I am going to deal with it. You need to trust me."

Olly nuzzled against him over the side of the bath, leaving wet patches on his clothes.

"I do trust you. I do."

Joe flicked water at him. "Come on. Time to dry off before you shrivel up like a prune."

Olly looked down automatically. "Too late." He palmed his wrinkled cock beneath the water. "Oh, you poor thing! He definitely needs some loving attention, Sir."

"He?" Joe rolled his eyes. "No, don't tell me. I don't need to know."

Joe helped Olly stand up, then wrapped a huge, fluffy towel around him. The warm water had helped but Olly still ached everywhere. His arse was sore where the plug had been forced into him, and his face still burned at the memory of Joe extracting it. His cheek was bruised purple and black down one side, and his wrists were ringed with the same mottled colours where he'd fought the belt around them when Mark had tied him down. Worst of all was his back. He'd been whipped before, willingly, but never so mercilessly. Joe had told him that his skin was broken in a couple of places.

Olly whimpered as Joe patted him dry. He was being so gentle but it still hurt. He followed meekly when Joe led him to Carey's guest room.

"Lie down on the bed, beautiful. I'm going to find some ointment for your back."

Joe pulled the door closed behind him. Olly crawled onto the bed and positioned himself carefully on his front, hugging two of the biggest, squashiest pillows he'd ever come across.

He didn't remember much of the journey back from Mark's house. He had hidden his face against Joe's chest and concentrated on the strong arms holding him close. That was all that had mattered. They had come to Carey's because they were fairly certain that Mark didn't know where he lived, and it was closer than Joe's place. Though Carey also had a small flat at the club, this was his home—a modern apartment with an underground garage and security in the lobby. Joe apparently had a key, because they went up in the lift while Carey stopped to talk to the security guard and give him a description of Vickery in case he did show up.

Carey's apartment was all high ceilings and light. Though modern, it still felt homey and there were books and photographs on every surface. Olly managed a smile when he realised that many of the pictures were of Alistair.

Heath had suggested a hot bath and had even gone to run it while he and Joe had cuddled on the sofa. There was an enigma. Joe's best friend was bloody scary. Not only was he physically imposing, he oozed dominance from every pore. He was gorgeous too. Olly wondered if he had a partner. The spark of attraction wasn't there for him—Joe was his perfect man—but he couldn't imagine a stunning specimen like Heath being alone. Olly was a little nervous around him, but he had shown him nothing but kindness, and Olly had realised that Heath was more like Joe than was initially apparent.

He could feel himself drifting off to sleep. He was so tired. Now the tension was gone from his body, it was as if the will to stay alert had gone. He heard the door open, then the side of the bed dipped a little as Joe sat next to him. When Joe started to rub soothing cream onto his sore back, he snuggled deeper into the pillows and sighed happily.

"Tell me if I hurt you love."

"S'good." Olly knew he wasn't that coherent, but the gentle strokes on his skin were pushing him further towards sleep. He gave in and let the comforting darkness take him.

Joe carried on smoothing the lotion into Olly's back. He loved the soft, sensuous feel of his skin and hated to see it marred by the welts left by Vickery's whip. The only marks on Olly's body should be his. Two of the strokes had bitten deep enough to break the skin, but the cuts had already closed and he was as sure as he could be that they wouldn't scar permanently.

He ducked his head to breathe in the scent of Olly's newly washed curls. The tumble of gold fell in wild disarray across his face, so Joe pushed it away to expose a defined cheekbone and the velvet lobe of one ear. He was very tempted to press kisses against the skin, but he knew that Olly desperately needed to rest. He got up and pulled the curtains to shut out the light, then crept towards the door. He took a last look at his sleeping angel before slipping away, leaving the door open in case Olly had bad dreams and cried out.

Carey's lounge was the focal point of his home and that was where Joe found Heath, stretched out in a deep leather chair, long fingers encircling a mug of coffee.

"Hey. How is he?"

"Sleeping."

"He's beautiful, Joe, and very brave."

"I know. I'm not sure I deserve him."

"Don't be bloody ridiculous." Heath looked genuinely annoyed. "You've been looking for 'the one' for so long, it's about time you gave yourself a break."

Joe grunted. "I want you to get to know him under better circumstances. He has the potential to be quite a handful."

Heath chuckled. "Then you'll be the one to bring him in line and he'll love you all the more for it."

Joe paced up and down the room, studiously ignoring the knowing smile on Heath's face.

Carey stomped into the room and threw himself onto the couch. "You're wearing down my carpet, Joe. Sit down, for pity's sake. Security guys are briefed, though I doubt our Mr Vickery is going to discover that Olly's missing until this evening. I can't wait to see him at the club tonight."

"Me either." Heath's grin was just a little bit evil.

"That fucker deserves everything that's coming to him." Carey's voice was full of suppressed fury.

Joe frowned. "I want him in the hands of the police without having to involve Olly. He's been through enough, and I don't think he could handle reliving everything again. You know what it's like. Even the most understanding cop would ask questions about his past, the lifestyle... Even with his injuries, it would be difficult to prove he didn't consent. It would be Olly's word against Vickery's."

"And that is why tonight is so important. It will work, Joe, you'll see." Heath curled his fingers into a fist and thumped the arm of his chair for emphasis.

There was a slight creak from the door behind them. Joe turned to find Olly leaning against the frame, wearing just a pair of very skimpy briefs.

"I woke up and you weren't there, Sir..." He looked confused, scared and ridiculously young.

Carey licked his lips suggestively and Joe glared at him before wrapping Olly up in his arms. "Let's get you back to bed, sweetheart. At some point you and I must have a conversation about who gets to see you in your underwear, okay?"

"Yes, Sir."

Joe could hear both of his friends chuckling behind him.

"Get some rest, Joe," Heath ordered. "You didn't sleep last night and you'll need to be alert later on."

Heath's suggestion was sensible and Joe didn't argue. He guided Olly back to the bedroom, trying to ignore the warmth of the boy's bare skin pressing against him.

Joe lifted Olly back into bed and pulled the covers over him. He stripped down and slipped under the covers too. Immediately, Olly scooted across and cuddled against him. Just the closeness of Olly's body, his warmth and silky skin had Joe's cock filling. He shifted so that Olly wouldn't feel it, but Olly had other ideas. Joe groaned as Olly caressed his belly lightly, then wrapped his fingers around his Master's length and began to stroke.

"Fuck me, Sir." Olly pleaded. "Need you in me."

"You're not ready for that, Olly." Joe had to grit his teeth as Olly kept his hand moving, but he didn't have the will to push the boy away. It felt so good.

"Please! I need you to own every part of me."

Joe wrapped his bigger hand around Olly's small one and stopped his movement with a squeeze. "Believe me, love, I own every inch and I don't need to fuck you to prove it. You're mine and that means doing as you're told, so go to sleep."

"But…"

"Enough. You've earned yourself a punishment, Oliver." Joe kissed him to soften the words.

"Oh, goody." Olly cuddled closer with a happy sigh and Joe realised that he'd been played.

"Brat." He ruffled blond curls affectionately. Within seconds Olly was peacefully asleep and Joe was left with a stiff, aching problem. Awkwardly, he extracted himself from Olly's limpet-like grip. There was sleepy grumbling from beside him, but Olly didn't wake.

Joe crept into the bathroom and applied a hand to his aching cock. He wondered at his own restraint. It would have been so easy to pin Olly to the bed and take what was being offered so freely, but Joe wanted the first time he made love to Olly to be perfect. That wasn't going to happen until he was convinced that Olly was fully recovered from his ordeal. The boy was special, and there was no way Joe was going to risk damaging him.

Chapter Twelve

"I want to come." Olly stuck out his lower lip and pouted in the best way he knew how.

"No. Absolutely, categorically no." Joe's tone left Olly in no doubt that the subject was not up for debate. He chewed on his lower lip anxiously.

Carey gave him a reassuring smile. "I'm not letting Alistair come either. You can keep each other company."

Olly glanced at where Alistair was sitting cross-legged on a sofa, bare feet sticking out of faded jeans, the sleeves of his dark red sweater pushed up to the elbows. He looked completely at ease that Carey had made the decision for him. Alistair patted the seat next to him. "It'll be fun, Olly. We can raid the fridge and watch horror films until they come home."

Olly blinked away tears that were too quick to rise. He was wearing Alistair's clothes and still felt a bit bleary-eyed from sleeping the day away — it was all too unsettling. He was scared and didn't want to be away from Joe for a minute. Just the thought of his gorgeous man being in the same place as Mark Vickery brought him out in a cold sweat.

He looked up as Joe's broad frame blocked out the light. Joe cupped his face, then gave him a thorough kissing. Olly parted his lips willingly, letting Joe take what he wanted. Stubble grazed his face as Joe pulled him close. He was almost out of breath when Joe finally released him.

"I need to know you're safe, Olly."

Olly nodded and gave Joe a hug. "I know. But you could get hurt…"

"Not a chance." That was Heath's deep voice. "Don't worry, Olly, Carey and I will keep an eye on him for you."

There wasn't a trace of teasing and Olly felt his anxiety ease a little. He curled onto the sofa next to Alistair and looked at the three tall, handsome men in front of him. Heath looked the most intimidating and very sexy in black leather trousers and a snug black T-shirt. Carey was in leather as well, but wore a loose, grey silk shirt, untucked. Joe looked devastatingly attractive in black jeans that sat low on his slim hips, and a long-sleeved black T-shirt with seams edged in silver.

"Is everything in place, Carey?" Joe sounded a little gruff and there were tiny lines of tension around his eyes.

Carey sneered with a twist of his lips. "Yes. If he shows up, and I know he will, he won't suspect a thing. Christian knows what to do and I've rung several friends to make sure they show up and play along."

"He's an arrogant son of a bitch. When he discovers that Olly is gone he'll probably try your place, but then he'll go to The Underground. He'll think that you'll go there with Olly to show him off, because that's what he would do." Heath said with certainty and the others nodded their agreement. Olly crossed his fingers and hoped that Mark would be as predictable as they all seemed to think.

"Are you going to tell us what you're planning?" Olly wasn't sure he really wanted to know, but he had to ask. He and Alistair had been kept carefully out of the intense discussions that had been going on that evening, and neither of them had been around during the day.

"When it's all over, sweetheart. Until then you just have to trust me." Olly looked into Joe's glimmering blue eyes in an attempt to detect any sign that he was being fobbed off. All he saw were compassion and concern.

"I'll be here when you get back, I promise." Olly gave up the fight and settled back on the sofa.

Alistair and Carey exchanged glances. Neither of them spoke, but Olly knew that the look held a whole conversation. Alistair had his instructions, Olly was sure of that, and letting him anywhere near the door wasn't going to be part of the night's activities.

Carey beckoned to Alistair, who went immediately to him. "Behave yourself, Alistair. Look after our guest."

"Yes, Sir." Alistair's tone was soft and restrained. He tilted his head back so that Carey could kiss him and smiled as Carey gripped his hair tightly, holding him close. Olly felt warm at the sight. The two men were so obviously in love, and he was glad for them.

Heath gave him a cheery wave and followed Carey towards the front door. Olly turned to Joe and found himself enveloped in a fierce hug.

"Be good." His deep voice cracked a little, and Olly couldn't bring himself to speak. He just nodded and watched as Joe left and pulled the door closed behind him.

For a moment Olly didn't know what to do, he felt so lost. Then Alistair grabbed his hand and pulled him back to the sofa.

"Come on—you choose a film. We need to distract ourselves."

"How can you be so cheerful? Aren't you afraid for Carey?"

Alistair tilted his head to one side thoughtfully. "Carey takes care of me. He can definitely take care of himself. Nope, I'm not scared and I hope they teach that bastard Vickery a lesson. He gives Dominants a bad name, and he shouldn't be allowed to hurt anyone ever again."

"I wish I knew what they're up to."

"No doubt we'll get all the gory details later. Joe and Heath are amazing, but I wouldn't want to be their enemy. Vickery has no idea how much trouble he's in." His tone was mildly gleeful and Olly couldn't help but smile.

"They're all a bit overprotective, aren't they?"

"Get used to it! Joe's likely to cause a riot if you so much as break a fingernail. Carey once sacked a bartender at the club because he didn't like the way the poor guy was looking at me. He had to hire him back the next day and apologise!"

Suddenly Olly felt shy. "I'm not good enough for him."

"Who says so? Anyway, that's Joe's decision. You must be very special to him, Olly. Carey told me he hasn't been with anyone for a long time."

"He's played with you, though, hasn't he?" Olly beat back feelings of jealousy.

"Only with Carey watching. He can really handle a paddle, you know."

Olly felt his face heat and he scuffed his foot into the carpet. Alistair rescued him from his embarrassment by shoving him playfully back onto the couch. "Film time! We need snacks. Lots and lots of sugary snacks — that'll teach those overgrown macho men not to leave us behind!"

* * * *

Joe surveyed the crowd gathered on the dance floor at The Underground and adjusted the black leather mask across his eyes. The place was packed, bodies gyrating to the pounding beat of heavy rock music. Dry ice swirled lazily at knee height while red lights strobed across the room, highlighting bare skin and gleaming leather.

"I don't think I've ever seen so many people here." Joe edged back into the shadows of the booth he shared with Heath.

"Word gets around. You're well respected, Joe, and nobody likes what Vickery is doing. There's not a single decent Dominant who wants subs subjected to the kind of treatment he deals out. It gives us all a bad name. The Underground has always had an excellent reputation, and the members don't want that to change."

Joe gave him a worried look. "What if this all goes wrong?"

"It won't. Carey could give masterclasses in cunning plans. He's a devious sod and he loves every minute of this. Not only that, he's going to make a bloody fortune tonight—just look around you!"

Joe nodded slowly. He wondered if he was the only one feeling the palpable air of expectation. Everyone knew that something was going on—they just weren't sure what.

The Underground was known for its spontaneous theme nights. Members often showed up only to be instructed at the door that there was a 'no shirt' rule or that a charity auction for willing subs was taking place. Tonight they had been met by a demurely dressed Christian handing out masks with a glint in his eye.

"Good evening, Mr Dexter, Sir—Mr Anders. It's very nice to see you. Masks are required this evening. Leather for Dominants, velvet for submissives. Anyone wearing a velvet mask and no collar is available to play with. Enjoy the night and if there is anything I can help with, do let me know."

"Thank you, Christian." Joe had watched Heath as he had employed his best stern expression and Christian had tried not to melt into the floor. "Has the member we are expecting arrived yet?"

"Yes, Sir."

"And which mask did he select?"

"Velvet, Sir. It's been a busy evening and I may have inadvertently switched their meanings."

Christian's cheeks had turned a little pink as Heath leaned towards him. "Well done. I think that masks won't be the only thing switching tonight."

They had put their own leather masks in place and taken the back stairs to the gallery overlooking the main dance floor. From one of the private booths they had an excellent view, while cleverly arranged lighting ensured that no one down below was able to see them.

One of the waiting staff, dressed only in a net thong and the silver mask that marked him as an employee, delivered a tray of drinks to their table. Heath put a hand gently on the boy's bare shoulder and pushed until he knelt next to him.

"What happened to the rest of your uniform tonight?"

The young man kept his eyes firmly fixed to the floor but spoke confidently. "Mr Hoffman requested it, Sir. He wanted the table staff to be more…distracting tonight. It wasn't compulsory, Sir, but everyone's helping."

Heath chuckled. "Carey thinks of everything, Joe. Look at them! They're virtually naked — enough to stop any hot-blooded Dom from thinking straight."

Joe nodded. "Relay our thanks to the staff when you get a chance. You all look spectacular."

"Pleasure, Sir. Olly was sweet to everyone." He climbed gracefully to his feet and scurried away.

Joe was first to notice the subtle change in the atmosphere and the increasing noise level from the dance floor. He leant forward slightly to get a better look.

"They have him, Heath."

Heath sipped his drink and stood up to lean on the balcony rail. "They do. And he's not happy about it. Shall we head downstairs?" He and Joe both removed their masks.

The crowd parted as they crossed the dance floor to stand in front of the raised stage where a tall, bare-chested man was threatening two leather-clad Doms with a bar stool, just like a lion-tamer who'd realised that his beast was not as domesticated as he'd assumed. His velvet mask was slightly askew and his hair dishevelled. The remnants of his shirt lay at his feet.

The two Doms, both enormous men who wouldn't have looked out of place on a rugby pitch, stood admiring their handiwork.

"You're wearing a velvet mask, boy—that makes you fair game tonight. Weren't you listening when you came in?"

Mark Vickery, his face purple with rage, wielded his makeshift weapon wildly and spat obscenities at them.

"You're not a very well trained sub, are you?" One man yanked the stool away from Vickery while the other grabbed his arms and held him still. His captor grinned as the crowd around him laughed. "Someone cut his trousers off. I want a better view."

"Use this." Joe's quiet, authoritative voice cut through the noise of the excited crowd. He held out a gleaming scalpel, which an onlooker enthusiastically employed to slice the leather away from the prisoner's legs, leaving him clad only in a pair of red briefs.

"And those."

Fabric parted, and Vickery was left completely exposed to the crowd, and to Joe's steely gaze.

"Not much to shout about." Heath's tone was derisive.

Vickery was apoplectic with rage, spit running down his chin. He looked rabid and completely out of control as he struggled violently.

"You're dead, Dexter! You stole my property. Let go of me, you fucking ape—"

Joe slapped his face, once. The sound slashed across the now silent room.

"That's the last time I'm going to touch you, Vickery. You disgust me. You chose a submissive's mask. It's about time you realised that submission deserves respect. It takes a huge amount of courage to give yourself to another man. It's a gift that should be treated with the care and reverence it deserves. Perhaps this little humiliation will teach you restraint, though I doubt it. So just in case you think you can walk out of here and go back to your old ways, I've arranged for a few artistic photographs to be taken. It's amazing what Photoshop can do these days." A young guy with a complicated-looking camera appeared and started snapping away enthusiastically. "I'm sure your employers and your family will be delighted to receive pictures of you looking so…ecstatic."

Vickery spat at his feet. "That fucking idiot on the door told me velvet was for Dominants."

Joe stared at him coldly. "You must have been mistaken."

He turned his back on the struggling man and paused. Speaking very softly, he managed to sound absolutely terrifying. "If you ever come near Oliver again, if you contact him in any way, if I even see you within shouting distance of him, those pictures will be in the mail." Then he walked away with Heath at his side.

The crowd merged behind them, and soon all they could hear were the mingled sounds of laughter and cursing as Vickery was chivied towards the exit.

Back in their booth on the balcony, Joe raised a glass. "To revenge."

"And isn't it sweet?" Heath clinked his glass against Joe's.

Carey joined them and downed his orange juice in one swallow. "Are you sure I can't let them mark him up just a little bit?"

Joe frowned. "No. I want him humiliated, not damaged. That would make us as bad as him. Losing his clothes will damage his ego, nothing more, but for him that's going to be worse than any beating."

"I hope your photographer got all the right angles, Carey?" Heath grinned.

"He's a photography major—I think he's planning on turning this into a class project."

Joe leant back into the padded seat and sighed. "You know, I'm not sure that the threat of blackmail is going to be enough to keep him away from Olly. He may not show his face around here anytime soon, but I'll still be watching my back."

Heath nodded, his expression serious. "You could be right. We should head back to The Edge in the morning and let Olly start getting used to his new life."

Joe nodded. "Agreed." Then his serious expression dissolved into a smile. "But that was fun, wasn't it? And that man really does have a very small dick."

Carey chuckled in agreement. "About the size of a cocktail sausage. I made sure Christian was on a break. As soon as Vickery's out the door his membership will be rescinded. Of course, he's not going to be very comfortable without any clothes and I do believe the local police are planning a drive-by right about now. I'm sure he'll enjoy a night in the cells."

"Carey, you evil sod. Remind me never to piss you off." Heath looked across at Joe. "Let's go. If they've been doing their best to achieve a sugar high, we'll probably have to peel Alistair and Olly off the ceiling by now."

Carey stood up. "I'm coming too. I can't wait to see the look on Olly's face when you tell him about tonight."

Joe smiled. "Thank you. Both of you. This will mean so much to Olly."

All he wanted to do was get back to Carey's place and wrap Olly in his arms. Then he would spend some time tasting every inch of his lover until Olly begged to come. If he begged really, really prettily, Joe thought he might relent and grant him permission — in a couple of days' time. He chuckled to himself. Suddenly life felt good.

Chapter Thirteen

Olly stood on the east beach of the little island that was home to The Edge, Joe and Heath's corporate training business. Of course, it was his home now too. He had spent three blissful months exploring and getting to know his new surroundings. He loved being near the sea and had spent hours reading on the little pebbled beach, which was edged with trees and very private. It also gave him plenty of opportunity to lie there, stare at the clouds scudding past and imagine all the things he would like Joe to do to him.

He picked up a couple of flat, smooth pebbles and skimmed them into the water. The first landed with a dismal plop, but the second bounced six times before disappearing.

"Yes!" Olly jumped up and down in excitement. That was the first time he had managed to get the angle right. Realising what he was doing, he stopped jumping and looked around to make sure nobody had been watching his antics.

There was a small part of him that wished someone had been. Joe had been gone for almost three weeks and Olly missed him horribly. He knew it was for a good cause, but that didn't make the empty, lost feelings go away. Heath was doing his best to make him feel better and keep him occupied, but it wasn't enough. Olly needed Joe the way he needed air.

He scuffed his feet, making indentations in the shingle, and stared at the water. Joe had gone back to London to make all the arrangements necessary to wind up his practice there and move it north. That meant finding alternative treatment for patients unable or unwilling to travel. He also had to talk to all his contacts who fed him consulting work and convince them that he wasn't moving to another planet. He had lined up a new tenant for his shared office space, but there was all the moving to do. He was keeping the house, as he and Heath travelled frequently to London when they were drumming up business, but he was having some additional security installed as a precaution since the place would be empty a lot more often.

Olly sighed. It was all necessary, but taking such a long time. The only consolation was that once it was all done he would have Joe with him all the time. He was desperate to convince his lover that there was no longer any need to hold back. Joe was his Master — Olly belonged to him. Olly just needed him to act like it! Joe had been patient, kind and — for a Dominant — undemanding. Olly longed to see his forceful side. He wanted to be ordered around, tied up and preferably fucked into the next county. Several times.

When a hand grasped his shoulder he nearly had a heart attack. He had been daydreaming, but how the hell anyone had managed to creep up behind him on the pebbles was a mystery. Before he could react, an arm wrapped tightly around his chest holding him still. A warm kiss brushed his neck.

"Joe?"

It was part exclamation, part question. He gasped as his captor sucked hard on his skin. That was definitely going to raise a bruise!

"I hope you weren't expecting anyone else, Oliver?"

Joe's deep voice sounded very stern and Olly's legs felt just a little weak. Joe would hold him up, though—he didn't need to worry about that.

"No! Of course not, Sir! But you weren't here and I didn't know you were coming back and it's wonderful but I'm a little shocked, but it's a good shocked. That sounded really bad, didn't it—?"

"Olly, stop talking."

Olly bit his lip. "Yes, Sir."

Joe spun him around. "I take it you're pleased to see me?"

Olly nodded and raised his eyes coyly. "I was thinking about you, Sir."

The corner of Joe's lip twisted a little. "Oh, were you now? And what exactly were you thinking about?"

Olly felt his face heat and suddenly he found the pebbles beneath his feet absolutely fascinating.

"When I ask you a question, I expect an answer."

Joe pressed a knuckle beneath his chin, raising his head.

Olly took a deep breath. "I was thinking about you tying me down and fucking me till I scream, Sir."

He stood absolutely still as Joe brushed a curl away from his eyes and ran a finger down his cheek. "And did that make you hard, sweetheart?"

Olly nodded. His cock was rigid and determined to make its presence felt. Joe reached out and cupped him through his jeans. Olly whimpered pitifully. He needed Joe's permission to come, but all the training in the world couldn't stop his body's response to that gentle touch. He jerked against Joe's hand and gasped as the sticky warmth of his cum coated the inside of his underwear. Joe massaged him through the denim and he spasmed again and again until he was utterly drained. If Joe hadn't grabbed him, he would have fallen.

Olly leaned into Joe's chest. "Sorry, Sir."

"There's no need to apologise for something I made you do, Olly. That would hardly be fair, would it?"

Fairness hadn't been a part of Olly's previous relationships. He let Joe's words work their way into his consciousness and relaxed. He'd made Joe happy, done what he wanted, and that felt good.

"Are you going to fall over if I let go of you?" There was just a hint of amusement in Joe's voice.

Olly looked up at him and pouted. "It's your fault my legs are jelly, and now you're laughing at me."

There wasn't a trace of repentance on Joe's face. His light blue eyes sparkled with humour. "Well, I fully intend to turn the rest of you into a similar state. Do you have a problem with that?"

"No, Sir! My legs are fine." His legs might be recovering slowly, but his cock was trying to break the world record for revival and was already starting to stiffen again. The movement reminded Olly of how sticky he was. "I'd really like to take a shower first, though."

"Oh, I think that can be arranged." Joe encircled Olly's wrist with a tight grip and pulled him back in the direction of the main house. Olly followed, unresisting, relishing the feeling of being held. He had a suspicion that Joe had already planned every second of this little adventure. All he had to do was follow his lover's lead. That was okay. That was his natural place in the world and nothing could have been better.

Unlike Heath, who had a small apartment in the main house, Joe's living accommodation while he was on the island was in a small converted building to the rear of the property. Originally a carriage house, it consisted of one large living room downstairs with a tiny galley kitchen, and a spacious bedroom and bathroom on the top floor. Honey-coloured stone had been left exposed and heavy oak beams criss-crossed the ceilings. The original rough floorboards had been polished and varnished, then covered with a scattering of rugs. Olly adored it and it already felt like home.

Joe didn't let go of his wrist until they were both standing in the bedroom. He could feel the indentations on his skin where Joe's fingers had gripped him tightly, and hoped that the bruises wouldn't fade too quickly. He loved the idea of carrying Joe's marks on his body.

"Take your clothes off."

It was an order, snapped out with little patience. Everything about Joe oozed dominance. The way he stood, the glint in his eyes, the set of his mouth. It made Olly shiver with excitement. His fingers were clumsy as he hurried to obey, stripping off until he stood bare and exposed to his Master's critical gaze.

"Legs apart. Hands behind your back."

Olly needed every ounce of his self-control to keep still as Joe walked around him. He left him standing there, itching to touch himself, while he went to the little bathroom and turned on the shower. To Olly it felt like he was gone for hours, though he knew it was only seconds before Joe returned.

"You may shower. When you're done, I want you back here in exactly this spot. Don't bother to dress. You won't be needing clothes."

It took a few moments for Joe's words to register in Olly's brain, but then he managed to get his legs moving in the right direction. As he washed his hair and soaped his body, he could think of nothing but what Joe might have planned. He felt more alive than he had in months.

He dried himself quickly and rubbed at his hair until it was just damp, then looked critically at his reflection in the steamy mirror. He attempted to comb some order into his curls before shaving and cleaning his teeth. That would have to do. Joe seemed to like him just the way he was, so why try to change?

He padded into the bedroom and stopped breathing. Joe had changed his clothes and was wearing a pair of dark blue leather trousers that hugged his body nicely. He wasn't wearing anything else. Olly made a conscious effort to slow his breathing before he started to hyperventilate. Christ, the man was sex on legs! Olly knew how strong Joe was, but the sight of all those rippling muscles was destroying his ability to think. He forced himself to move and resumed his stance in the middle of the floor.

"Please remember to breathe, Oliver. I'd rather you be conscious when I fuck you."

Olly took a ragged gulp of air but, for once, no words came to his lips. He bowed his head and tried to stay calm. Of course, when Joe's next move was to fasten thick leather cuffs around first one wrist, then the other, his composure disintegrated and he whimpered.

"You remember your safe word?" Joe was checking the fit of the cuffs. They were tight enough that Olly could feel them properly, but not so restrictive as to bruise or cut off his circulation. Olly nodded.

"Good. Because I'm not going to stop this time. Not unless you say that word. Understand?"

It was repetitive and unimaginative, but he nodded again. His tongue felt swollen and dry in his mouth and talking was out of the question. Joe wrapped leather around his ankles and needy little noises that would never grow up to be words started to squeeze from between his lips.

The leather ring that Joe fastened around the base of Olly's aching cock was the same dark blue as Joe's trousers.

"If you come before I say you can, you won't sit down for a week."

Olly wasn't sure what excited him more—Joe's commanding tone or the thought of the punishment he might earn. He started to squirm, shuffling his feet, trying to relieve some of the pressure in his swollen balls.

"Keep still. I won't tell you again." Joe softened the words with a firm pat to his arse. "Having beams in this room is one of the reasons I chose it. They are useful for more than just holding the roof up."

Olly looked up and wondered how he had managed not to notice the chains that were hanging above his head. He was sure they hadn't been there when he'd gone into the shower. It didn't matter. They were there now and Joe was lifting his arms so that the metal rings on his cuffs could be attached to the chains. The height had been measured very cleverly. His arms were stretched wide and taut, but not so much that he was pulled onto his toes.

Olly felt a light tap on his leg. "Lift your foot." Joe pulled away the rug beneath him, revealing metal rings set flush into the floor. He pulled them up until they stood proud, then set about chaining Olly's ankle cuffs to the rings.

Soon his body formed a perfect X. His cock jutted forward, clearly very pleased with what was going on. Chained in place, Olly felt a kind of dreamy contentment. Joe was in control and would keep him safe. He trusted him absolutely. Reassurance wasn't necessary, but when Joe kissed him with just the lightest brush of his lips, any doubts that might have been hiding in his subconscious disappeared.

Olly watched curiously as Joe placed a small table to the side of him and a low stool right in front of his legs. If Joe sat there his mouth would be right in line with Olly's cock, and that opened up a whole world of delicious possibilities.

Joe disappeared into the bathroom and returned carrying a small bowl of water, an aerosol can and a razor. Olly swallowed nervously. Was Joe really going to do this? Olly pictured the silky golden curls that bedded his cock. He couldn't imagine how he would look without them, but the thought of Joe shaving his most intimate parts was a massive turn-on. His cock twitched and he was grateful for the leather ring around its base, because without it there was no doubt that he would have come the instant Joe applied the razor to his skin.

Joe didn't ask him if he minded, didn't even look at him. He just squirted a generous amount of foam into his hand and spread it across Olly's groin.

"I've been looking forward to this for weeks." He began to shave the short hairs away, swishing the razor regularly in the bowl. "You will be so sensitive by the time I'm done. Can you imagine what it will feel like when I lick your bare skin?" His tone was conversational and controlled.

Olly moaned, "I'm glad you're enjoying yourself, Sir."

Joe's grin was merciless. "This is what it means to be owned, Oliver. Your body is for my pleasure and nobody else will ever touch you again." He pulled a section of skin taut and slid the razor across it, carefully following the line of the hair. He pushed Olly's straining cock to one side, then the other. Olly knew there would be no need to shave his balls—they were already completely hairless, always had been—but Joe checked anyway, stroking every piece of skin diligently. After a little more tactile inspection, he moved his shaving gear behind Olly's stretched body and sat down again.

Olly's muscles clenched as Joe pulled his arse cheeks apart and dragged a finger across his hole. "Hmm. No hair here, either. That's a shame. Still, I wouldn't want to waste all this foam." Olly heard air being expressed from the can, then Joe slicked the soft, creamy stuff along his crack and massaged it around his entrance. He pressed a finger inside Olly, who tried to thrust back and drive him deeper. Joe added a second finger and twisted and turned them both inside Olly's sensitive channel.

"Joe, please! Sir!" Olly thrashed in his chains, desperate for more. Then the fingers were gone and he felt empty. He heard sounds then—wonderful, comforting sounds of a zip descending and a foil packet ripping. Joe pressed the slick, blunt head of his cock against his entrance and grasped Olly's hips with strong hands, holding him still. When Joe thrust into him in one deep, powerful motion, Olly screamed his delight. Joe's reaction to the sound was to withdraw and plunge deeper, harder, again and again. He had no mercy. His hips pistoned and Olly felt the slap of flesh on flesh. He felt so full, so complete as Joe finally claimed what was his.

When Olly thought it was impossible for Joe to pound him any harder, his Master's pace went up a gear. He couldn't breathe, couldn't swallow. His hearing and sight seemed to have shut down. The only sense that meant anything was touch. He screamed again when Joe reached around him and squeezed his balls. Olly was so sensitive to every contact. The kiss of the air on his denuded skin bordered on painful. Joe flicked open the stud on his cock ring and issued the one command that he was capable of obeying.

"Come."

Olly's body spasmed and he shot hard and fast. Everything burned. Joe's thrusts speared his depths, as his Master came inside him with a triumphant shout. Olly felt wetness on his cheeks before the flashing lights in his eyes exploded into darkness.

* * * *

He had been dreaming, and it'd been the most amazing dream. Joe had done all the things he had been wishing for over the past few weeks. Olly grumbled to himself and tried to force his eyes open. Five seconds later, reality slammed into him like a sledgehammer. *Not a dream. Real!* It had been real. He knew it because his body was telling him so, from the deep ache in his arse to his sore arm muscles and bruised hips. He burrowed under the duvet with a happy sigh.

Cooler air caressed his face and he tried to pull the covers back up, only to have them yanked away completely. Joe leaned over him with a chuckle. "I've never fucked anyone into oblivion before. How are you feeling?"

Olly pouted. "Cold. Give me back my covers."

Joe shook his head. "I prefer the view this way."

"Why don't you get in here with me?" Olly suggested hopefully. For a moment he thought Joe might refuse, but he just shrugged, shucked off his leathers then stretched out next to him. Olly immediately rested his head on Joe's broad chest and nuzzled there. A strong arm circled him and held him tight. "Are you sore?"

Olly gave a disbelieving grunt. "You have to ask?"

Joe chuckled. "You weren't complaining at the time."

"That's because I lost the ability to speak."

"Brat. Next time I'll gag that pretty mouth of yours."

Olly slung one leg across Joe's thighs and realised that his Master was hard again. "How long was I out?"

"Over an hour." And in that hour Joe had released him from bondage, cleaned him up and put him to bed. Olly tried to press even closer to Joe's warm skin. "Freshly fucked is a good look on you, Olly."

"It was amazing. You were amazing. How did you decide I was ready, Sir?"

"It wasn't difficult, Olly. Before I went away, I thought that you were about to strap me down and ride me if I didn't take you soon. I just wanted to get things more settled and be back for good. I didn't want to do this, then go away again."

Olly giggled. "The riding thing—it did cross my mind."

He was just about to go exploring beneath the covers when Joe's mobile phone began to vibrate and jiggle its way across the bedside table.

"It's Heath." Joe answered the call and listened intently for a couple of minutes.

Access to only one side of the conversation meant that it made little sense, but Olly got the gist that something was up as Joe's hold on him tightened.

"He did what? When? Wait there, I'll be over in a minute."

"What's going on, Joe?"

Joe was already clambering out of bed.

"There was an anonymous package in the mail. Heath cut himself opening it—there was a scalpel inside."

Olly could only manage a whisper that Joe probably didn't hear. "Oh, no."

Chapter Fourteen

Ice-cold fury filled Joe's veins. No man had the right to hurt what was his, and Olly was definitely his. He'd claimed him and he had every intention of wrapping a collar around his neck so that the rest of the world would know it too. He pulled on clothes at random, hardly caring what he looked like. The other man he loved — though in an entirely different way — had been hurt and Joe needed to get to him. He yanked on his company fleece and pulled his boots on, only then noticing that Olly was also getting dressed.

"What do you think you're doing?" he growled.

"Coming with you, of course."

"No, you're not."

"Yes, I am."

Joe grabbed hold of Olly's wrist. "No. I'm going to lock you in here, nice and safe."

"Joe! I'm a nurse, remember?"

All of Joe's instincts fought to deny the truth — that Olly would probably be of more use to Heath than he would at that moment.

"Fine. But you stay in my line of sight at all times."

Olly smiled angelically and kissed him. "I love it when you get all overprotective."

Joe scowled, knowing that he was overreacting but unable to stop himself. "Let's go before I change my mind and chain you to the bed."

Olly trotted down the stairs behind him. "Can we do that later? Please?"

Joe was very tempted to sling Olly over his shoulder and do exactly that, but it would have to wait.

They ran through the courtyard to the main house and in through the front entrance, which was closest to Heath's office. Joe pushed open the door and blanched at the sight of blood dripping dramatically from Heath's clenched fist. Olly pushed him gently to one side and knelt on the floor in front of the chair Heath was slumped in.

"Joe, can you fetch a first-aid kit, please." Olly didn't turn around to check that Joe was doing as he'd asked—he was completely focused on his patient. Joe took less than a minute to return with a green plastic box full of supplies.

"What do you need?"

"I need to take a look at the wound. Heath, can you open your hand for me?"

Heath was a bit pale, but otherwise looked a lot less shocked than Joe felt. He opened his hand and pulled away the handkerchief he had been pressing against the cut that ran from the base of his thumb towards his wrist.

"Are there some gloves in the kit, Joe?"

Joe passed Olly a pair of latex gloves and he slipped them on. He probed gently at the wound and smiled. "It's quite deep, but it hasn't damaged anything important. I think I can just clean it and close it up with dressings and tape. We can have another look in the morning. But you'll have to have it wrapped quite tightly, Heath, to stop you moving it around and reopening the wound. It's either that or a trip to casualty."

He rummaged in the first-aid box, picked out what he needed then set to work. Joe pulled up another chair, accepted that Heath was not about to lose a limb and started to think a bit more clearly.

"Where's the envelope? Was there anything else in it apart from the scalpel?"

"On the desk. There was nothing else, no note or anything. It was wrapped in layers of tissue and it sliced through the wrappings into me almost as soon as I picked it up." Colour was returning to Heath's face.

Joe picked up the small, padded envelope, which had a handwritten label addressed just to The Edge.

"We could get this handwriting checked—he hasn't bothered to hide it."

Heath shook his head slowly. "No point. It's a pretty clear message. Vickery wants us to know that this was from him." He winced as Olly doused his hand in liquid antiseptic. "Fuck, Olly! Are you trying to kill me?"

"Baby." Olly carried on, ignoring Heath's prize-winning scowl and Joe's snort of laughter.

"I don't know what *you're* laughing about. I thought he was supposed to be all sweet and submissive?" Heath muttered grumpily.

Joe smirked. "He just needs a firm hand. Preferably across the backside."

Joe could see Olly's cheeks pinkening and wondered if that thought was making him hard. He gave himself a mental slap. He really had to get his mind off Olly's beautiful little arse and back to the present.

"What are we going to do about this?" Joe rested his elbows on his knees and steepled his fingers.

"I'm not sure there's much we *can* do. I'll call Carey and see if he's heard anything, but short of going back to London and confronting Vickery…"

"Fuck! I hate this." Joe closed his eyes and massaged his temples.

Olly finished dressing Heath's hand and scooted back to sit on the floor at Joe's feet.

"There's something I think I should tell you. Something that might help." Olly's words were whispered and there was a tremor in his voice. Joe leant forward and ruffled his hair.

"What is it, sweetheart?"

"When Vickery had me, he told me something. What happened to me at the prison… He planned it all. He paid those men to… He paid them to…"

Olly began to sob as the memories flooded back. Joe lifted him onto his lap and held him tightly, whispering soothing words into his ear until he calmed. Olly took gulps of air and gradually relaxed. Joe and Heath exchanged horrified looks that soon turned to anger.

"If we could get proof, he'd be finished." Heath looked thoughtful. "I'll call my Dad – he might be able to help."

Joe nodded. "He certainly has all the right contacts. If anyone could find a way, it would be your old man."

Olly snuffled. "Am I missing something? Is Heath's dad a hit man or something?"

Heath had a coughing fit.

Joe kissed the top of Olly's head. "Heath's father is a judge, Olly."

"Oh. Oh! Sorry, Heath, I didn't mean to imply that members of your family are likely to be bloodthirsty criminals. I'm sure they aren't. I mean, you do look a little intimidating, but you're nice. Sometimes. And looks don't mean anything, do they? I mean, you are very good-looking. Not like Joe, of course, but—"

"Olly, if you carry on digging that hole you'll need a ladder to get out." Joe couldn't hide his amusement at the disbelief on Heath's face.

Olly buried his head into the curve of Joe's neck and hid. "Sorry." The word was muffled and a bit soggy.

Heath stood up, careful not to put any weight on his injured hand. "I know it's still early, but I'm going to turn in with a mug of cocoa and a couple of ibuprofen."

Joe could feel the vibrations of Olly's silent laughter. "I think you've just shattered a few more of Olly's illusions."

"I think young Oliver might need a lesson or two in appropriate behaviour for a submissive. I hope you both have a very educational evening!" Heath stalked from the room and Olly dissolved into laughter.

"I'm sorry, Sir! It's just that... Heath and cocoa? Really?"

"Under all that brooding angst there's a big softy lurking, but you will never, *ever* let him know I told you that."

"What's it worth?" Olly looked up from beneath thick, golden lashes.

"How about you not spending the rest of your life in chastity?"

Olly got a little paler. "Okay, Sir. That sounds like a good deal." He squirmed on Joe's lap, which did nothing for Joe's concentration.

"However, a little denial does have its advantages." Joe picked Olly up and slung him over his shoulder. Olly struggled and protested until Joe gave him a sharp tap on the arse. "Keep still or I might drop you on something sensitive."

He hefted Olly's body to make him more comfortable, then strode across the hall. He punched a code into a keypad and went through the door that led to the parts of the building used for The Edge's more 'bespoke' courses. There were several doors leading off the corridor facing him. Some opened into ordinary classrooms but others granted access to spaces kitted out as playrooms. They were used to demonstrate the safe use of various pieces of bondage equipment, and to allow clients to practise their techniques in a secure environment.

Joe headed to a room that looked like a doctor's surgery. It was clinically white, and the only equipment was a large, black leather chair that contrasted sharply with the stark walls. He put Olly down and watched as the boy looked around him nervously. Olly knew all about The Edge's sideline in courses for men into the BDSM lifestyle. It was a very profitable part of the business, and Joe hoped that one day Olly would be able to help out with some of the classes. This was the first time he had brought him to the rooms with a clear intent to play.

"What are we going to do, Sir?"

"You are going to take your clothes off. I am going to watch." He'd half expected Olly to hesitate or question him, but he didn't. He stripped off quickly and efficiently, then knelt at Joe's feet.

Joe took a moment to admire the lines of Olly's slender body and smooth skin. He didn't have the frame to carry heavy muscle, but was nicely toned.

His cock looked spectacular, stiff and straining. Joe wrapped his hand around it and squeezed. "You'll keep yourself shaved for me from now on, Oliver."

Olly whimpered, "Yes, Sir."

"Let's make you a bit more comfortable." Joe picked Olly up and deposited him in the chair, placing his ankles in metal stirrup cups that spread him high and wide. "Beautiful." He loved that Olly was so completely exposed and vulnerable to his every whim.

He stroked one finger along the length of Olly's arm then grasped his wrist, dragging it above his head. At the top of the chair a loop of leather had been fixed. He pulled Olly's other hand up, then cinched the leather around both wrists. "Excellent. But now we have a little problem." He flicked the head of Olly's leaking dick. "For what I have in mind, this just won't do."

He perched on the edge of the chair and played with Olly's hair. "Have you ever seen one of those clever wine coolers that you freeze, then slip over the bottle like a sleeve?" He pressed a finger to Olly's lips. "You don't need to answer, love—just think about the concept for a moment while I fetch something from the fridge." He waited for a moment until realisation dawned on Olly's face and the boy started to pull on his bound wrists.

"Sir! You wouldn't?"

He gave an evil chuckle. "I most definitely would." He opened the cupboard door that concealed an integrated refrigerator and pulled out what looked like a ridged fabric tube. "This is adjustable, but will fit you nicely, I think. It's covered, so there's no danger of losing any skin." He slid the tube over Olly's cock then tightened it with a Velcro strap. Olly gasped and arched his back.

"Fuck! Oh—it's so cold, Sir. Take it off! Please!"

Joe shook his head implacably. "I haven't heard your safe word, Olly." He went to another cupboard and rummaged around for a while, smiling as he listened to Olly's moans and curses. He found what he was looking for and returned to stand over his wriggling lover. "You look perfectly delicious, Olly, just how I like you. Restrained, wanting, frustrated...and all mine."

"I'm glad you're having fun, Sir!"

"You've probably realised by now that I don't do anything without good reason, and your...discomfort is for a good cause. I have a present for you."

Olly was gritting his teeth. "Why do I think it's not going to be gift-wrapped and tied in a pretty bow?"

"Because you are an astute young man, Oliver."

"Astute? I'd prefer 'cute', 'adorable' or 'devastatingly sexy'."

Joe placated him with a chaste little kiss. "How about all of the above? Now, stop talking and let me concentrate." He slid the icy sleeve from Olly's cock and put it to one side. "Well, that worked remarkably well."

Olly tilted his pelvis and strained to look down. "Oh, my God! You've killed him, Sir!" His dick lay limply curled against his thigh.

"I'm sure 'he' will recover. However, I need him in his current condition in order to fit him into this." Joe held up a metal contraption of gleaming steel loops linked to a thick shackle. Before Olly had time to protest, Joe slipped the device onto his cock, closed the shackle and locked it with a small padlock. He checked for any rough edges but the metal was smooth, and a perfect fit. The shackle gripped the base of Olly's cock and the rings circled his shaft at regular intervals, linked by a steel joining piece. The device ended in a crossed metal cap that hugged the end of Olly's cock snugly. He released Olly's ankles from the stirrups and unstrapped his wrists. "There. All done."

Olly sat up and looked miserably at his imprisoned cock. "You are a very cruel Master, Sir."

"Yes, I am, Olly. Having your body so completely within my control is deeply arousing. I'm going to take you back to bed, tie you up and fuck you until you scream." He handed Olly his jeans. "Get dressed, sweetheart."

Olly dressed slowly. "Is there anything I can do to make you change your mind, Sir?"

"About fucking you?"

"Oh, no! That sounds perfect, Sir. I meant this." He pointed at his metal-bound cock before he zipped himself up.

"Do you think I'm likely to change my mind?"

"No, Sir." Olly chewed on his lip.

"No. Exactly. Let's go." He took a firm hold of Olly's slim wrist and pulled him towards the door.

Joe couldn't wait to have Olly naked and bound in his bed. Every step of the journey back through the house and across the courtyard took an age. Olly trotted behind him, uncomplaining. Joe wanted to scream "Mine!" to the world but he settled for a deep, satisfying kiss.

"Go to the bedroom. Wait for me. I want you naked and kneeling, Oliver."

Olly disappeared up the stairs as Joe pulled the door closed and locked it. For the next few hours he would make sure that Olly had no room in his thoughts for anyone but his Master. Vickery was the stuff of nightmares. Joe was determined that the boy he loved would have only sweet dreams that night.

Chapter Fifteen

The next day, Olly sat cross-legged and completely naked on the bedroom floor and contemplated his metal-bound cock. He shook his head sadly. "It's not your fault. You didn't do anything wrong. I'll be really good today and I'm sure Joe will let you out later." He lay back and stretched out, putting his hands behind his head. He had a perfect view of the discreet metalwork embedded in the heavy oak beams, and that made him smile.

Lots of things made him smile now. He was in love. He was happy. Joe was all his dreams rolled up into one scrumptious, dominant package. Even the fact that his Master had a thing for denial couldn't depress his mood. Knowing that Joe held the key to the contraption around his cock made him feel ridiculously content.

Of course, that didn't mean that he didn't really, really want to come, because he did. The previous night, Joe had demonstrated remarkable stamina and taken him twice more, both times with a great deal of enthusiasm. Olly's arse ached, but in a good way. He had slept the dreamless sleep of true exhaustion and now felt wonderfully rested.

He had woken late to find Joe's side of the bed empty and cold. Joe had left a note on the bedside table that read, 'Teaching this morning, Olly. Meet me for lunch at one.' Then Joe had drawn a soppy little heart that had made Olly feel warm inside. If the spectre of Mark Vickery had not been hanging over their heads, everything would have been perfect.

He got up, then padded to the bathroom for a shower. The mundane routine of washing, shaving and cleaning his teeth became a whole new experience when all he could think about was the weight of the cage around his cock. It wasn't uncomfortable, but it was impossible to ignore. Joe would know that, of course. Thinking about what he couldn't have just made Olly want it more.

Perhaps if he got himself ready for his Master, that would earn him some credit. He found a string of fat anal beads in the bedside cabinet and coated them with lube. Pushing the three round balls into his channel was a challenge, but he did it. He felt really full and knew that he would be nicely stretched for Joe by that evening. Of course, he was also torturing himself through self-inflicted stimulation. His poor cock jerked in its cage and he gave it an apologetic look before pulling on his underwear and getting dressed.

Olly wore the staff uniform of black jeans and a matching fleece with 'The Edge' embroidered on it. He didn't like to stand out, and he did help around the place even if he wasn't on the payroll, so he didn't feel like too much of a fraud. He strolled across to the main building and ventured into the staff restaurant, which was buzzing with lunchtime activity even though it was the weekend. He took a quick look around, but there was no sign of Joe.

Olly felt a little lost. He checked his watch to make sure he wasn't early, but he was right on time. It wasn't like Joe to be late—he was a stickler for punctuality and Olly had been punished several times for his tardiness. Of course, he usually made sure he was one or two minutes late just so that Joe would have an excuse to punish him. His cheeks warmed at the memory of the last spanking that little trick had earned him.

Someone came up behind him and squeezed his shoulder. Heath's growly tones followed. "Why are you standing around like a lost lamb, Olly?"

"Hi, Heath. Joe asked me to meet him but he's not here."

"His class probably overran. Why don't you go and find him? You know the code, don't you?"

It was Saturday, so Olly knew that Joe would be teaching the small group of Dominants that had booked in for that weekend's 'Understanding Submission' course.

"Yes, I do. Is that okay?"

Heath nodded. "Of course. He loses track of the time when he gets into some deep and meaningful discussion with a client. He's probably having an in-depth debate on the psychological impact of silk versus leather for blindfolds."

Olly put on his best innocent expression. "Oh, silk is always best, Sir. Much more sensual against the skin. It ties nice and tight but doesn't chafe. It tells you that your Master loves you and cares about how you feel." He couldn't hold back his giggles as Heath gave him a look of utter disbelief.

"If I didn't know that Joe would have my balls, I'd bend you over my knee right here, you little brat. Now get lost, before I decide to take the chance!"

Olly fled. He made his way to the private wing where he'd been just the previous evening and wandered down the corridor. It was strangely quiet, and he wondered if he had managed to miss Joe somehow. There were small glass panes in each of the classroom doors and he peered into each of them as he went by, but they were all empty. *Strange.* That only left the white room with the big leather chair, the one kitted out as a dungeon, which he loved, and the room that housed the whipping post. Not that anyone actually got whipped in there. It was a safe place for people to practise and learn to control their strength. Some whips were difficult to handle, and they weren't the kind of toys to use unprepared.

The doors of the last three rooms didn't have windows. Olly pushed open the first, but the white room and the big leather chair were empty. The last two doors stood side by side at the far end of the corridor. Tiny flickers of light showed beneath the one leading to the dungeon so Olly pushed it open, a little nervously.

He caught sight of Joe's blond head and heaved a sigh of relief. He pulled the door shut behind him and moved into the shadows. He didn't call out because it was apparent that Joe was talking to someone.

The room was cavernous, painted black and hung with all manner of restraints. Alcoves housed spanking benches, slings and various other pieces of equipment, though Olly could only make out shapes in the dim light. The room was kept deliberately dark, with just a few strategically placed halogen bulbs set into the ceiling. Olly couldn't see whom Joe was talking to and the room seemed to soak up sound, so he only caught the occasional word. Joe was moving, though, taking slow steps, gradually stepping back towards the door and the place where Olly stood, concealed by the darkness.

A tall figure appeared out of the gloom. Olly thought he recognised him as one of the weekend's course members. He'd only seen them briefly when they'd arrived, but the man seemed familiar. He was tall, with close-cropped black hair and a dense beard. There was a small gold hoop in one ear and a glittering stud in his nose. His neck showed the tops of tattoos that disappeared beneath his dark grey shirt.

Olly's eyes adjusted to the darkness and he could see that the stranger held something shiny in his hand. It glinted dully. Icy cold gripped his heart, and his head pounded. It couldn't be. He squinted hard, trying to look past the dyed hair and unfamiliar beard.

It was someone he'd hoped he would never see again. It was Mark Vickery, and he was holding a scalpel.

The disguise was brilliant. If it hadn't been for the cruel eyes, Olly would have been fooled. The tattoos and piercings were clever — not things that would ever be associated with an eminent surgeon. Olly knew that Joe could look after himself, but Vickery was holding the scalpel as though he had every intention of dissecting Joe into tiny pieces. Shivers of fear crept along Olly's spine.

Moving as slowly as he could, Olly edged along the wall, feeling his way carefully. A few more steps and Vickery would be close enough to see him. He needed to find a weapon. This was a dungeon, for pity's sake — it must be full of lethal implements. Olly was scared but there was no way on earth that he would let Vickery hurt Joe while there was anything he could do about it.

"If it wasn't for those beautiful golden curls, Oliver, you would be very difficult to see in that dark outfit." Sarcasm dripped from Vickery's tongue like acid.

"Olly!" Joe turned towards him, distracted, and Vickery lashed out. The scalpel flashed, Olly screamed and Joe pressed a hand to his face as red droplets scattered through the air like rain. Olly sank to his knees, devastated that he had provided Vickery with an opportunity to attack.

His hand closed around something cold and hard. Heavy chain clinked and he wrapped his hand tightly around the links. Joe didn't retreat—he lashed out with his feet, driving Vickery back into the darkness. Olly could hear low grunts as the two men fought, then cursing as Vickery crashed into something and fell. For a moment there was just the sound of heavy breathing. Olly wanted to call out to Joe, to find out if he was all right, but he didn't dare. He clambered to his feet and pressed back against the wall, dragging his makeshift weapon with him.

Then Vickery was in front of him, just inches from his face. He was sweating and dishevelled. Saliva flecked his chin. Olly cringed and cowered away from him.

"You're mine, Oliver. Did you really think I'd let you go so easily?" Vickery licked his lips slowly.

"You're insane," Olly whispered. "You'll never get away with this."

"Oh, I think I will. I'm going to take you overseas to a place where no one will ever find you. It'll be just you and me from now on. I think you'll enjoy being my slave, boy."

Olly felt the heat of tears slide down his face and cursed his own weakness. Where was Joe? How badly was he hurt? He summoned up every scrap of courage, tightened his grip on the chain in his hand and swung it with all his strength towards Vickery's head.

He'd got his hands on a pair of iron manacles and the ends swung hard and heavy into Vickery's face. Blood spurted from his lips and nose, but he kept coming. Olly dropped his improvised weapon and tried to run, but Vickery slammed into him from behind, knocking him into the wall. Pain shot through his shoulder and he collapsed to his knees with a cry. Fingers tangled into his hair and pulled viciously.

"Get your filthy hands away from him, you piece of shit." Joe's high kick connected with Vickery's head, and he crashed to the floor and lay still.

Olly scrambled his way over to Joe and held tightly onto his lover's legs, too shaken to attempt to stand. Joe knelt next to him and gathered him into a tight hug. "It's over, sweetheart, it's all over. You're safe now." Joe carried on whispering words of reassurance into Olly's ear and eventually he felt calmer. His nurse's training kicked in.

"I should check on him. Make sure he's still breathing. And your face! How bad is it?"

"It's just a scratch. Nothing a plaster won't fix. I'll find something to tie this idiot up with."

Olly knelt at Vickery's side and felt for a pulse in his neck. It was there, hammering away strongly. He was breathing steadily. Olly thanked God that he wouldn't have to deliver mouth-to-mouth. There was just enough light to see the dark blood smeared across Vickery's skin, but Olly didn't feel an ounce of sympathy. The man was alive and that was so much more than he deserved.

Joe returned with a set of handcuffs, which he used to fix Vickery's hands to the leg of a spanking bench. He removed the prone man's belt and used that to bind his ankles.

"There. That should hold him. Let's go and raise the alarm. I'm sure Heath would be delighted to come down and keep watch over him." Olly leaned into him as Joe slipped an arm around his shoulders, and together they went to find Heath.

* * * *

By early evening, things had calmed down. The local police had come and gone after taking statements from anything that moved. It still made Olly giggle uncontrollably when he remembered the look of shock on one young constable's face when he'd got his first sight of the dungeon. Shock had turned to curiosity, and Olly was convinced that they would be seeing him again.

Vickery had regained consciousness to find a very pissed off Heath standing over him. Unsurprisingly, he had become a bit more subdued and the police had carted him off without any trouble.

Olly had cleaned up the cut on Joe's face, which was scarily close to his eye. Later, as they sat in Heath's lounge, he checked the wound.

"I think you'll have a scar," he mused as he applied a fresh dressing.

"Why does it sound as if you like that idea?" Joe pulled his squirming boyfriend into his lap.

"Scars are kind of sexy," Olly admitted, "and I'll always remember how you came to my rescue."

"I feel like an idiot," Joe admitted. "How could I not have recognised him? He was sitting in my classroom all morning."

"I didn't either, and neither did Heath. It was a good disguise." He fidgeted in Joe's lap. Being so close to Joe was causing some problems down below, and now he didn't have any distractions, every movement reminded him about the beads up his arse.

"Stop wriggling!" Joe kissed him into stillness.

Heath chuckled. "I think you two need some alone time. At your place. I need to call my dad back—he left a message earlier."

Joe didn't need telling twice. He deposited Olly onto the floor, grasped his wrist tightly and tugged him towards the door. Within minutes they were back in Joe's bedroom—*their* bedroom, Olly reminded himself—and Joe was undressing him purposefully.

"I should really be punishing you for putting yourself in danger today. You should have hidden, not tried to fight him."

Olly pouted. "So it's all right for you to get hurt, but not me?"

Joe nodded and pointed at the bed. "That's right. That's how it works. Your tone isn't very respectful, Oliver. Perhaps you do need a lesson. Get on your hands and knees."

The position made the cage around his cock feel like a lead weight. Olly felt his face heat. Now he had his head down and arse up, Joe was going to see what he had been doing.

"Well, well." Joe's hand connected with his arse with a resounding smack. Olly yelped. The anal beads pressed hard against his prostate and sent bolts of lightning to his poor, defenceless cock.

"What exactly have you been up to, Oliver?" Another smack. Olly whimpered.

"Would you like me to take them out?" Joe smacked him twice more in quick succession. His arse felt as if it were on fire.

"Yes, Sir! Please!"

There were more smacks before Joe obliged. Olly lost count of exactly how many, but he knew with absolute certainty that his balls were going to explode if Joe didn't remove the chastity device soon. Joe withdrew the beads carefully and slowly as Olly twitched and moaned. He took his own sweet time sheathing his cock in latex and applying a glistening coating of lube.

"Please, Sir!"

"What is it, Olly? I'm busy."

"Aren't you going to take it off?" Olly knew he sounded desperate but he didn't care.

"Take what off?"

Olly moaned at the teasing and pointed at his cock. "This thing, Sir. Please! I'm too young to die."

"Whose decision is it whether it stays or goes, Oliver?" Joe sounded very stern.

"Yours, Sir." Olly pressed his forehead against the mattress and gritted his teeth.

"Exactly."

When Joe flicked his tongue around Olly's needy entrance a few seconds later, Olly screamed. It took all his willpower to stay still as Joe teased and tortured him mercilessly. When Joe stabbed his tongue through Olly's protective ring of muscle, Olly sobbed with pleasure and frustration. It was a heady combination. It barely registered when Joe finally flipped him over, undid the padlock on the chastity device and set his cock free. He hardened so fast he nearly blacked out from the sensation. He knew that incoherent sounds were coming from his mouth, but had no hope of controlling himself.

Olly felt his knees being pressed back and wide. Then Joe was inside him in one smooth, hard thrust that had him arching and straining to take him as deeply as possible. Instinctively he held his legs back to give Joe better access, but when his Master began to move with determined, forceful thrusts of his hips, Olly lost the ability to control any part of his body.

Joe wasn't gentle. He hammered home his claim with force, holding Olly in place so tightly that he knew his hips would be bruised. Olly didn't care — the sensations Joe was delivering were euphoric. His world shattered into a million fragments of light. There was nothing but the power of Joe's penetrating strokes, the burn that flooded his body and the explosive build of an orgasm he could do nothing to contain. The moment Joe wrapped a hand around his cock, Olly came. He didn't have permission, but the release was worth the severest of punishments. His vocal chords froze in a silent scream as waves of ecstasy coursed through his body.

He opened his eyes just as Joe reached his climax. Olly gasped as Joe pushed deep inside him. His lover's pale eyes were full of love and Olly's name was on his lips as he came. It couldn't have been more perfect.

Chapter Sixteen

Joe watched in amusement as Olly pottered around the dungeon, tidying away equipment and stowing toys. He had a flogger in one hand, a length of thick chain in the other and a heavy spreader bar under his arm. He was humming softly and his body swayed in time to his own rhythm. Over the last few weeks he had gradually relaxed. All the little signs of tension and fear that had been there before were gone. Joe felt his stomach knot. He couldn't help but wonder if Olly would want to leave and spread his wings now that he no longer needed a protector. Their little island home was isolated, and Olly was very young.

"I'm done, Sir. Can we get some lunch now? I'm starving." Olly grinned cheekily and sank to his knees at Joe's feet. His expression when he looked up was adorable—coy and shy with a big dose of mischief.

Joe ruffled Olly's curls. "You did really well today. The class loved you."

"It was more fun than I imagined it would be." Olly tilted his head to one side thoughtfully. "They were all very nice."

For someone who had spent the entire morning being tied up in a variety of less than comfortable positions, Olly was remarkably cheerful. Joe had been a little reticent about allowing him to help out with the bondage classes, but having a willing victim made the experience a lot more useful for his enthusiastic students. Olly had worn a plain black T-shirt and shorts so that his limbs were accessible. There was no way that Joe was going to allow him to wear anything less in a room full of other Dominant men. As it was, he'd had to rein in his possessive instincts every time another man had wrapped a cuff around one of Olly's slim ankles or wrists.

"Would you like a little appetiser before lunch, Sir?" Olly's pretty blue eyes were firmly fixed on his fly.

Joe flicked open the button on his waistband but didn't touch the zip. He leant back against a convenient pillar. "No hands."

Olly immediately put his hands behind his back and leant forward to grasp the tag of the zip in his teeth. It slid down easily and Olly nuzzled Joe's crotch, moving aside the fabric that blocked access to his cock.

Joe took a deep, controlled breath and braced himself as Olly wrapped warm, soft lips around his sensitive tip. He had been hard for what seemed like hours. Just watching Olly in bondage had been enough to keep him right on the edge, and several times that morning he had almost thrown his paying students out so that he could sink himself into Olly's sweet little arse.

He clenched his jaw as Olly began to lick and suck enthusiastically. He might be easily distracted in other situations, but Olly always found incredible focus when he was giving head. Joe loved that single-minded attention to his needs, and fuck, did it feel good!

Olly gave Joe's cock a rest and began to suckle his balls, mouthing them gently and muttering happy little sounds. Joe caught hold of his hair and made it clear where he wanted Olly to be. Olly planted a kiss on the tip of his leaking dick before lapping at the juices hungrily. He shifted on his knees a little, then took Joe into his throat in one movement. Joe's thigh muscles went rigid as Olly deep-throated him with ease. He tightened his hold on Olly's hair, giving him the only warning he was going to get that Joe was about to come. Olly knew that signal and sucked harder, allowing his teeth to scrape just a little. Joe's hips jerked and he came in a hot gush down Olly's welcoming throat. His legs were like jelly and he was really grateful for the solid wooden post supporting him.

Olly licked his lips and looked up through golden lashes. "Thank you, Sir."

"You're welcome, Oliver." He pulled Olly to his feet and wrapped him up in a hug. Far too soppy, but he didn't care. "Thank you too, sweetheart—I needed that."

Olly snuggled against him, getting as close as he could. "I know, Sir. You've been looking a little...uncomfortable all morning."

Joe could feel him laughing against his chest. "Brat." He sighed. "I suppose my condition was obvious to everyone else too?"

"Oh, no, Sir—they were all too busy looking at me like I was the best dessert on the menu!"

"Oh, they were, were they? I think you and I need to have our own lesson in here this evening, so that I can remind you exactly who your Master is. Now put some more clothes on—we're joining Heath for lunch."

* * * *

It was later than usual by the time they tidied themselves up and reached the staff restaurant. Heath was already eating and just raised one dark eyebrow as they joined him. Olly giggled and Joe shrugged. "Sorry, we got a little...distracted."

"You don't sound sorry." Heath's eyes twinkled. "I hear the class was a spectacular success. Your group were all talking about it when they got up here."

"That's great. Any negatives?" Joe always wanted to improve on anything they were doing at The Edge.

"Only one." Heath grinned wickedly. "Apparently Olly was wearing far too much clothing!"

Joe glared and stopped his retort by shoving a forkful of pasta into his mouth. Olly was looking very pleased with himself too. That, he would have to deal with later.

Heath pushed his plate aside. "I have some news. I spoke to Dad this morning and the police have persuaded two of the prison rioters to testify against Mark Vickery in return for shorter sentences. Olly will still have to give evidence, but there's absolutely no doubt that our dear doctor is going to go down for a very long time."

"He'll probably plead insanity." Joe frowned.

"He'll try. All the preparations he made at his house to keep Olly captive, the fake tattoos and piercings, the deliberate disguise... Far too much premeditation for him to get away with that one."

Joe nodded. "He's certainly one case I wouldn't like to analyse." He looked over at Olly, who was glancing between him and Heath with worried eyes. "Don't be scared, love. Heath and I and Carey and Alistair will all be there with you."

"I just want it all to be over. I don't want him hurting anyone ever again."

Joe gave Olly's shoulder a light squeeze.

"Dad's also asked me if we can take on another one of his projects."

Joe grinned. "Well, the last two have turned out fine." Heath's dad occasionally sentenced someone to work at The Edge instead of sending them to prison. They were usually young men who just needed a sharp nudge in the right direction. The last two that had come along had ended up staying, and were both now working in the kitchens as trainees under the watchful eye of Emile, the irascible French chef, and doing very well.

"When's the new boy due?"

"Not for a couple of months, but if you're okay with it I'll let Dad know."

Joe nodded. "We can always use the extra help." They carried on talking about the business and how it was growing. Bookings for the normal corporate courses were full for months, and the weekends now had a waiting list. Word of the less public side of The Edge had spread rapidly and two London clubs, including The Underground, now insisted that prospective members sign up for a course as part of their probation.

"May I be excused, Sir?" Olly pushed his chair back. "I'm working for a few hours this afternoon."

"Of course. I'll see you later." Joe watched Olly all the way to the door. Olly had found himself a part-time nursing job on the mainland at a private hospital for wounded military personnel. He covered for the regular staff when they were on leave or training, and loved every minute.

"He's amazing, Joe. You're very lucky." Heath looked a little wistful.

"I know. I hope he doesn't get bored with me."

"Bored? That boy adores you! If you can't see that, you're denser than you look!"

"Well, we'll see tonight, won't we? Is everything organised?"

Heath grinned. "Carey and Alistair will be here by five. The catering crew are setting up in the dungeon. You just have to get Oliver there."

Joe smiled. "That won't be a problem. He's already expecting a trip down there later. He won't suspect a thing."

"And you're sure he won't mind me being there? It's different with Carey — he has Alistair."

"I would trust you with Olly's life, Heath. He would be devastated if you weren't there."

* * * *

Joe was waiting when Olly returned that evening. Though he understood Olly's need to work and be independent, that didn't stop him from missing the boy when he wasn't around. He preferred to have him in sight at all times, but accepted that it was important for Olly to know that Joe trusted him to behave himself when he was away from his Master.

"We have a date in the dungeon, brat. You've got half an hour to prepare yourself for me. There are clothes laid out for you upstairs."

Olly's cheeks pinkened nicely and he lowered his eyes. "Yes, Sir." As he disappeared up the stairs, Joe couldn't hold back his smile. He had been planning this evening for some time, and now it was here he couldn't wait to get started. He was very tempted to follow Olly up the stairs and into the shower. Holding Olly's pliant body against the wall and plundering his arse while he was slick and dripping was one of Joe's favourite pastimes, but not tonight. Tonight he'd have to be patient.

When Olly came down the stairs precisely half an hour later, Joe had to remind himself that he was supposed to be in control. He schooled his face into calm and resisted the urge to drool. Dark blue leather hugged Olly's slim legs, and a silk shirt in the palest blue brought out the colour of his eyes. His curls shone gold in the lamplight, and there was a touch of clear salve on his lips that made them shine.

"Fuck, you're beautiful!" Joe couldn't stop himself.

Olly blushed and chewed on his lip. "Thank you, Sir. These clothes are wonderful."

"Just a couple of finishing touches." Joe brought out a pair of leather cuffs that matched the blue of Olly's trousers and buckled them around his wrists. He checked the fit, then cupped Olly's neck with one hand. The lightest of pressures brought Olly closer and they kissed, deep and tender. There was no aggression, no dominance, just a gentle exploration that heated Joe's cock into iron rigidity.

He had dressed deliberately plainly in plain black leather trousers and a soft pullover. He thanked the Lord for the foresight to wear something that wasn't too tight.

"One last thing." From his pocket, Joe pulled a length of dark blue silk. He tied it firmly around Olly's eyes and stood back to admire his work. "Perfect. We are going to the dungeon now, love. Trust me to guide you."

Olly just nodded and held out his hand. Joe took it and stroked the palm with his thumb while he took a few deep, steadying breaths.

The short walk to the main house and down into the basement made Joe glow inside at the trust his lover placed in him. Olly didn't hesitate or stumble once— he allowed Joe to lead him with absolute faith that he would be safe. Joe's protective instincts kept him nervous until they reached the door to the dungeon without incident.

"We're here, sweetheart. Are you ready to play?"

"Just tell me what to do, Sir. I love you." Olly whispered the words but to Joe's ears they were a shout of joy. He opened the door, led Olly forward and turned him around so that they were facing each other.

"Kneel." His voice sounded ragged.

Olly sank gracefully to his knees and bowed his head, waiting for Joe's next command. Joe knelt in front of him and unbuttoned Olly's shirt. He slid the silk from Olly's shoulders and put it to one side. He could see that Olly was breathing quite fast, and pressed a hand against his smooth chest.

"There's nothing to be afraid of, Olly. I will never harm you." Carefully he pulled Olly's arms behind him and linked the cuffs together, then he moved to kneel in front of him and gently unzipped his fly. Olly's perfect cock sprang eagerly free, jutting pale against the dark leather of his trousers. Joe stroked him a couple of times until a bead of pre-cum glistened at his tip. Then, reluctantly, he let go and stood up.

Feeling almost as if he were floating, he acknowledged the three other men in the room. Heath, tall and imposing in black leather, stood directly behind Olly. Carey, with Alistair kneeling quietly at his feet, stood to one side, a huge smile on his face. He handed Joe a slim velvet box, which Joe took with shaking hands. Heath untied Olly's blindfold and pulled the strip of silk away.

Joe watched anxiously as Olly glanced around in confusion, then relaxed as Olly's eyes met his and stayed fixed there.

"I've asked our friends to be here tonight, Olly, to bear witness." He paused and smiled gently down at his beautiful partner. "You are bound to me." He touched Olly's shackled arms. "Exposed to me." He stroked Olly's rigid cock. "Mine to do with as I will. I want to make a lifetime commitment to you. I offer you protection, guidance and love." He knelt in front of Olly and opened the box in his hand to reveal a delicate silver chain with a pendant shaped like a miniature padlock. "Will you accept my collar, Oliver?"

It took all his courage to wait for a reply. Olly's eyes glistened and a tear rolled down one smooth cheek.

"Oh…yes, Sir, I will. Of course I will! I love you so much!"

Joe took a shuddering breath and leant forward to fasten the chain around Olly's neck. Then he kissed him, wrapping Olly's hair around his hand and making his ownership absolutely clear. He unfastened Olly's wrists and pulled him into a hug, to the sounds of applause and whistles from their delighted friends. Olly was sobbing and laughing at the same time, hanging on tight. Joe could have stayed there all night but eventually they had to pull apart. He tucked Olly's dick back into his trousers and zipped him up carefully.

"I'll deal with him later, sweetheart. That's enough exhibitionism for one lifetime. For my eyes only from now on, okay?"

Olly nodded and scrubbed at his tear-streaked face.

"Come on, you two lovebirds, you're neglecting your guests. There's a feast waiting for us." Carey gestured at a table laden with food. He shook Joe's hand. "You are a lucky man, Joe Dexter."

"And you are a devious sod, Carey—something for which I will be eternally grateful."

Heath gave Olly a hug. "Behave yourself, brat. If Joe gets too soft on you, I'll be there to remind him that he's in charge."

Olly pouted. "We need to find you a boyfriend—you have *way* too much time on your hands."

That stunned Heath into indignant silence. Carey gave Olly a hug of his own and examined the pendant. "You've earned this, Olly. I wish you every happiness."

Alistair kissed him full on the lips. "Feels good, doesn't it?" He fingered the slim strip of leather around his own neck.

Joe listened and watched and glowed with pride.

* * * *

The five of them ate and drank and talked until the early hours. When Joe caught Olly yawning behind his hand, he scooped him up and carried him back to their bed.

Olly toed off his boots, shrugged off his shirt and crawled onto the bed to sit propped up against the pillows. He had a cheeky grin plastered across his face. "I'm not really tired, Sir."

"It's been a perfect day." Joe stripped down to his underwear and joined him. He pulled Olly against his chest. The feeling of skin on skin pulled a moan from him that he just couldn't hold back. He stroked Olly's curls and kissed him, tasting his lips, nipping and sucking at the succulent flesh.

He lifted Olly so that the boy could rest against him and encircled him with his arms, kissing and nibbling at his neck. He worked his hands across Olly's smooth chest, stroking the silky skin until he reached a rosy nipple. He flicked a finger across the hard nub before taking it between a finger and thumb, rolling it delicately. Olly gasped and pressed against him, arching his back. Pleased with the reaction, Joe pinched a little harder, then switched his attention to Olly's other, neglected nipple and gave it the same treatment. Olly writhed and moaned his pleasure.

"Sir, please, don't stop!"

"I decide what you need, Oliver, remember?"

Joe fiddled with Olly's zipper and released his straining cock. It jutted hard from his body, the tip already glistening with moisture. Then he returned to torment Olly's nipples and smirked as the boy spread his legs wantonly.

"You are not to come without my permission."

Joe rubbed his thumb across Olly's slit, teasing him mercilessly. He dragged a nail the length of Olly's cock and rolled his tight balls in the palm of his hand. Olly was shaking against him, needy little cries escaping his kiss-swollen lips. Joe pressed two of his fingers against Olly's mouth until Olly accepted them. The boy suckled him greedily, making his fingers nice and wet.

"Time to turn over, Olly. Take off your trousers, get on your hands and knees."

Olly scrambled out of the clingy leather with difficulty and got into position while Joe slid off the bed and removed his underwear. His cock was dark and thick with arousal. He knelt behind Olly and rubbed a damp finger against his hole, applying persistent pressure until Olly's body surrendered to him. He added a second finger and thrust them deep, before exploring the inner surface of Olly's channel. When he found the sensitive bundle of nerves he sought, Olly sobbed and pushed back against him desperately.

"Please, Sir! Have some mercy!"

Joe pulled his fingers out and slicked his cock with lube. "Our tests all came back negative, Olly. There need be no more barriers between us." He lined himself up, grasped Olly's narrow hips and pushed forwards with one smooth, hard thrust.

Olly yelped, "Oh! Sir, that's feels so good... I'm so full!"

Joe revelled in the feeling of Olly's hot, tight channel caressing his dick. He started to move slowly.

"Harder, Sir, please!"

"Patience!" But Joe couldn't hold back anyway. His hips pistoned, Olly's hands twisted into the sheets and the pillows muffled his screams.

"No!" Olly shouted as Joe withdrew.

"Turn over, Olly. I want to be looking into your beautiful eyes when I come."

Frantically Olly spun over and rested his legs over Joe's shoulders. As he pushed forward to penetrate deeply, Joe took Olly's hands above his head and pinned them tightly. He thrust harder and deeper than ever before, knowing that he was close. Olly panted and whimpered, muttering "Please..." over and over.

"Come!" Joe issued the order and fired his own release hot and deep into Olly's willing body. Olly obeyed—he could do nothing else. He came in hard spurts across his own abdomen, racked with spasms as his body gave in to its need.

Joe collapsed against Olly's shuddering form, softening slowly within him. He released the boy's wrists, which would definitely display his marks in the morning, and smiled. Olly stole a cheeky kiss.

"I love you, Sir."

He looked sleepy and adorably sated.

Joe slipped away to fetch a warm cloth, then cleaned them both up. He climbed back into bed, pulled up the covers and wrapped Olly in a tight hug. He played with the chain around Olly's neck and nibbled his soft earlobe.

"I love you too, beautiful. You're mine now. Always."

Olly entwined his fingers with Joe's beneath the covers.

"Yours, Sir. Forever."

LIVING ON THE EDGE

Dedication

Amy — this one's for you, with my thanks. You made me a better writer.

Chapter One

The car sped along the motorway, its interior lit by flashes of neon orange and red from signs warning drivers to take a break, not to drink and drive and to slow down in the rain. Esther looked at her husband, Adam, who was driving. His forehead was creased into a frown, his eyes narrowed in concentration. It was dark, the rain was kicking up more spray than Niagara Falls and every truck they passed seemed to be generating a tidal wave of watered-down mud. In the passenger seat, Esther rearranged the rolled-up pullover she was leaning against, but it was impossible to get comfortable and she couldn't relax anyway. She glanced into the rear-view mirror and pursed her lips. The cause of her anxiety was slumped in the back seat, the side of his face pressed against the cool window glass. His unusually pale eyes were open but unfocused, as though he were deep in thought. In the dim light it was impossible to see true colours, but his hair was dark and somewhat unruly, falling across his face in tousled waves.

"How long are you going to keep up the silent treatment, Aiden?" Esther spoke sharply and her husband cast a resigned glance in her direction.

"Leave him be, Esther. He doesn't have to talk if he doesn't want to."

"He brought this on himself, Adam. If it wasn't for me, he'd be rotting in jail right now."

"I know. And he's going to have a whole year to regret his actions."

"He's twenty years old. He should know better."

"Yes, dear."

A pained sigh came from the back of the car.

"For fuck's sake, Sis. Lay off. You've committed me to a year of purgatory. Stop trying to justify your own actions."

"Even you must accept that this is a better option than prison."

"I'd have been out in six months. This is double the sentence. Thanks a lot."

"You ungrateful brat. The things I do for you…"

Aiden rolled his eyes. "I didn't ask you to help, Essie. Stop acting the martyr."

"We're here."

That stopped the bickering as they pulled off the motorway into a gloomy, unwelcoming service station.

"Esther, relax. Aiden, think about it. What do you think would happen to someone who looks like you do in prison?"

Aiden scowled but then muttered an apology under his breath. Esther shook her head and looked at her little brother. Adam was right, but it wasn't Aiden's fault that he looked the way he did. He was prettier than she was with his beautiful, unusual eyes, fine bone structure and soft, dark hair. Sometimes it was hard to believe that they were related. Aiden was the only member of the family who wasn't stocky, sandy-haired and freckled. He was slim, pale-skinned and, at five foot eleven, relatively tall. She loved him deeply, but the last year had challenged even her tolerance for his behaviour.

It had all started three years ago, on Aiden's seventeenth birthday. He had decided, against her better judgement, to come out to their somewhat old-fashioned parents. There had been no histrionics, no judgement, just a quiet disappointment that had gradually eaten into Aiden's soul.

He'd been a brilliant student, a year ahead of his peers, and as soon as he could arrange it he'd left home for university. To start with he had emailed his sister regularly, choosing to keep in touch with her rather than face awkward phone calls with his technologically challenged mother and father. He'd seemed to thrive in the rarefied academic atmosphere, embracing the demands of studying maths and IT at the same time.

Then, in his third year, the emails had started to tail off. They'd become shorter and less informative. Esther had gone to visit and had found Aiden holed up in a darkened room with a computer and an intimidating man whose name she had never learnt. Though clearly shocked to see her, Aiden had taken her out to dinner, made all the right noises about studying and enjoying himself, then had sent her on her way. It was only when she'd got back home that she'd realised he had actually told her little of substance, and that she still had no clue as to what he was up to.

The first she'd learnt of exactly how much trouble he was in was when their mother had called her, mildly hysterical, to tell her that that Aiden had been arrested for hacking. Six months of hell had followed. Aiden had refused to talk about what he had done or why. He'd been released into Esther's care on bail, pending trial, and was banned from being anywhere near a computer. The university had allowed him to finish his degree remotely and that was what he had spent six months doing—painstakingly writing his dissertation by hand and avoiding all mention of the impending trial.

Esther had attended court in the expectation that the trial would take weeks, but to her shock Aiden's lawyer had entered a guilty plea on his behalf. Aiden hadn't met her eyes once as the lawyer had made a statement pleading for leniency. Then the judge had asked for both the defending and prosecuting councils to meet in his chamber. What had emerged was a choice—six months in prison, or twelve months' attachment to an organisation of the judge's choosing for community service. The latter depended on payment of a bond and that was where Esther had come in. She had agreed to post the bond, which meant that if Aiden reneged on the conditions of the sentence, she stood to lose her house and business.

Aiden hadn't been given any choice in the matter. The deal was made and the result was the sulky attitude in the back of the car. He'd been released into their custody, provided that they travelled to meet his custodian for the next year immediately. The alternative had been a prison van, so, ever practical, Essie had bundled her husband and younger brother into their car, dismissed the policeman who had walked them to the vehicle and set off into the darkness.

Cold, damp air swept through the car as Esther opened the back door to let Aiden out.

"Child locks, Essie? Seriously?"

"Act like a child, you get treated like one." Esther grimaced. She was starting to sound like their mother and that wasn't good. Aiden's raised eyebrow and sardonic grin said that he knew exactly what she was thinking.

"Shut up, Aiden."

"I didn't say anything!"

"You were going to. Now, a Mr Anders is supposed to meeting us in the café. He's escorting you the rest of the way."

Adam locked the car and they headed inside, Aiden trailing miserably behind them. It was late and there weren't many customers in the slightly grubby restaurant. Aiden watched his sister as she scanned the seating area. At the back of the room, someone waved in their direction. Esther marched them over and held out a hand.

"Mr Anders? I'm Esther Locke. This is my husband, Adam." They shook hands, then Esther grabbed Aiden's arm and pulled him forwards. "And this is my brother, Aiden Keller."

Aiden pushed down his inclination to make a sarcastic remark and looked up through his hair, then up a bit more. Christ, the man had to be six foot five. Eventually he hit a pair of steel-grey eyes and a stern expression.

"Heath Anders. Sit down, Aiden. I'll be with you in a minute." Heath's voice was deep and soft but his words carried an air of command. Aiden found himself sliding obediently into a chair while Heath gently manoeuvred his sister away from him. The discussion that followed was brief, and Aiden couldn't hear what was said. After just a couple of minutes Esther gave a small smile in his direction and a brief wave, then she and Adam walked away without looking back.

Aiden swallowed hard. Esther hadn't even said goodbye. He lowered his eyes, blinking back the sting of tears.

"I find that prolonged departures do nobody any good."

Aiden looked up to see Heath towering over him.

"Would you like something to drink before we continue the journey?"

"Coffee. Please." The please was added a little belatedly, but there was something about Heath's stance that made Aiden think that rudeness would not be tolerated.

Heath's lips twitched. "Stay here."

Aiden watched as he walked away. Broad shoulders topped a body wrapped in a dark fleece and black jeans. Every movement spoke of restrained strength. He moved confidently with a measured, unhurried pace. Aiden couldn't stop his gaze from drifting down to a very nice arse—the guy was exceptionally well put together. It wasn't difficult to imagine what it would be like to be held down by Heath, and somehow Aiden knew that held down was what he would be. Heath didn't look the type for caring and sharing. He was so obviously dominant that it oozed from every pore.

"Probably straight." Aiden hoped he had only thought the words rather than said them out loud. It was hardly appropriate to be thinking about the man in that way. Still, if he had to be stuck in some godforsaken place as slave labour for twelve months, at least there would be something nice to look at. *Twelve months. Fuck.* It felt like a life sentence, and Aiden wondered for the millionth time if what he had done was worth it.

Heath returned, levered his long legs beneath the table and placed a large cup of steaming coffee in front of him. Aiden's hands shook just a little as he ripped open a sugar sachet and sprinkled a few grains into his drink. The fight with the miniature milk cartons proved a bit more challenging until a large hand closed around his own, took the annoying little pot away and opened it for him. The burning sensation would have been less if Aiden had plunged his hand into an open fire. Skin on skin contact with Heath short-circuited his brain and turned his cock into a very hard problem.

He shifted uncomfortably. "I don't need your help." He fought the second milk carton and sprayed white liquid across the table.

"Of course you don't." Heath wiped up the mess with a serviette. "Look at me, Aiden."

Aiden suddenly found the tabletop very interesting indeed, but there was something about that voice that stripped away his resistance. Slowly, unwillingly, he raised his eyes.

"Better. I have one ground rule that we need to get out of the way. I know you don't want to be here. Well, suck it up—I don't care. You did something wrong and this is punishment, not a fucking day trip."

Aiden blinked and clenched his fists beneath the table.

"From this point on, you do what I say, when I say it. Disobey me and you will be punished. Do as you're told and we will get along just fine."

"So, you say 'Jump' and I say 'How high'? Is that how this works?" Months of frustration and worry brought sharpness to Aiden's voice.

"How high, how far and what kind of fucking landing is required."

Aiden watched the steam rise in lazy swirls from his cup. "So who made you my lord and master?"

He tried not to twitch as Heath growled at him. "The misguided judge who saw fit to save you from the hazards of a custodial sentence."

"It was my first offence. That old bastard could have let me off with a fine."

"And what exactly would you have learnt from that? And just so you know, that old bastard is my father."

Aiden paled and shoved his chair back. "So this is some kind of convenient arrangement for providing you with free labour?"

"Don't be such a fucking drama queen. It won't hurt you to find out what hard work feels like. I didn't ask to be lumbered with your useless, childish arse, believe me."

Aiden tilted his chair back on two legs and scowled. "Whatever."

Before he knew what was happening, a hand was wrapped in his collar, heaving him from his chair then shoving him unceremoniously towards the door. There weren't many cars in the car park, and despite the fact that he was being roughly manhandled towards it Aiden couldn't help but admire the sleek Jaguar they headed towards. Heath pushed him into the passenger seat with a grunt. Aiden was still marvelling at the cream leather and polished walnut when he felt cold metal close around his wrist.

"What the hell...?"

Heath smiled serenely and locked the other cuff around the door handle.

"You can't do this!" Aiden yanked furiously on the cuffs, wincing as the metal dug into his skin.

Heath shut the door with a solid clunk, then got into the driver's seat and started the engine.

"You need to get used to the fact that I can do whatever the hell I like with you. The next time you say 'whatever' to me, I'll gag you."

Aiden banged his head back against the seat in frustration. He glared uselessly at Heath, but got no response other than a satisfied smirk. He closed his eyes and took a few calming breaths. After what he'd been through recently, surely he could deal with this power-crazy bastard? He sneaked another peak. He might hate Heath's guts already, but he couldn't deny the man was gorgeous. He watched Heath's thigh muscles tensing under tight black denim as he changed gear, then took a sideways look at the strong hands clasping the wheel. No white knuckles there—Heath was sickeningly relaxed and in control of the situation.

Control. Now, there was a word to conjure with. Aiden let the thought of being controlled by Heath seep into his mind. His half-hard cock started to swell in appreciation of its owner's daydreams and Aiden suppressed a curse. With one hand chained to the door, he couldn't even fold his hands demurely in his lap to hide the growing bulge. He muttered a silent prayer that Heath was the kind of driver who kept his eyes strictly on the road.

He exerted pressure on the handcuffs in the hope that the pain of metal digging into his wrist would deflate his errant cock. It had the opposite effect. He couldn't stop thinking about what it would be like to be forcibly handcuffed by Heath in the bedroom. On his knees. Naked. *Shit.* Now he was fully and painfully hard, and there was absolutely nothing he could do to hide it.

The stress is driving me crazy, he thought. Sure, he'd had bondage fantasies for as long as he could remember, but this was hardly the time or place, or indeed the man to be having them about. He was stuck in a car heading for a year of purgatory, and only a handful of people knew that he hadn't actually done anything wrong. He should be scared, anxious or at least mildly pissed off. Instead he found that he was weirdly looking forward to spending more time with a man who took great pleasure in putting him in his place.

Chapter Two

Heath focused all his attention on the road. It was a foul night, and that seemed to be a good enough reason not to look at the young man in the passenger seat next to him. This was not the first time that his dad had asked him to take on someone who would otherwise have gone to prison or spent an unproductive few months washing graffiti off walls. His father believed that young people should fulfil their potential, and if that meant forcing them to recognise that they had some, so be it.

Heath's business was convenient for his father's purpose. It was based on a small island reached by a narrow causeway. The nearest town was twelve miles away. He ran high-end corporate training courses aimed at powerful people looking for an edge to keep them at the top of their game. It was difficult to find good people willing to work there because of the isolation, so Heath had built a small, close-knit team, most of whom lived on the island during the week and went home on their days off. An extra pair of hands belonging to someone who didn't have the option of refusing menial tasks was usually very useful.

This time, though, Heath just knew that Aiden meant trouble. From the first moment he had set eyes on him, there had been no question. *Big fucking trouble.* He remembered the conversation with his father.

"Son, this boy wouldn't last thirty seconds in prison before he was warming the bunk of some Neanderthal. He's a prison riot waiting to happen. He's also scarily bright. He'll be good for you. I mean, for the business... Good for the business."

Heath had assumed that his dad had been exaggerating, though as a judge he wasn't usually prone to flights of fancy. He had dismissed that little slip of the tongue with good humour. He had to have the only dad who felt the need to set up prospective partners for his gay son. Anyway, it had been a while since he had taken one of his dad's cases, so he'd said yes. He was already regretting it.

Aiden was no exaggeration. He was absolutely beautiful. Far too pretty to be left without protection. Heath tried to ignore the stirrings in his lap—he already felt an irresistible urge to keep Aiden safe. He tried to convince himself that that was all it was. Who was he kidding? Just the thought of any other man laying a hand on that slender body made him want to growl. Aiden didn't come across as the sweet, submissive type he usually went for—in fact, he was one big piece of attitude. There was something, though...underneath the sarcasm Heath was catching hints of vulnerability. All Aiden needed was a strong hand, someone to open his pretty eyes to the joy that could come from submitting to another man.

Heath relaxed his hands on the steering wheel and allowed his lips to curl into a small smile as he recalled Aiden's expression when Heath had locked the handcuff around his wrist. Delicious. Hurt bewilderment to cold fury in the time it had taken Aiden to register metal around his flesh. Heath had fastened the cuff tightly. He'd wanted Aiden to know that he was restrained and helpless. Three hours in the car thinking about the fact that he was at someone else's mercy would do him good.

Heath blinked and scrubbed a hand through his short, dark hair. He'd only known Aiden for an hour and already he was finding it hard to keep images of him out of his head. He couldn't help but wonder what he would look like naked. Aiden's arms were slim and toned — would the rest of him match up? Did he have much body hair? His unkempt waves were very dark, so it was likely, but that could be easily remedied. He had a narrow waist and hips — if anything, he was slightly underweight. Nothing that good food and hard work couldn't put right. Heath caught himself licking his lips. Fuck, what he wouldn't do to have Aiden naked and displayed for his inspection.

"What kind of business do you run?"

Heath jumped at the unexpected sound of Aiden's voice. It was soft and low, with no trace of the petulance he had detected earlier.

Heath glanced sideways and noted the tension that tightened Aiden's lips and creased the skin around his eyes with tiny lines.

"Didn't they tell you at court?"

"Nobody told me anything. My sister collected me from the police at the courthouse and we came straight to meet you. I haven't been home, didn't get the chance to ring anyone. They wouldn't even let me pack anything."

"And your sister? Esther, is it?"

"Too busy tearing me a new one to answer my questions."

"She put up the bond for you, though." *That must count for something*, Heath thought.

"Yes. That's why I'll be a good little boy and do as you say."

The petulance was back, but now Heath realised that it was just a cover-up for the fear that Aiden must be feeling. To be told nothing of where he was going or what he would be doing must have been horrible.

"The Edge has many facets, but mainly we run intense corporate training courses. Some with an outdoor adventure theme, others based on business psychology. Occasionally we diversify into related areas." He didn't expand on that. Now was not the time to be introducing Aiden to the less public face of The Edge. He would find out soon enough.

"Why The Edge?"

"Because sometimes that's all it takes to gain a competitive advantage. The tiniest change in management style or attitude can make an enormous difference. Our customers come to us because they want that edge."

Aiden fell silent.

Heath glanced at him. "What, no more questions?"

Aiden stared at the road ahead through wipers barely clearing the windscreen of the driving rain.

"What's the point? Will you answer them?"

Heath knew he must have dozens of burning questions, but was too afraid of exposing his worries. Aiden wasn't the type to want to appear vulnerable. He was all prickly corners and sharp edges. Heath bared his teeth in a feral grin. Fuck, it was going to be fun smoothing down some of those rough bits.

"I'm not making any promises."

Aiden jerked on the metal cuff attaching him to the door handle. "Was this really necessary?"

"Nope. But it was fun. The look on your face was priceless." Heath kept an absolutely straight face and waited for the explosion.

"Bastard." The word was little more than a whisper from between clenched teeth.

"You're not the first person to say that and I doubt you'll be the last." Heath was completely unfazed.

Aiden turned his head away and Heath gave a mental shrug. He turned on the CD player and increased the volume a little.

"What's the band?"

"Within Temptation." Heath glanced at Aiden's slim fingers, which were tapping out the tune on his knee. "Do you know them?"

Aiden shook his head and the dark waves of his hair bounced against his shoulders. "No. I like the sound, though."

Was there no part of Aiden's body that didn't have the power to turn him on? Heath sank his fingernails into his own palm in the hope that it would discourage the enthusiastic swelling of his cock. *There should be a fucking law against any man looking that good.*

"Why don't you try and sleep for a while?"

He caught the glance that Aiden shot his way. He had sounded a bit brusque, but... *For pity's sake, give a man a break.* There was no way he was going to survive another two hours in such a small space with Aiden if the young man remained conscious. Heath was pretty certain there were laws against using the hard shoulder for the kind of relief he had in mind. Soft lips wrapped around his cock, slender fingers stroking his balls... Christ, he needed to get a grip. Oh, and that was not the thought he needed right then. He'd grip that soft, shiny hair and make sure Aiden couldn't escape... He could use those handcuffs in so many interesting ways...

A small snuffle drew his attention and he realised with some relief that Aiden had done as he had suggested and was napping, his dark head resting against the seat. With the lines of worry smoothed from his skin, Aiden looked innocent and very beautiful. It took all Heath's willpower to keep his eyes and his mind on the road.

Aiden was under his protection, his responsibility for the next year. Heath would just have to learn to keep his hands and his dreams to himself.

Chapter Three

Aiden didn't wake until the low growl of the car's engine disappeared from his subconscious. For one wonderful moment, he had no idea where he was, then it all came flooding back with a vengeance. Reflexively his hand jerked and the chain attaching him to the door handle clinked. He squeezed his eyes shut again, not wanting to face the misery of his own reality.

It was very quiet in the car—too quiet. Aiden forced his eyes open. Heath was gone. He squinted out of a window into the darkness, but couldn't see much through the water that still ran in sluggish rivulets down the glass. He could just make out the outline of buildings up ahead, but there was no sign of life. He sat there for a couple of minutes, wondering what the hell was going on, before the crunch of footsteps on gravel betrayed the presence of someone walking towards the car. The door swung open, taking his arm with it, and a blast of frigid air sent a shiver the length of his body. Heath's dark head appeared, his hair sticking to his forehead in soggy tendrils. He unlocked the cuff around the door handle, pulled Aiden out of the car then locked the free cuff around Aiden's other wrist.

"What the fuck are you doing?" Aiden tugged on the short chain indignantly and scowled as he caught the sparkle of amusement in Heath's dark grey eyes.

There was a heavy thunk as the car door slammed shut, then Heath gripped Aiden's shoulder, firmly but not roughly.

"It's raining, in case you hadn't noticed. I suggest you save the inane questions for inside."

Aiden didn't notice the water dripping down his face, soaking his thin shirt. All he was aware of was the pressure of Heath's fingers on his shoulder and the grip of cold metal around his wrists. The combination was intoxicating. Heath rested his other hand gently on the small of Aiden's back and applied pressure. Aiden managed to force his legs into motion, walking only where he was guided. His aching cock rubbed against the confines of his clothing with every step. He didn't want to move too fast in case the contact between his back and Heath's hand was lost. That small patch of warmth was safe, secure. He wanted to lean back against it and let Heath take his weight.

"Watch the steps."

The moment Heath removed his hand, Aiden felt bereft and scared. He was exhausted—the emotions of his arrest, the trial and now the nagging fear of the unknown were taking their toll. It was warm inside and his body reacted to the change of temperature with uncontrollable shivers. Heath pushed him towards, then up two flights of stairs. At the top were two closed doors. Heath used a large, old-fashioned key to unlock the one to the left and pushed it open.

"In."

Aiden stumbled over the threshold and stared around the small room. It didn't take long to look over the bed—made up with sheets and blankets—a small chest of drawers and a plain wooden desk with a single shelf above it. In the corner of the room, through another door, he glimpsed a tiny bathroom.

"This is your room." Heath undid the handcuffs and propelled him to the edge of the bed. "Sit."

He disappeared into the bathroom and came back with a large blue towel, which he wrapped around Aiden's shoulders.

"Are you hungry?"

Aiden shook his head silently.

"Well, it's close to midnight. Get dry, get some sleep. I'll be back to get you in the morning."

The door shut quietly behind him and Aiden grimaced as he heard a key turn in the lock.

"Just fucking great. I might as well have gone to bloody prison." Even as he muttered the words he knew they weren't true. The towel around his shoulders was testament to that. He sniffed and rubbed his eyes, putting the slight watering down to tiredness. He pulled the towel close around him and breathed in the fresh, clean smell. Why had Heath bothered? Perhaps the man *did* care.

Aiden shook his head, scattering water droplets across the floor. "Idiot. He doesn't give a toss about your sorry arse."

He rubbed his hair vigorously, then bounced experimentally on the edge of the bed. It was nice and firm. The sheets were soft and everything smelt clean. It wasn't so bad.

He shucked off his damp clothing, placing jeans and shirt on the back of the wooden chair. After only a moment's hesitation he stepped out of his navy briefs and let the air play across his bare skin. He stretched slowly, feeling the kinks in his muscles loosen bit by bit. The wooden floor felt warm beneath his bare feet as he paid a quick visit to the bathroom, where he was happy to find toothpaste and a cellophane-wrapped brush.

Five minutes later, he turned out the light and slid beneath the sheets. If he couldn't sleep, at least he could fantasise about Heath…but within minutes he was dead to the world.

Chapter Four

"Holy fuck!" Heath had stared at the security monitor on his desk and tried to convince himself that he hadn't been deliberately spying on Aiden. It had just been bad timing. The system was set to rotate around the various cameras and had just happened to be focused on Aiden's room at the very moment Heath had sat down. Of course, pressing the pause button to stop the feed moving on to the kitchens had been all his own work.

It had been no good. He'd had to unzip his fly — the pressure had been getting unbearable. His fingers had felt huge and clumsy as he'd fought to release his rigid dick while Aiden had stripped and stretched on the screen in front of him. Aiden had the most delicious body, lean and toned, his skin the colour of fresh cream. Heath had imagined what it would be like to lap at that cream. There wasn't an inch of Aiden's body that he wouldn't like to lick, kiss and bite until Aiden screamed with pleasure.

The angle on the screen hadn't been perfect. He'd seen the curve of a hip, a slim thigh, arm and shoulder. Then Aiden had turned towards the bathroom and Heath's cock had jerked hard as he'd got the perfect view of an arse that would doubtless feature in his dreams for weeks to come. Heath had wrapped his fingers around his aching dick and stroked quickly. He'd been consumed by a tumult of emotions. Lust had been close to the top of the list as Aiden had disappeared into his bathroom, but the overriding impulse had been possessiveness. Heath had shuddered and come into his hand, absolutely certain in the knowledge that sooner or later, Aiden would belong to him.

Now, he cleaned himself up and leant back in his chair, stretching his long legs out. It was late and he wasn't usually much of a night owl, but tonight he couldn't settle. He switched off the monitors and flicked through the pile of mail that had been left on his desk. There was nothing that couldn't wait. He was just about to give in to the temptation that glinted golden in the decanter across the room when the office door opened.

"I saw the light. You're up late."

Heath smiled as his business partner and oldest friend strolled into the room and perched on the edge of his desk.

"Checking up on me, Joe?" He gestured at the glinting decanter. "Would you like one?"

Joe drummed his long fingers on the edge of the desk. "No, thanks. I have plans for Olly tonight."

Olly was Joe's very cute, very submissive boyfriend. Heath knew that Joe would never drink if he were planning a scene with him.

"Well, don't let me keep you two apart. I'm fine."

Joe grunted sceptically. "Your usual icy demeanour is thawing round the edges, Heath. Something's on your mind. I'd guess it would have to be our new houseguest. You did collect him this evening, didn't you?"

Heath gave his friend a calculating look. Joe knew him far too well. He took in the neat blond hair, classic good looks and long, lean frame. Joe was his best friend, but he was also potential competition for Aiden's affections. Thank God that Joe was utterly smitten with Olly. Joe might be one hundred per cent Dominant in their relationship, but Heath knew damn well that Olly could wind Joe around his cute little finger. Jesus, he had it bad. Why the hell was he considering his best friend as a possible rival?

Joe chuckled. "Well, well. It's about time the great Heath Anders found himself a new challenge. This should be very entertaining." He swung his long legs off the desk.

Heath scowled. "I never said I had any interest in him."

Joe just raised an eyebrow. "You didn't have to my friend. It's written all over you, along with a bloody great warning beacon screaming 'hands off, he's mine'."

Heath got up, stomped over to the decanter and poured himself a generous finger of brandy. "Fuck off, Joe. Don't you have an appointment with a certain twinky arse?" He knocked the drink back in one and coughed as the burning liquid hit his throat.

Joe didn't look in the least bit offended. His blue eyes gleamed with amusement as he headed towards the door. "Sweet dreams, my friend. Don't forget we have an early start in the morning. I assume I can leave it to you to rouse the sleeping beauty?"

"Fuck, Joe, how do you know what he looks like?"

"I don't, but he must be bloody spectacular to have you in such a state. You always did like the pretty ones."

Heath made a less than friendly gesture, his smile wry as Joe closed the door behind him. Aiden was beautiful. Heath would trust Joe with his life, but he wasn't so sure about the twenty men arriving in the morning for a corporate bonding week. He would have to think very carefully about how to keep Aiden away from them. He already knew that he didn't want any other man looking at him in the wrong way, let alone getting close enough to touch. They might all be ramrod straight, but he wouldn't be taking any chances. Aiden was enough to tempt anyone out of the fucking closet.

He gave serious consideration to a second brandy, but dismissed the idea and slipped the stopper back into the decanter with a clink. With a group of important clients arriving in the morning, he had to keep a clear head. A hangover was not going to improve what he was pretty certain was going to be a shitty day.

He pushed the door of the study closed and climbed the same set of stairs that he had taken Aiden up earlier. He paused outside Aiden's door for a moment, but there was no sound. He turned to the door on the right and pushed it open. It was no coincidence that Aiden had been given the room opposite his—the moment he'd set eyes on him across the service station, Heath had sent a message back to the island to have it set up.

His own accommodation was a great deal more spacious, however. Though many of the staff chose to commute to the island, Heath opted to live on site. His door led to a small, self-contained apartment that suited his need for privacy but provided everything necessary for him to live comfortably when there was no one else in residence. There was a small kitchen, comfortable lounge and a big bedroom with a bathroom leading off it. Everything was decorated in muted shades of cream and green with splashes of darker contrast here and there in cushions and throws. On the walls were a small number of artworks, pieces that he had picked up at small gallery shows by new or undiscovered artists. He bought what he liked rather than for reasons of overblown reputation, and his taste showed in the quality and depth of the work. In the lounge, the pictures were landscapes, stormy seas and wild moorland, but in the bedroom there was something very different. He pushed open the door and smiled, as he always did, at the large painting hanging directly above his bed.

He was lucky enough to count Garrick Balen as a friend. Now, there was one young artist who did have a huge reputation, and Heath knew he would never have been able to afford his work if he'd had to buy it like everyone else. But this picture had been a gift. It was a portrait of a kneeling man with his arms stretched high above his head, chained and helpless. The image was impressionistic, showing only hints of his body, a curve of muscle here and there, just enough for the observer to know what the artist had intended to depict. What Heath loved the most, though, were the eyes—lowered but so expressive, hinting at love. They were the same unusual colour as Aiden's, a bright jade green.

He looked at his neatly made bed and imagined Aiden displayed there for his pleasure. Black leather would look stunning against his creamy skin. Heath shook his head. "Get a grip, you idiot. Time for a cold shower."

He could look, but he knew he couldn't touch. Well, not in the way he wanted to. It would be a whole year before he could act on his desires—while Aiden was obliged to obey him, Heath would have to maintain a professional distance.

As hot water washed away the remains of the day, Heath cursed his luck. What were the chances that he would find a man so perfect, yet so untouchable? Still, a year might seem like an eternity, but it would give him plenty of time to test Aiden's willingness to submit to him when the time came. The bigger challenge would be keeping other men away from him, particularly if he ever came into contact with the less public side of the business.

Chapter Five

Aiden woke confused and groggy, with a thumping headache to compound his misery. He stayed still for a while, allowing his brain to stick a few cells together enough for him to master logical thought.

"Fuck!" Sitting up was not the best course of action he could have taken. He felt a little sick. He was also a bit shivery and his body couldn't decide whether hot or cold was the better option. His watch had been taken away at the courthouse and there was no clock in the room so there was no way of knowing the time, but it was light outside. The blinds at the single small window were up, something he hadn't even registered the night before.

His body drove him to the bathroom, but he didn't dare look in the mirror. He felt awful and imagined he must look equally bad. If he dressed, it would have to be in the previous day's clothes. He didn't have the slightest idea what to do, so he crawled miserably back into bed and waited for what the day would bring.

He must have drifted back to sleep, because the next time he woke the light was blocked by Heath's broad-shouldered frame standing over him. The sheets and blankets on his bed had slipped down to his hips, and he was suddenly very aware of Heath's steely eyes on his body. Self-consciously, he started to pull the sheets up.

"No."

That was it. Just one word, and it was enough to stop him moving. He wondered fleetingly if Heath practised mind control.

"What do you mean, no?"

Heath didn't speak. His expression was set and stern. God, he looked glorious. Then he shot a hand out and yanked the bedcovers down to the foot of the bed, leaving Aiden totally exposed.

"What the hell?" Aiden blushed furiously and scooted up the bed, attempting to cover his half-hard cock with his hands. All his blood seemed to be rushing south and there was nothing he could do about it.

"Move your hands."

It was an order. Plain and simple. Every atom of Aiden's body screamed resistance, but his hands didn't seem to be connected to his brain—they moved to grasp the edges of the bed. He didn't have to look to know that his cock was swelling into iron hardness, standing proud from his body. He could feel the cool sensation of air hitting the moist tip. His balls felt tight against his body. Christ—he thought he might come just from knowing that Heath was examining him with a predatory look on his face.

Time must have slowed, because Heath seemed to be staring at him forever before he spoke.

"Very good. I expect obedience at all times. There are fresh clothes on your chair. Get dressed and come downstairs. My office is off the main hall." Then he turned and left.

Aiden felt even more feverish than he had before. His skin was slick with sweat that was rapidly cooling. His dick throbbed and he felt...shit, he had no idea how he felt. Aroused, confused, indignant, bewildered... He didn't know where to start.

He resorted to the basics. He took a shower, shaved, scrubbed his teeth, finger-combed his hair and dressed in what proved to be a uniform of sorts. The clothes were identical to those Heath wore—black cargo pants, black polo shirt with 'The Edge' embroidered on it in silver thread, thick socks, undershorts and light walking boots, all black. There was also a zip-up fleece with the same logo across the back. Everything fitted perfectly, and Aiden had to wonder where they had got his sizes. He shrugged. What did it matter? It wasn't as if he had a choice, and his own clothes had disappeared.

He took the fleece off again because he felt really hot, and headed down the stairs. There was only one open door off the main hall, but he hesitated and knocked rather than walking straight in.

"Come in, Aiden." Heath's deep voice seemed to echo in his ears. He held the doorframe, momentarily giddy, then forced himself to walk into the room. Heath was sitting behind a large desk, scribbling rapidly on a pad in front of him. There wasn't another chair so Aiden stood still with his hands clasped loosely behind his back. If Heath wanted to play power games and make him wait, so be it. It wasn't as if he had anywhere else to go.

"Did you sleep well?"

Aiden looked up into steel-grey eyes and searched for sarcasm. It seemed to be a genuine question.

"Yes, thank you."

"Good. I'll take you to breakfast and then we will go through your duties." He paused. "You're very flushed, are you feeling okay?"

"I..." Aiden didn't want Heath to think he was making excuses already, but he did feel a bit peculiar.

"Don't bother lying to me, Aiden." Heath was around the desk with a hand on his forehead before Aiden could stutter a response. "Fuck, you're burning up. Why didn't you say something?"

Aiden thought about their earlier encounter and rolled his eyes. "I had other things on my mind, okay?" He took an unbalanced step sideways and felt the room closing in. Oh, shit, he was going to faint like a girl. The last thing he felt before he did just that was a strong arm around his waist, keeping him safe.

Chapter Six

There were colours, lots of colours. Red and orange and black interspersed with flashes of light that brought blinding pain with them. Aiden was vaguely aware of coolness on his forehead, warm blankets around his body, a steadying arm as he staggered to and from the bathroom. When he finally regained full consciousness and blinked his sore eyes into sight, the world became confusing again. Perched on the end of his bed was a pretty blond with the biggest, bluest eyes he'd ever seen.

"Am I dead?"

The blond grinned. "Well, I'm definitely not an angel, so unlikely. You've been in and out of reality for two days though, so I'm glad you're back."

"And you are...?"

"Sorry! I'm Olly. Mr Anders—Heath—asked me to look after you while you were ill. I'm a nurse." His laugh tinkled across the room as Aiden stared hard.

"A nurse? A real nurse?"

"Would you like to see my certificate?" Olly's blond curls bounced as he stood up and thrust a thermometer into Aiden's gaping mouth.

"Close, please. Quiet." He held up a slim hand and checked his watch. "My, it's nice to boss someone around for a change!"

Aiden rolled his eyes and waited impatiently until Olly pulled the thermometer from his mouth and checked it.

"Excellent. I was beginning to wonder if it would ever get back to normal."

Aiden struggled to sit up. He felt sticky and dirty and his throat was sore, but there was no pain. "What the hell happened to me?"

"Well, Mr Anders obviously had a dramatic effect on you, because you fainted in his office. Doesn't surprise me, he is gorgeous, though fainting does seem like a bit of an extreme reaction. Not my type, of course, but definitely hot as hell. He sounded the alarm and had you brought up here. He spent the whole of the first night watching over you—wouldn't leave. I think he likes you. Do you like him too? You'd make a beautiful couple if you can put up with him. Mind you—"

"Stop!" Aiden groaned. "Do you ever stop talking?"

Olly tilted his blond head to one side thoughtfully. "Joe likes to gag me, so probably not."

He'd said it as if it was the most ordinary thing in the world. Aiden wondered if this was all some crazy dream. "Who's Joe? No, don't answer that, I need a shower more than an answer."

He made to get up, then realised that he was naked beneath the blankets. "Uh, who undressed me?"

Olly giggled. "I offered, but Heath, I mean Mr Anders, wouldn't let me. He did it himself."

Aiden flushed bright red at the thought of Heath's hands on his body.

Olly giggled again. "You don't have to be shy, Aiden. I really am a nurse. I've seen it all before, promise."

Aiden didn't move and grasped the covers tightly to him.

"Fine. I'll start the shower for you and leave you to it, if you promise not to faint again."

Aiden nodded slowly but stayed put. Olly turned the water on and steam began to fill the small bathroom. Aiden managed a nod of thanks and tried not to laugh at Olly's obvious reluctance to leave. Eventually, Olly gave in and pulled the bedroom door closed behind him with a pretty pout. Aiden gave a sigh of relief. It wasn't that he didn't like Olly — quite the opposite in fact — but he needed time to process what had happened to him. The hot water felt wonderful, and as he washed away the clammy feeling from his skin he felt much better. He dealt with the idea of Heath undressing him by blanking it from his mind.

As he dried off and dressed, his stomach rumbled and he wondered how long it had been since he'd eaten. He was a bit wobbly, but otherwise okay. There was a knock at the door.

"Can I come in or are you still feeling shy?"

Olly didn't wait for an answer and was soon pressing a cool hand against Aiden's forehead.

"Stop touching him, Olly."

A tall man dressed in the same uniform as Olly and Aiden joined them. There was something about the way he stood that made the black cargos and fleece look like high-end couture. He oozed confidence and power from every pore. He held out a hand. "Aiden, I'm Joe Dexter, Heath's business partner."

His grip was firm, but he didn't squeeze too hard. Aiden was very aware that this guy had no need to prove himself to anyone. So this was Olly's Joe, was it? He was strikingly good-looking, with short, light blond hair and light blue eyes. There was just a small scar below his left eye to mar otherwise perfect skin.

"Olly tells me you're feeling better, and now I can see that for myself. Olly, take him to lunch, make sure he eats and then turn him over to Heath. Try not to talk him to death."

Joe ruffled Olly's curls affectionately, and Aiden watched in amusement as Olly's body seemed to melt backwards into the larger man.

"Yes, Sir."

"Good boy."

Joe turned to leave and Aiden raised an eyebrow at the exchange. Theirs was obviously not your average business relationship.

Olly gave him a mischievous wink. "Come on, food time. If I deliver you to Mr Anders in less than perfect condition, I'll be scrubbing out the toilets with a toothbrush."

Aiden followed him out of the door. "Why would he care what condition I'm in?"

Olly snorted. "They told me you were some super-intelligent computer whiz. Try switching that brain into gear and think about it."

A slow blush stole across Aiden's face.

"Ah. Now he gets it." Olly chuckled in delight all the way down the stairs.

Chapter Seven

Heath stood behind his desk and glowered at the young man in front of him. He felt vaguely angry that Aiden was so pale and drawn.

"Olly tells me that he thinks you had a nasty virus. Do you feel well now?"

"Better, thank you. I...I'm sorry I fainted on you."

Heath allowed a small smile to touch his lips as Aiden shifted uncomfortably from one foot to the other.

"Well, we'll adjust your work schedule for a few days to make sure you are fully recovered." He sat behind his desk with some relief. It was apparent that he couldn't be in the same room as Aiden without developing an aching erection. He was going to have to spend more time away from him, or he'd lose his mind. He looked up into those beautiful jade eyes and schooled his expression into coldness.

"This afternoon I'll have Olly show you around the island and introduce you to the staff you'll be working with. You will spend time in the kitchens, the garden and with the outdoor instructors. I will give you a timetable, which you will follow. This is a busy place and I don't have time to keep a constant eye on you, so I'm going to give you a choice." He opened a drawer and pulled out a device that looked like a small black plastic box attached to a rubberised strap. "Do you know what this is?"

"A wireless tracker?"

"Correct. Now, I can't force you to wear this, but if you do you'll have the freedom of the island. That's the range of the device. Try to leave and an alarm will go off, and believe me, if you make me track down your wandering arse you won't enjoy the consequences."

"And if I refuse?"

Heath frowned. "Then you'll be locked in your room every night and escorted at all times during the day."

"I can't imagine that that would be very easy to organise?"

Heath scowled at the amusement on Aiden's pretty face. "Are you deliberately trying to piss me off? I can have you up to your neck in crap twenty-four hours a day if I want to. I suggest you cooperate."

He could almost hear the cogs whirring in Aiden's brain. It was quite apparent from his expression that co-operation was not at the top of his 'to-do' list. Inside, Heath smiled—he loved a bit of resistance. Watching Aiden submit eventually would be all the more pleasurable for a bit of a fight. Aiden had spirit, but he was definitely submissive. He just didn't recognise it for what it was.

"Fine. Put the bloody thing on me."

"Put it on yourself." Heath threw the band at him. There was no way on this planet that he was going to kneel at Aiden's feet to put the tracker on.

Aiden dropped to one knee and slipped the strap into the locking mechanism.

"Tighter." Heath tried not to drool at the sight of Aiden looking up at him indignantly. "It will chafe more if it's loose."

Aiden pulled the strap until the device was snug against his skin, then looked up again.

Heath nodded his approval. Was that pleasure he saw flash in Aiden's green eyes? Just another sign that he would be a wonderful submissive if such a small indication of satisfaction made him happy. He was very graceful as he climbed back to his feet, but there was tension in his stance. Not surprising, considering his situation.

Heath considered for a moment whether to keep his young charge off balance, or whether to ease off and let him relax. His heart said one thing, his head another. This was going to be a nightmare. There was no way he could touch Aiden until his sentence was complete, but keeping his distance was going to be one hell of a fucking challenge.

He followed his head. "You take orders well. Get used to it. There will be a lot of people ordering you around from now on. If a member of my staff tells you to do something, you do it."

"Even Olly?" Aiden's lips twitched mischievously and Heath shook his head slowly. This wasn't going to be easy.

"Olly couldn't tell a dog to sit without sounding apologetic, but yes, even Olly."

There was a hesitant tap on the door. "Come in, Olly." Heath resigned himself to the hurt puppy look he knew he was about to be faced with. "I didn't say anything that wasn't true, now, did I?"

Olly pouted prettily before his face broke into a huge smile. "No, Sir. I'm sorry I overheard. I didn't mean to."

"Do you think you can manage to show Aiden around without losing him?"

Olly put an arm around Aiden's shoulders. "Yes, Sir, it will be my pleasure."

Heath controlled the growl that rose from his throat as he watched another man touch his property. It wouldn't do to frighten Olly when he didn't have a harmful bone in his body, and besides, Joe would probably dismember him if he did.

"You will report to me here every evening at eight p.m., Aiden. I'll see you tonight." He looked for acknowledgement, hoping that Aiden would respond appropriately.

"Yes... Sir."

Heath glowed inside. That one whispered word on Aiden's lips was all he could have hoped for. Aiden's eyes were cast down and there was a pretty flush on his face that said more than any words. What had it taken for him to call him Sir?

Then the doubts came. Perhaps he had just been following Olly's lead. Heath drilled into Aiden with his eyes, willing him to look up. As if under a spell, Aiden lifted his bright green eyes from under impossibly thick lashes and in that moment Heath knew, without a doubt, that Aiden felt the same attraction that he did. Fuck, they were both in deep trouble.

Chapter Eight

Aiden's head swam as Olly treated him to a running commentary on every aspect of the island, its buildings, the staff and the courses they ran. The place was bigger than he'd thought and he was glad he'd accepted the tracker without too much fuss. He might even get some time to himself if he was lucky — there were certainly plenty of places to escape to.

Bad choice of thoughts. Escape was not on his agenda. His sister might be a pain in the arse at times, but there was no way he would let her down or risk her money. Alone time would be good, though. He was not afraid of his own company and doubted that many of the staff would want to be friends with a convicted criminal.

Olly might be the exception. He cheerfully chattered away and treated Aiden the way he would anyone else he might have just met. Aiden grinned. Where his own personality tended towards healthy cynicism, Olly was definitely a 'glass half full' kind of person. Aiden found himself warming to the smaller man and even started to ask him a few unprompted questions.

"As you'll be working in lots of different places, I'll take you to the main ones first. You need to get your bearings so you can find your own way around."

They started in the kitchen gardens where a gruff, elderly head gardener held out a gnarled hand and shook Aiden's firmly before squeezing his arm hard.

"Strong lad then? Good, 'bout time they gave me some young muscles to do the heavy work around here."

Aiden looked around the immaculately laid out plots with genuine admiration. "This is amazing, Mr…uh…?"

"Call me Jacob, lad, we don't stand on ceremony around here. No time for airs and graces. Do you know owt about growing things?"

"I can tell the difference between a weed and a vegetable, but that's about it. Sorry."

Jacob's bronzed face cracked into a smile that exposed a prominent gold tooth. "Well, that's a start, and a step up from Olly here. He's not allowed near my plants, so if you catch him in here, you have my blessing to turn the hose on him."

"Jacob! It was only one time and I thought they were dandelions—I really did."

Olly looked completely crestfallen until Jacob tousled his hair and handed him a punnet of strawberries. "Fresh from the greenhouse. I know how much Joe likes these, though he would never admit it."

Olly bounced up and down in excitement. "Thanks, Jacob, these will make his day!"

Aiden tried not to laugh, but he caught Jacob's twinkling eye and couldn't stop himself.

"Hey! Whose side are you on?" Olly protested half-heartedly.

"When's my new assistant starting then, young Oliver?" Jacob wisely changed the subject.

Olly bore a grudge for all of ten seconds. "Tomorrow morning at seven. But you have to share him, Jacob. He's only yours until midday."

The old man shrugged. "Better than nowt, I suppose. Bright and early tomorrow then, Aiden. Don't be late, or I'll have you up to your ears in the compost heap before you can think up an excuse."

He turned back to his work and Olly started off towards the grounds. "How was I to know they were some weird kind of lettuce? They looked like dandelions. Some people have got memories like elephants." He grinned at Aiden. "Maybe you'll muck up even worse and Jacob will forgive me."

Aiden laughed. "It's quite likely. Now, where are we going next?"

"Assault course. We're going to meet Georgia Jones. She heads up the outdoor adventure team." He paused and looked curiously at Aiden. "Are you into women? You know, as well as men? I know you like men 'cos I've seen the way you look at Mr Anders."

"God, Olly, you have a vivid imagination. But to satisfy your rampant curiosity—no, I'm not into women. Why?"

"Well, Georgia's scary, but I'm reliably informed that she's hot too."

"What do you mean, scary?"

Olly looked a bit nervous. "She was an instructor in the army. She's used to bossing men around and I think she enjoys it. She shouts a lot."

Georgia proved to be short, blonde and Scottish. Her hair was cropped into a short, gamine style and her brown eyes shone over her snub little nose. She looked Aiden up and down critically. "You don't look much like a master criminal. More like an escapee from some emo rock band. Still, help is help. I hope you're fit, because you'll be demonstrating the kit for the courses we run and helping me safety test everything. We are so busy these days that the rest of my team are too involved with leading their own courses."

Aiden looked at some of the ropes, scramble nets, walls and tunnels that seemed to stretch for miles into the distance and swallowed. It all looked a bit intimidating. A slap on the back from Georgia propelled him forwards a couple of steps. "Don't look so scared—you'll do fine! You should see some of the lumbering idiots we get clambering over this lot every week. If you've got time to come back later, I'll train you up on a few of the obstacles and see how you get on."

Aiden looked at Olly questioningly.

"I'll send him back when we've finished the tour, Georgia. Couple of hours, okay?"

"Sure. See you later, Aiden."

As he followed Olly back towards the house, Aiden wondered at how everyone he'd met so far had been nothing but nice. He'd been half expecting the cold shoulder, but apart from some obvious curiosity, everyone seemed to be welcoming.

"Kitchens next. Be warned, the place is a hellhole. Emile runs it like a prison, but the staff all seem to worship him. Bloody good food, though."

"Emile?"

"Chef. French. Temper like a silverback gorilla and about the same size. He has a staff of twenty, including the waiting team. Exclusively male. He doesn't approve of women cluttering up his kitchen, apparently. Personally, I think he could do with a woman's touch in there."

They went down some stairs into the basement and Olly pushed open a swing door. Aiden's senses were assaulted by a cacophony of sounds, sights and smells — shouting, the clattering of pots and pans, steam swirling from huge sinks. Bright fluorescent strip lighting threw everything into stark relief. There were half a dozen white-clad men chopping, slicing, stirring and banging oven doors. Amidst the chaos, a huge man was waving a ladle and shouting orders in French.

"Emile!" Olly had to bellow to make himself heard.

Suddenly, Olly disappeared as the chef folded him up into a huge hug. Aiden feared he might have to fight his way in to rescue him before he suffocated, but eventually Olly emerged, red-faced and panting, balancing his strawberries precariously.

"Olly, *mon petit*, have you seen the light and come to cook *avec moi*?"

"Sorry, Emile, no. But I've brought you something better! This is Aiden. He's new. Oh, and could you put these somewhere so that Joe can have them later?"

Emile gestured, and a harried cook relieved Olly of his berries.

"Aagh! The criminal! Pah, he's just a boy."

A kitchen assistant dropped a baking tray with a clatter and Olly ducked as a piece of crockery, thrown by the irascible Emile, flew over his head and hit the wall close to the unfortunate boy's head. Aiden tried to make himself smaller and therefore less of a tempting target for missiles. Emile ignored them both and swore about the consistency of a sauce that someone else was carefully stirring.

"Don't worry — his bark's worse than his bite." One of the staff gave Aiden an encouraging smile. "He's a pain in the arse, but he'll defend this kitchen to the death if he has to." He turned back to his station and began chopping some kind of herb with the sort of speed that made Aiden wonder how he still had a full complement of fingers.

Olly tried to attract Emile's attention again. "Emile! Aiden will be working for you after evening service, okay?"

"Pah! 'Ow can I teach him anything about food when he is elbow deep in hot water?"

"You can teach anyone, Emile." Olly smiled sweetly and Aiden almost called for a bucket.

"You are a criminal, yes? Can I trust you near my kitchen knives?"

Aiden flushed. It was the first time anyone had hinted they might not trust him, and he had got used to the idea that nobody cared about his past. "I'm not that kind of hacker," he replied belligerently.

Olly fell about laughing. "He doesn't chop up people, Emile, he hacks computers!"

"Why would anyone want to hack up a computer? You make no sense, Olly."

By now, Aiden was smiling too. "Don't worry, Emile. I'm not dangerous, I promise."

"*Bon*. There is no more to say. Let me get back to cooking..." Instantly he was swearing and brandishing a ladle like a weapon, Olly and Aiden completely forgotten. They pushed their way out of the kitchen, took one look at each other and dissolved into hysterics.

"Maybe I should try to develop that reputation?"

Olly shook his head. "Oh, my God! That man's priceless. I hope you weren't too offended?"

Aiden went quiet. "No, but it did remind me why I'm here. I'm not supposed to be enjoying myself, Olly."

"Oh, don't worry—once I've shown you round the rest of the building and you've done your stint with Georgia, I have to take you back to Mr Anders. He'll make sure you know you're being punished." Olly twisted a blond curl coyly around his finger. "Of course, being punished by him could be fun."

Chapter Nine

Over the next five weeks, Aiden settled into a routine. Having some regularity to his life was welcome, and it gave him time to think. After an early breakfast, he spent the mornings with Jacob in the garden, which he enjoyed. If the weather was dry he'd be digging, planting, wheeling barrowloads of compost around — all the tasks that Jacob's aging back and knees no longer allowed him to do in comfort. If it was raining, they would be in the greenhouses transplanting seedlings or sorting out one of the many storage sheds. It was hard, dirty work, but Aiden found that he enjoyed the fresh air and listening to Jacob's tales of his misspent youth.

Lunch split the day, and Aiden usually found Olly waiting for him in the staff restaurant to gossip about the latest course intake. He liked to rate all the men on a scale of desirability, where Joe, of course, was the only ten and the majority of visitors barely climbed beyond a three.

The only times Aiden came into contact with the corporate guests was during the afternoons, when he helped Georgia and her team with various outdoor activities. One of his jobs was to run the assault course as a demonstration, then later on he would check ropes and planks, rake sand pits and run the ride-on mower over any overgrown areas. Georgia made no dispensation for bad weather, so rain or shine, he spent his afternoons getting sweaty and attracting a significant amount of mud.

He had an hour to shower, change and eat before his daily meeting with Heath at eight. Then it was Emile's turn to boss him around in the kitchen, where he was usually put to work washing up the delicate glass and silverware that couldn't be put in the industrial-size dishwashers, or mopping the floors and emptying the bins. At eleven he'd fall into bed, exhausted, and if he dreamed, he didn't remember.

The briefest part of his day proved to be the toughest. Half an hour in close proximity to Heath was more challenging than anything Georgia, Emile or Jacob could throw at him. Aiden often had to spend a couple of minutes outside Heath's door, schooling his expression and calming his shaking hands, before he could knock and go in. He had trained himself to tap on the door at precisely eight o'clock. Heath had no tolerance for a lack of punctuality. He was also a stickler for good manners and an appropriate measure of deference. Of course, Aiden's idea of appropriate and Heath's were at opposite ends of a very long scale.

At the end of his first week, he'd stood in front of the desk in Heath's office as Heath had unfolded his tall frame from behind it with an impatient grunt. Aiden could still remember every word.

"You are an affront to my eyes and you're making my office untidy. For fuck's sake, stand up straight."

Aiden had known his trousers had been splashed with mud and there'd been a small graze on his cheek from a mishap on the assault course, but he hadn't thought he'd looked that bad. Heath's tone had still sent some kind of invisible signal to his brain, and he'd pulled his shoulders back.

"Hands behind your back."

Heath's grey eyes had dared him to disobey. Aiden had grasped one wrist with his other hand and had attempted to keep still. Heath's kick to one of his ankles had pushed his legs a little farther apart.

"How did this happen?" Heath had touched his cheek with cool fingers, and Aiden had flinched as if he'd been stung. Heath's grip on his wrist had tightened enough to bruise, and he had felt his cock stiffening.

He'd stammered out an answer. "I slipped in the mud and caught the corner of a support on the scramble nets…Sir." Using that word had inevitably made his cock even harder. He'd prayed that Heath wouldn't brush against him or look down. With his hands behind his back, he'd had no way of hiding his body's reaction.

Heath, of course, had done both.

Heath had taken a slow step back, his grey eyes glinting. "You will stand like this when we meet each evening."

Aiden's face had burned. One touch. That had been all it had taken to turn him into a trembling wreck. Then Heath had stroked his hair.

"Good boy."

He'd found the will to glare, hoping that it would disguise the glow that had suffused his entire body at the knowledge that he had pleased Heath Anders.

Four weeks later, he still dreaded this daily meeting. It was torment to be alone with Heath and not be able to act on the desires he harboured. His body didn't help him to keep his secret, and Heath seemed to revel in the ability to make Aiden hard with just a flick of his fingers or the brush of his knee. He would look pointedly at the tented fabric and smirk, but never say anything directly.

Over the weeks, he had coached Aiden to stand just the way he wanted him, and now Aiden found himself dropping naturally into a stance that was overtly submissive. As the days passed, Aiden managed to keep still for longer, controlling his desire to fidget. Stillness and calm seemed to please Heath, and his approval made Aiden tingle in all the right places.

Tonight, though, he was late, and he didn't have time to collect himself before he knocked on the door. He heard a muted, "Come in." Heath's voice sounded sterner than usual, but maybe it was just his imagination. Aiden had to force his body to relax and be still, but he couldn't rid himself entirely of a vague sense of unease.

"You're late."

"Sorry, I—"

"You don't speak unless I tell you to. You're late, and that demands punishment."

Heath circled him slowly and Aiden found a spot on the wall to fix his eyes to so that he didn't twist his head to follow Heath's movements.

"How do you think you should be punished, Aiden?"

Heath's deep voice slid sensuously across Aiden's senses. He swallowed, his throat and mouth suddenly parched. He had only been two minutes late, and he'd been helping Olly. He wanted to protest his innocence, but it was as though his vocal chords had been cut. He ducked his head, allowing his hair to fall across his eyes.

"Nothing to say?" Heath used his knuckles to tilt Aiden's chin up and a small moan escaped Aiden's lips. His cock ached for another touch, any touch.

He shook his head slowly. He could feel pre-cum gathering on the tip of his cock, dampening his shorts. His balls felt hot and tight. Why the hell did his body respond this way when he should be pissed off? Instead, he felt eager anticipation for what Heath might have in store for him.

"Very well. You obviously need a reminder that breaking my rules has consequences. Go and do your kitchen shift. I'll put some thought into exactly how you should be dealt with. I'll expect you back here at ten, prompt."

Aiden chewed on his bottom lip. He raised his gaze cautiously and almost gasped at the expression of predatory lust on Heath's face that he hid a little too slowly. His stomach flopped over a couple of times and he felt in desperate need of an ice pack for his groin. It was a huge relief when Heath dismissed him to the kitchen.

Aiden pulled the heavy office door closed behind him and leaned against it for a moment, eyes closed, waiting for the rapid beat of his heart to calm. Gradually, a sound he didn't recognise seeped into his awareness. He opened his eyes and tried to pin down the direction the sound was coming from. There was a grandfather clock across the hall ticking away, which was distracting, and for a moment he thought he'd been imagining things. But then he heard it again. A small whimper.

The only door that was ajar led to Joe's office, directly opposite Heath's. Soft light spilled around the edges of the dark wood. Quietly, Aiden moved across the hall, trying to convince himself that this wasn't spying. He wasn't exactly taking the most direct route to the kitchens. If he didn't move a bit faster Emile was going to wrap the nearest metal utensil around his head, but his curiosity got the better of him.

He didn't dare get too close to the door, and that meant that his view was restricted to a narrow strip. He gulped and took a shaky step back. Olly, his hands cuffed behind his back, was bent over Joe's desk, as naked as the day he was born. His face was turned away from the door and Aiden could now clearly hear his small moans of pleasure. Suddenly, the splayed tails of a flogger landed across his arse, darkening the shade of red that already stained both smooth, round cheeks. Aiden couldn't see who was landing the blows that followed, one after another, evenly spaced, smacking leather against skin. He knew it had to be Joe and it was confirmed when Aiden heard his voice, low and reassuring.

Aiden felt frozen in place. He knew he should turn away, but he couldn't. He watched as Joe stroked Olly's sore arse, then squeezed and kneaded the flesh. Then Joe dragged his finger up and down Olly's parted crack, grazing his hole.

"Please, Sir! More!" Olly's whisper was quiet but desperate. Joe smacked his hand down on Olly's exposed arse.

"I decide when you deserve more, Oliver. Do you want to be put back in chastity?"

"No! I'm sorry, Sir, I'll be good." Olly was sobbing with frustration.

Aiden's face burned. The scene playing out before his eyes was so hot. He was painfully aroused, but it had nothing to do with Olly or Joe. His imagination had Heath holding that flogger, and it was his own skin stinging from the kiss of leather, his own hands straining against metal bondage. Fuck, if he watched any longer he was going to come. He forced himself to turn away. He needed a dose of French swearing and culinary violence to bring him back down to earth.

As he walked stiffly away, Olly screamed out his pleasure, much louder than before. Aiden ran for the basement stairs.

Chapter Ten

Heath stretched out his legs and sank back into the soft leather of his favourite armchair. The latest corporate group had gone. The lounge bar was empty apart from him, Joe and Olly. Joe was sprawled in the chair opposite him, with Olly on the floor at his feet, leaning against his knee with a dreamy smile and slightly swollen lips. He looked thoroughly and happily fucked.

Heath sipped red wine from a glittering crystal glass and tried to ignore the smile on Joe's handsome face. A smile that was rapidly becoming a smirk.

He gave in.

"All right, all right. I know you want to say something, so just spit it out!"

Joe chuckled, the sound rumbling deep in his throat. Absently, he wound Olly's blond curls around his fingers. "So, did it work? Olly was very careful not to make him too late."

"Two minutes. Just long enough to justify punishment. Damn it, Joe, you should have seen his face. He wanted to protest, but he wanted punishment more. It was fascinating—the fight going on behind those eyes."

"He's not sweet and pliable like Olly, is he? He's defiant, rebellious… He must hate wanting to drop to his knees for you."

"And that makes him all the more difficult to resist."

"So why try? I know strictly speaking he's a prisoner here, but if you both want this…"

Heath sighed. "I can't, Joe, not until he's free. But I can start to train him—even if he doesn't know it's happening."

"Devious sod. Well, you'll be glad to know that he is drawn to open doors."

Heath swirled the wine in his glass thoughtfully. "He watched you, then? What exactly did he see?"

"I don't think he could see me. Just Olly, taking a thrashing over my desk."

"Good. I want his imagination working overtime when he comes to me later for his punishment."

"Devious. And evil." Joe raised his glass in a mocking toast. "Any time you want us to help out again, just say the word. It was a pleasant early evening interlude."

"I'm not sure Olly's arse echoes that sentiment."

"His arse is mine, to do with as I please." Joe grinned. "And I've given him a cushion."

Olly lifted his head and shifted onto his knees between Joe's spread thighs. He looked up adoringly. Joe gave him the slightest of nods and Olly leant forward and tackled his zipper with even, white teeth.

"Oh, for pity's sake, don't you two ever let up?" Heath swallowed the last of his wine and stood, scowling down at his friend.

Joe sucked in his breath as Olly wrapped his lips around his now exposed cock. "This could be you too. Though Aiden might be more inclined to bite it off."

Olly almost choked on a combination of swollen cock and laughter, but didn't look up.

"Brat." Joe stroked his hair gently.

Heath rolled his eyes and stalked from the room, shutting the door behind him just a little too firmly. He didn't begrudge his friends one second of their happiness—it had been hard earned—but it had been a long time since anyone had looked that way at him, and he wanted it again. The problem was he wanted it from Aiden and that meant that his fingers would be well exercised for some time yet.

He headed back to his study and tried, unsuccessfully, to settle to some paperwork. His attention continually strayed to the clock and every minute felt interminable as he waited for Aiden to return. He ran his tongue over his lower lip in anticipation. Would Aiden obey and take his punishment, or would he refuse? Heath hadn't planned how he would deal with the latter scenario. His instincts were good—he knew a natural submissive when he saw one. If he were wrong... Well, he'd cross that bridge if he came to it.

There was a nervous tap at the door and Heath smiled a slow, feral smile.

"Come in, Aiden."

Aiden was wearing just his uniform polo shirt and trousers, no fleece. His face was a little flushed and his hair dishevelled. Two hours in Emile's kitchen would do that to anyone. He faced Heath but kept his eyes firmly fixed on the floor.

Heath took a moment to admire the shape of the Aiden's arms, slim but firm. He had filled out nicely after almost two months of decent food and hard exercise. The toned muscle suited his slender frame. Heath wondered what the rest of him looked like under all that concealing black. Perhaps he should rethink the staff uniform—it just wasn't clingy enough to give much away. He allowed himself a smile. If everything went to plan, he'd soon be seeing everything he wanted to.

He made his voice deliberately gentle. "So, Aiden, would you prefer to have your punishment now or in the morning?"

Aiden looked startled and a little scared. Heath kept his silence until Aiden realised that he had to speak because there was no other option.

"Tonight...Sir." He hesitated, as if uncertain whether that was enough, then added a whispered, "Please."

Heath just nodded, took a step forward and grasped his slim wrist firmly. He applied just enough pressure to make a point but not enough to hurt, then tugged Aiden after him. His skin was so soft and smooth, warm to the touch. He resisted the urge to stroke Aiden's inner wrist with his thumb. He wondered if it was one of Aiden's erogenous zones, if he would respond to it being wrapped in a supple leather cuff. *Fuck.* Mentally he reprimanded himself for visualising things that had an inevitable effect on his cock.

Aiden trailed after him, unresisting and unquestioning, until they reached the men's locker room. The large shower area was a pristine, white-tiled square with showerheads on three walls. Heath dropped Aiden's wrist and pretended not to notice when he caressed the red marks left by his grip. He circled the room, turning each shower fully on as he went.

"Now you're going to clean it, inch by inch." He pulled a small scrubbing brush and a bottle of cleaning fluid from a cupboard and threw them into the centre of the shower area. "Without getting your clothes wet." Then he took a seat on a changing bench, crossed his ankles and waited to see how long it would take Aiden to realise that this punishment wasn't as simple as it seemed.

Slowly, a pretty flush spread its way across sharp cheekbones. "You son of a bitch. You can't do this." His voice was scratchy, as if his throat were dry.

Heath quirked one eyebrow. "Can't I?" He watched, delighted, as Aiden visibly trembled.

Aiden glared back at him and just for a moment Heath thought he might refuse, but then he pulled his shirt off over his head, muffling a "Fuck you." Boots and socks were next, then trousers — pushed down and kicked away. Heath had to clamp his mouth shut to stop himself from drooling at the sight of all that smooth, pale skin over toned muscle. Despite his dark colouring, Aiden had very little body hair. Nothing on his chest and just the faintest tracing leading beneath his black shorts. He hesitated for just a moment before turning his back and yanking off his underwear.

Heath nearly came there and then at the sight of Aiden's perfect, smooth, tight arse. What he wouldn't give to bend Aiden over his knee right that minute and give him the spanking he deserved. How pretty those cheeks would look with his mark on them.

Aiden grabbed the cleaning tools, took a step into the showers and dropped gracefully to his knees. For the next hour Heath was in a heaven of his own making as Aiden scrubbed each tile, even though they were all perfectly clean already. Water glistened on his skin. His hair darkened and hung in dripping tendrils around his face. Every movement tensed muscles in his thighs and buttocks. Tantalising glimpses of plump, smooth balls were an occasional treat, but Aiden kept his legs stubbornly closed and his back to his audience. It wasn't until he had scrubbed every tile and stood with a groan that Heath knew he would see what he really wanted to.

"I assume I'm done, or do you want me to repeat that utterly pointless process?" Aiden snapped.

Heath just smiled calmly. "You're done."

Aiden turned with more than a hint of defiance, stalked from the shower room and grabbed a towel to wrap around his waist. It took long enough for his erection to be clearly visible to Heath's satisfied gaze. That was all he needed to know. There was no doubt that Aiden was thoroughly, and beautifully, turned on by domination.

Heath smirked. He needed to get to his own room, and fast, or his balls were going to explode.

"Get dressed and go to bed. I'll decide on your punishment for swearing at me tomorrow."

Aiden's expression was a perfect combination of naked need and rebellious disbelief. Heath was left with the ideal image to take to his bed and an urgent appointment with his hand.

Chapter Eleven

Aiden pressed his forehead against the cool tiles and muttered a string of curses under his breath. He stroked himself roughly, taking out his anger and frustration on his iron cock. It didn't take long before he came with a gasp, but it was a while before he picked up his discarded towel and cleaned himself up.

He sat on one of the wooden benches, eyes unfocused, staring off into the distance. His head was full of confused thoughts and images. He should feel humiliated, indignant and bloody angry, but all he did feel was a warm inner glow. Kneeling naked beneath the water, knowing that Heath's grey eyes were following his every move, had been incredibly erotic. He could think of several ways that it could have been even better. A nice, fat butt plug, a studded cock ring…chains on his ankles. He shook his wet hair, trying to shock some sense into himself. What the hell was wrong with him? He dressed slowly and headed up to his room, suddenly exhausted. Heath had had no right to subject him to such a punishment, but all he could think about was what the next one might be.

Getting Heath out of his head proved to be impossible, and his dreams were coloured by a montage of highly erotic and sometimes improbable scenes. When he awoke, a little shell-shocked with only dim memories of his night of fantasising, his cock was painfully hard. The remedy, an icy shower, did little to improve his mood.

He joined Olly at their usual breakfast table, gulped down a glass of juice then scooped cereal rapidly into his mouth. Olly looked at him from over a newspaper with raised eyebrows. "What's eating you this morning?"

Aiden chased the last cornflake around his bowl and sighed. "Didn't sleep very well."

Olly chuckled knowingly. "Perhaps you should tell Heath how you feel and get it over with?"

"What?" Aiden felt his face heat. "You talk some rubbish, Olly. My only feelings for Heath are bloody irritation."

"Oh, really? That's what it's called nowadays, is it?" Olly shook his blond curls. "Anyone with two brain cells to rub together can see the sparks flying between you two. Being submissive is nothing to be ashamed of, you know."

"I'm not...submissive." Even as the words left his mouth, Aiden knew they were a lie, and Olly didn't deserve that. "Am I?"

"Be honest, Aiden. When you are alone with Heath, how do you feel?"

"Nervous. On edge."

"Horny?"

Aiden bowed his head. "Fuck, yes. All the time."

"And do you visualise yourself screwing him into the ground?"

"No!" Aiden looked at Olly and sighed. He'd fallen for that, good and proper.

"No. Quite the reverse I imagine?" Olly tilted his head to one side. "And there's a part of you that hates that you want it."

Aiden scrubbed a hand through his hair and looked for any trace of amusement in Olly's eyes. All he saw was empathy.

"Aiden, submission comes in many forms. Joe makes me feel safe, cherished. I never feel better than when I'm kneeling at his feet or curled in his lap. Somehow, I can't see you doing that for Heath."

Aiden shook his head. "No. But what if that's what he wants, Olly?"

"He wants you. He likes a bit of resistance. Relishes the fight. For him, you're perfect. But he will make you obey him, Aiden, don't doubt that. He's even more Dominant than Joe. One of these days his restraint is going to crack. He's going to tie you down and fuck you into submission. He just doesn't want to touch you while there's any chance you feel you don't have a choice."

Aiden absorbed the words and felt some of the tension in his body disperse. He focused on buttering a piece of toast so that he didn't have to look directly at Olly again. He glanced up at the TV flickering away in a corner, catching a name that piqued his interest. He listened to the story, straining to hear over the noise of breakfast chatter and clashing cutlery.

The footage showed various men in suits being led from several different corporate buildings in the capital. The ticker tape on the screen shouted, 'Breaking news—eighteen people convicted of serious fraud, embezzlement, money laundering...' The list went on.

Aiden suddenly realised that Olly was saying something. "It's all over the papers, too. The biggest scandal to hit the city in years. Crime behind the façade of big business, and apparently it all came crashing down because of a system glitch in their computers that relayed hidden accounting information into the public domain."

Aiden pushed his chair back and stood. Olly was still talking, "Hey, isn't Tecnet Corporation one of the companies you hacked —?"

"I have to go." Aiden turned towards the door.

"It's the weekend, Aiden. Jacob's not here."

"I know, but he's left me a ton of work, and for some reason Heath doesn't like me to be around when the weekend course members arrive. I'd better make myself scarce."

He grabbed his fleece from the back of the chair and headed for the refuge of the gardens. Unfortunately, his timing was off and he crossed the main hall just as Heath arrived with a small group of visitors and their bags. Aiden froze and looked for the quickest and least conspicuous escape route, but it was too late — he'd been spotted. Not by Heath, but by a tall, dark man at the back of the group. He had a neat goatee and eyes that seemed almost black.

"Well, boys, look what we have here. It seems Mr Anders neglected to mention how gorgeous the staff are. Heath, I hope this delicious piece of arse will be assisting this weekend?"

Aiden wanted to sink into the ground as five pairs of eyes turned towards him. What the hell kind of corporate group was this? Without exception, they looked like they wanted to eat him alive.

Heath's voice was calm, but his eyes spoke of future retribution as he looked at the cause of all the interest.

"Aiden. Shouldn't you be in the gardens by now?" Aiden ran for the door, but still overheard Heath's next words. "Sorry, gentlemen. He is very much taken, and his Master is not known for his ability to share."

"He's not collared." That was a voice he didn't recognise.

"No. He is off limits, though."

Murmurs of "shame" and "the prettiest ones are always taken" burned in his ears, and suddenly the distant greenhouses felt like sanctuary.

Transplanting seedlings helped to focus his mind as he carefully extracted the tiny plants from large trays and moved them to individual pots. As he worked, slowly and methodically, he had time to think about The Edge and its clientele.

Other than Emile and some of the kitchen crew, the staff members at weekends were different. There were no women, for a start, and the average age dropped considerably. Heath always kept him away from the main house as much as possible, and he spent most of his weekends working in the gardens. There were no outdoor activities — everything took place in the main buildings.

There were parts of the house he'd never seen, controlled by keypad entry systems. He'd been kept so busy that locked doors hadn't really excited his curiosity, but now he began to wonder just what went on behind them. He shook his head. It really wasn't his business. He didn't want to attract any attention. But Heath had clearly talked about him having a Master, and a possessive one at that. *What the hell was that about?* His cock jerked as he realised that he half hoped it was true.

He cleared up his tools and moved outside. There were a couple of beds to dig over ready for late planting, then the roses to trim back. His mind drifted to the news story he'd seen on the TV. Olly had made the connection between his own conviction and one of the companies involved — but one could be coincidence. He wondered if anyone knew more about his case. If anyone realised that all those companies, rather than just one, had been his hacking targets, there would inevitably be questions he couldn't answer.

He straightened up and rolled his shoulders. He'd been at The Edge nearly two months. He could be gone in days. He bent over and ran a finger under the band around his ankle, shifting it into a more comfortable position. He couldn't wait to be rid of the bloody thing. He wasn't so sure about wanting to leave The Edge. It had its attractions, and his stomach knotted at the thought of never seeing Heath again.

"What the hell were you doing in the hall this morning?"

Aiden nearly jumped out of his skin at the sound of Heath's voice behind him. For a big guy, he sure could move quietly. He turned towards a steely gaze and swallowed. Heath's hair was tousled by the wind, his arms folded across his chest, which helped to display the muscle definition perfectly. He looked absolutely gorgeous. Pissed off, but gorgeous.

"I asked you a question, Aiden."

Aiden bridled. His body was betraying him, his cock hardening rapidly at Heath's tone, but none of this was his fault.

"What do you think I was doing? I was on my way here. Why does it matter?"

He took a step back as Heath growled his displeasure.

"I don't want you anywhere near our weekend clients. I've told you that before."

"Why not? Is it too embarrassing to have a criminal on your staff?" He could feel himself colouring as Heath closed the gap between them

"Don't be ridiculous, that's got nothing to do with it." Heath glowered sexily. "The men who come here at weekends are different from our usual visitors. You aren't safe near them."

"Because they're Dominants?" Aiden spat the words like a challenge as all the pieces suddenly dropped into place. "Like you?"

Heath's grey eyes darkened. "Who told you?" He took another menacing step.

Aiden rolled his eyes. "I worked it out all by myself, Heath. I can't believe it took me this long, now I think about it."

Heath's face was expressionless. "Then you understand why I don't want you anywhere near them?"

"No! I don't."

Then Heath was reaching for him, cupping his neck and pulling him in for a kiss that began gently, but rapidly turned into a scorching attack. Heath grabbed his hair tightly, holding him in place. He nipped at Aiden's lips and probed his mouth, pushing away his defences to explore and taste him. He could do nothing but respond, opening himself to anything Heath wanted to do. Tentatively, he did a little tasting himself. Heath's lips were so wonderfully soft, but they still bruised. Stubble scraped his vulnerable skin. He was running out of air. Could he come from a kiss? It was becoming more and more likely.

He gasped as Heath released him but cupped his face with his hand.

"You're mine, Aiden. Understand? Mine."

Then Heath turned and strolled away without looking back.

Chapter Twelve

That night after Heath and Joe had finished their customary review of the day, they settled down for a nightcap.

"Does something about this group seem off to you, Joe? There's one guy that asks a lot more questions than usual."

"Tall bloke with a goatee? Name's John?"

"Yes, that's him. He seems to have an unhealthy interest in the staff. Keeps asking questions about recruitment, training, that kind of thing. Do you know who recommended him?"

Joe wandered over to his desk and pulled out a file. No one attended The Edge's more specialist courses without a reference. "Owner of a club called Chainmale. It's genuine. We've had people from there before."

He returned to his seat. "Is he showing interest in anyone in particular?"

"No. And that's what worries me. If it was just a fixation on one of the boys I could understand it, but he's more interested in how long people have been here, that kind of thing. He's spreading his questions around too—I've had a couple of the boys come to me, saying that he's been asking about various people. I think he's looking for someone."

Heath frowned and Joe's brow creased with worry. "Aiden. He must be looking for Aiden. I think you should ring your father and see if he has any information he can give you about the case."

Heath nodded. "First thing in the morning, but we need to keep a close eye on this John…and Aiden." He paused, feeling Joe's eyes on him. "I kissed him, Joe."

Joe chuckled. "About fucking time. Did he deck you?"

"No. He was… It was… Oh, bloody hell."

Joe poured him another drink. "Here. I think you need this. You're in love with him, aren't you?"

"Since the first moment I saw him. Fuck, I'm becoming as sappy as Olly." He sipped his drink slowly, savouring the warmth that coated his tongue. "He knows what I am, Joe. He's worked out what we do here at weekends without anyone telling him. I told him he was mine."

"And what did he say?"

"I didn't give him the chance to say anything. But it's true, Joe. I can't bear the thought of another man getting anywhere near him, let alone touching him."

"Jesus, Heath. How many courses have you run on the importance of communication and trust? Follow your own advice!"

"This isn't a normal situation, Joe. Aiden is in my care. I've already abused my position by kissing him."

"Rubbish. He wants it as much as you do. I've seen the way he looks at you. Take a risk. Push him and see what happens."

Heath swirled the liquid around his glass. "Maybe. I'll think about it."

They sat in companionable silence for a while before Joe headed off to bed. Heath left the office shortly afterwards. He climbed the stairs slowly and stopped outside Aiden's door, Joe's words playing in his head. Then he was holding the handle and before he could change his mind, he opened the door.

The glow of a small bedside lamp lit Aiden's perfect features softly. The green glint of his eyes seemed brighter than normal. He was propped against his pillows, reading a paperback thriller, his dark, wavy hair stark against the white cotton. The bedspread covered him from the waist down, but it was the bare part that attracted Heath's attention. All that smooth skin and toned muscle.

Aiden's eyes widened and he dropped his book. Heath allowed himself a satisfied smile. Aiden was nervous, that was good. He pulled the door shut with a click and leaned against it.

"Have you thought about what I said to you earlier, Aiden?"

Aiden nipped at his lower lip before he spoke. "How could I not?" He looked down.

"Look at me."

Aiden jerked his head back up instantly and he coloured prettily.

"You were already mine, weren't you, Aiden? I was only confirming something you already knew." Heath let the silence grow.

"I…"

Heath watched as he pulled his knees up, holding the edge of the covers like a lifeline.

"Well, let's see, shall we?" Heath straightened but didn't move away from the door. He schooled his expression into coldness.

"Get rid of those fucking covers."

Slowly—oh, so slowly—Aiden pushed the covers down over his knees and let them pool around his ankles.

"Lie flat."

Aiden glared at him but then slumped down onto the bed and flattened his legs out, moving his hands to cover a rapidly filling erection.

"Hands above your head. You will never cover yourself in my presence."

Heath walked the length of the bed, running one finger up Aiden's calf and thigh. He slipped his belt off and used it to bind Aiden's hands to the headboard. God, he looked so perfect, stretched out for inspection.

Heath began to touch gently, trailing his finger across Aiden's collarbone and down the centre of his chest. Aiden twitched beneath his touch and whimpered.

"Keep fucking still." Heath rolled Aiden's tender nipple between his fingers and watched Aiden closely as he tried desperately not to move. He applied enough pressure to hurt a little and kept his focus on that one tiny spot for one minute, then another. Aiden was fully hard now, cock straining, a gleam of pre-cum at its tip, but still Heath played with that one tormented nub. He let go briefly, then pinched hard. Aiden yelped and his hips jerked upwards. Heath smirked and began the same process on Aiden's second, neglected nipple.

"Oh, God… Heath… Please!"

"Quiet!"

Heath revelled in the feel of silky, warm skin beneath his fingertips as he smoothed his hand across Aiden's belly, resting it there, absorbing the heat.

"You are mine. Your body is mine, to do with as I see fit. Your only role is to obey."

Heath traced the line between Aiden's hip and thigh, featherlight, tormenting mercilessly.

"Turn over."

He watched as Aiden struggled onto his front, the leather around his wrists digging into his flesh as the belt twisted with him.

"Spread your legs."

Heath stroked the length of Aiden's spine, tracing the ridges of bone, until he reached the top of his arse. It was firm, smooth, perfect. For a while he just admired its form and imagined what it would feel like to bury himself between those cheeks. He brought his open hand down hard, once, twice, then inspected the pretty red marks left behind.

Aiden cried out in shock, but didn't protest. In fact, he shoved his arse up, as if asking for more.

"Good boy. Up on your knees."

Tied as he was, this forced Aiden into a head down, arse up position, which had Heath practically drooling. It was a bloody good job Aiden couldn't see his face.

"Wider. Display yourself properly."

Aiden shuffled his knees apart, and now Heath could see his tight little entrance. Aiden's dick was straining, his balls pulled up tight against his body. Heath knew that it wouldn't take much to make him come. He resisted the urge to touch, and instead blew a slow stream of air onto Aiden's exposed hole.

"Aagh! Fuck!" Aiden came hard, shooting onto the sheets below him, hips jerking, arms straining against his bondage.

Heath stood back and watched. *What a perfect sight.* When Aiden's panting slowed, he stepped forward and released his wrists. Aiden collapsed, regardless of the stickiness beneath him, and moaned. Heath bent forward and whispered in his ear, "If you ever come again without my permission, there will be consequences." He kissed Aiden's trembling shoulder then sucked hard, raising a mark.

"Now tell me who you belong to."

"You, Sir." The words were barely a whisper, but they were enough.

Heath smiled and closed the door softly behind him as he left.

Chapter Thirteen

Aiden woke early and with a start. He lay still for a moment, listening for unusual noises, but there was nothing out of the ordinary. The dawn chorus was in full swing, but apart from hundreds of overly competitive birds, all was quiet.

Then he remembered the previous night. "Oh, holy hell! Was I dreaming, or did it really happen?" The light bruising around his wrists confirmed his fears. Just the sight of the marks Heath had created was enough to harden his dick. Aiden banged his head back against the pillow and cursed creatively, hoping that no one was watching the security monitors—they would think he had gone mad.

So what the hell would happen now? He had submitted to a man who was his walking wet dream, and loved every minute of the experience, but there was still a part of him that resisted. Somewhere deep in his mind, he needed to know that Heath regarded him as more than a toy to be played with, then discarded.

He showered and dressed in a bit of a daze, then took a long hard look at himself in the mirror. He felt different. Surely he must look different? He pushed his hair back from his face and made a mental note to ask Olly if there was someone on the staff who could give him a trim. Perhaps he'd even be allowed off the island if someone went with him. His green eyes had tiny flecks of amber around the pupils, something he hadn't noticed before. The clear jade colour was unusual, but his mother had told him that his great grandfather's had been a similar colour. At the time, she had been trying to reassure him. He'd been beaten up at school for being too pretty, and had come home with an impressive black eye.

He smiled wryly at the memory. He'd been no pushover and he had never been bullied again after that day. He'd put up with being called 'pretty boy' on the hockey field with good humour, and his skill had eventually won over even the most persistent doubters.

His lashes were thick and dark—a constant irritation to his sister, who had to spend a fortune on mascara. His normally pale skin had a warmer hue after hours spent working outside, but was still more cream than tan.

Aiden shrugged. What did Heath see when he looked at him? Did he think that now Aiden had taken that first tentative step towards submission, he would be willing to spend a higher proportion of time on his knees? That so wasn't going to happen.

* * * *

Olly looked at him suspiciously over breakfast. "You're acting all weird. What have you done? You're not digging an escape tunnel or something, are you?"

Aiden almost spat coffee all over the table in his attempt not to laugh.

"I'm not trying to escape, Olly. I promise." He gestured at his ankle. "This bloody thing keeps me nicely penned, doesn't it?"

"You could cut it off."

"What with? It's steel under the rubber. I'd end up cutting off my own leg, and then I wouldn't be able to run very far, would I?"

Olly pouted. "You're my friend now. I don't want you to go."

Aiden ruffled his blond curls fondly. "How did you get this into your head? I'm not going anywhere."

"Good. Pass the jam." Olly could switch topics the way he switched TV channels.

"It's Sunday — what are you doing today?"

Olly frowned. "There's that course in. Joe has to work all day."

"Well, I'm working in the garden. Do you want to help? There's a load of old terracotta pots to scrub out."

Olly's face lit up. "Do I get to boss you around?"

Aiden rolled his eyes. "I bet you've never asked Joe that question."

Olly giggled. "I might give it a try. He likes to have a good reason to spank me."

Aiden groaned. "Too much information. But you can tell me more about the less public side of the business while I work. Now I know about it, I might as well get the full story."

Olly grinned. "Well, that will be fun."

Aiden looked past Olly's shoulder, then lowered his eyes.

"You wouldn't be planning on having fun without me would you, Oliver?" Joe placed one hand on each of Olly's shoulders and squeezed. Olly pushed his chair back precariously on two legs and leaned into Joe's body. His eyes closed and Aiden could have sworn he heard purring. Joe stroked Olly's hair absently and fixed his eyes on Aiden.

"Heath wants you in the study, Aiden. You may as well come too, Olly." He pushed Olly's chair back to the floor, then kept one hand on his shoulder as he guided them towards the door. Aiden felt his stomach knotting uncomfortably at the thought of seeing Heath again, but with Joe looming close behind him he had little choice.

Heath was waiting for them, an unreadable expression on his handsome face. Aiden found himself held by his gaze, unable to look away. A small smile curved the corner of Heath's lips and suddenly, desperately, Aiden yearned for those lips to capture his own. He was so utterly distracted that he didn't notice that there was someone else in the room until a cough broke the silence. Joe pushed the door closed and leant back against it, his arms wrapped around Olly, holding him close.

"Hello, Aiden. Why don't you sit down?" The man who had spoken took a step forward, into the light. He was tall, though not as tall as Heath. His blond hair had been cut severely short. His pale blue eyes darted around the room, never resting anywhere for very long. He looked tense, coiled, as if he was about to pounce on something. He looked dangerous.

Aiden had met him before, all those months ago when he had been approached by the authorities who had asked for his help. It seemed like a lifetime ago.

"Agent Becket. What are you doing here?" Aiden knew his voice sounded a bit shaky and he hated himself for appearing weak, but this man's appearance could only mean trouble. He took a seat in front of Heath's desk and waited for an answer.

Becket perched on the edge of the desk and gave what Aiden assumed was supposed to be a reassuring smile. It didn't help.

"Aiden, I've apprised your colleagues of the situation. They know the real reason you are here."

"They aren't my colleagues, Becket, they're my gaolers. Or had you forgotten that little detail?"

Becket ignored him, "As you have probably seen on the news, things have developed. The worms you planted into various company systems did their jobs and we took down an extensive crime ring as a result. It worked like a dream."

"So I assume you're here to let me go? To give me my life back?"

Becket hesitated, and Heath stepped forward to stand next to him. "It's not that simple, Aiden. Agent Becket tells us that there is a contract out on you. It didn't take long for someone to make the connection between a mischievous hacker and the collapse of multi-billion pound criminal empire."

Aiden looked around the room. Olly's eyes were huge with shock. Joe was holding him tightly. Agent Becket's face was as cold as ever—the man had less emotional range than a black mamba. Heath... well he looked like he wanted to kill someone. Slowly.

"I get the feeling that I'm not going to like what's coming." Aiden felt sick. "This wasn't supposed to happen. Pleading guilty was supposed to give me anonymity. My name was never supposed to be connected with the trial. I agreed to take my punishment and wait it out until you took them down, then my name would be cleared."

"There was a leak. What can I say? I'm sorry it happened, but it did, and you are a target now."

"Do they know where I am?"

"We believe they know you're here on the island, but not what you look like. Someone has been asking suspicious questions recently."

Heath nodded. "He's still here—he's on this weekend's course."

"Then you need to get me away from here, Becket. I'm putting other people in danger." Aiden couldn't stop his hands from shaking. He pressed them hard into his knees, clenching his fists tightly.

Heath walked around behind him, put a hand lightly on his shoulder. He wanted so much for Heath to take him into his arms and hold him, but that touch would have to do. He prayed that Heath wouldn't move his hand away.

"If we do that, we won't stand a chance of catching them, Aiden. They'll just track you down again and again. Here, we are in control," Becket said firmly.

"So what are you saying?"

"You have to stay here. Act as if nothing has changed. We're going to draw them out."

"You mean you're going to stick me on a hook and dangle it to see what takes the bait? Charming."

Becket chuckled. "Still as fucking sarcastic as ever."

"At least take this bloody thing off my ankle?" He gestured jerkily at the tracker.

Heath's grip tightened a little. "No. It stays. Agent Becket and I have agreed that we still need to keep track of you."

Aiden twisted round to look at him. Heath's face was a picture of stubborn implacability.

Aiden gave up. "Fuck."

"Well, I can see that Mr Anders has you well under control, Aiden. Make sure it stays that way. As far as the world knows, you are still here, serving time. Understand?"

"Fine." Aiden crossed his arms and sighed heavily. At least Becket didn't know just how accurate his words were.

Heath cuffed him lightly. "Behave. Stop acting like a brat."

Joe laughed. "Well, I have a course to get back to. Now we know Aiden's not a criminal mastermind, perhaps he could take a look at the security camera feeds today — the computer's playing up."

Aiden glared at him. "Unbe-friggin'-lievable."

Agent Becket headed for the door. "Be good, Aiden. I'll see you again soon."

With Joe, Olly and Becket gone, Aiden was painfully aware of how close Heath was to him. He stood up and tried to edge away, but an iron grip around his wrist stopped him. A light touch tilted his jaw up, then Heath was taking his mouth and doing things with his tongue that made Aiden gasp. Heath pulled him close and kissed him deeply. Aiden didn't resist — he let Heath do whatever the hell he wanted to, and it felt amazing.

When they finally parted, Aiden felt dazed. His confusion increased when Heath twisted his arm up his back and shoved him forwards over the desk, pens and paperclips flying off onto the floor. Heath's weight was over him and he was undoing Aiden's trousers, shoving them and his underwear down, exposing him. With his clothing tangled around his ankles and one arm still twisted painfully up his back, he couldn't escape. His cock was rigid, pressed hard into the edge of the desk. He could taste Heath in his mouth, smell the shampoo in his hair and soap on his skin.

Heath slid a long wooden ruler off the desk next to his head, and Aiden knew what was coming. It was still a shock when the narrow piece of wood snapped across his arse, leaving a line of fire in its wake.

"That's for not telling me the truth." Heath's voice was rough. The ruler landed again. "That's for swearing." Two more blows landed and Aiden moaned, trying to rub himself against the edge of the desk. "Those were for suggesting you should leave." Heath massaged his sore skin and probed at his hole with a persistent finger before the ruler landed again, harder this time. Aiden cried out, but the pain was sweet and he craved more. "And that was just because I wanted to."

Aiden squirmed and struggled, but Heath held him down firmly, landing blow after blow until his arse felt as if it were on fire. He was desperate to come, but Heath leaned over him and whispered in his ear, "You don't have permission to come." Heath yanked him upright and spun him around. Heath tapped his swinging dick lightly with the ruler. "This is mine. You are mine. I'll deal with you properly tonight. Now get to work." He slammed the ruler down on the desk, then turned away, pausing at the door. "You so much as think about touching yourself before I say you can, and potential hit men will be the least of your worries."

As the door closed quietly Aiden slid to the floor, sobbing with frustration. "Bastard!" He spat the word out, but still relished his stinging lips, glowing arse and aching cock. It was the most exquisite torture. He groped blindly for his clothes and stood on shaking legs. It was going to be a bloody long day.

Chapter Fourteen

Heath needed to run. He did a quick change and headed out at a pace that was probably far too fast. Adrenaline was racing through his system and he needed to order his scattered thoughts. The circumference of the island was roughly five miles, so a couple of circuits would give him time to think.

He relaxed into a steady rhythm and tried to process everything that had happened. Agent Becket had shown up at dawn, asking for Aiden, and it had taken some convincing before Heath had agreed that he could see him. He had made Becket give him the whole story before he would send Joe to fetch Aiden from breakfast.

Aiden had been approached while still at university by one of his professors who consulted for MI5. Aiden was young, brilliant and a little rebellious — perfect for the job that had been needed. He had hacked the systems of several large corporations to plant a worm that had lain dormant, hidden for several months. At the same time, he had planted a joke virus that made the incursions look like a prank by a bored student with more brains than sense. To disguise the connection between the target corporations, the virus hit several unconnected organisations as well. Aiden had also agreed to be caught, to plead guilty and to accept whatever punishment the presiding judge saw fit to hand out. Then, once his worm had become active and done its job, he'd be exonerated.

He hadn't even been paid. His reward had been months of pressure and stress, and a family who believed he had gone off the rails. At the end of it all, a job in the secret intelligence service was waiting for him. Heath cursed as he ran. Aiden had been used, albeit willingly, and his future was apparently already mapped out for him.

He ran a little faster, muscles burning. Taking that ruler to Aiden's perfect arse had given him hope. There was no way Aiden would have submitted to that kind of treatment if he didn't have genuine feelings for him. Knowing the truth about Aiden only served to convince Heath that they were meant to be together. Aiden was strong, brave and loyal—all qualities that Heath valued, and that Aiden would need if their relationship developed in the way Heath planned.

He checked his watch and started to head back, slowing to a more comfortable jog as he approached the buildings. He paused at the gate to the walled gardens and watched for a few minutes. Aiden and Olly were sitting on the ground, surrounded by a huge pile of flowerpots and buckets of water. They were both laughing.

Heath's heart pounded. Aiden was so beautiful. He couldn't stand the thought that he was in danger. His every instinct was to lock him away and keep him safe. Leaving him out in the open like this was far too dangerous.

He ran through a quick mental list. Joe was teaching until lunchtime — that was another hour. Heath would pick up the afternoon sessions until four, then the course members would depart for the mainland. Aiden would be safe where he was, for now.

He stretched slowly, allowing his body to cool down gradually. Olly and Aiden were flicking water at each other like a couple of kids. It was good to see them relaxed, even if it was only likely to be for a short time.

As if he had sensed someone watching, Aiden looked directly towards him and their eyes met. Even over the distance, the connection between them felt intense. Then Aiden smiled and Heath felt the fist around his heart tighten. Fuck, he was stunning.

He moved quickly out of view. He couldn't keep looking or he would be forced to go over there, grab Aiden and take him somewhere where he could do all the things to him that he desperately wanted to.

Christ, he was the one who was supposed to be in control. He needed to get a grip. He'd be no use to Aiden if he wasn't thinking clearly. He jogged slowly back to the house, hoping that a cold shower might shock some sense into him.

Chapter Fifteen

Surrounded by flowerpots, with Olly laughing and flicking water at him, Aiden had felt happier than he had in an age. The sun had been weak, but in the shelter of the walled garden it had warmed his skin. Not as warm as his arse had been feeling, however. He'd shifted carefully. Every movement had reminded him of Heath's tender attentions. The trouble was that every jolt of pain had also stiffened his cock and made his balls ache. Heath had ordered him not to touch himself. That had made him even harder. Disobedience hadn't even crossed his mind.

Some kind of sixth sense had made him look up towards the gate. Heath had been standing there, staring hard in his direction. Bloody hell, the man was gorgeous. Before he'd even realised what he'd been doing, Aiden had smiled, and it had stayed on his face even when Heath had moved away.

Olly glanced at him, then at the figure moving away from the gate. He chewed on his lip, then grinned. "You've got it bad, haven't you?"

Aiden sighed. "But why, Olly? Why do I feel like this? He's been an absolute bastard."

Olly rolled his big, blue eyes. "You're as submissive as I am, Aiden. That means you like being ordered around. You just can't admit it to yourself. And now Heath knows that you're innocent, there's nothing to stop him claiming you."

"He kind of already has…"

Olly squeaked excitedly. "You mean you and he have —?"

"No! Jesus, Olly. I overheard him telling the course members that I had a Master, that I was taken. Then he told me that I was his." He paused, blushing. "And I accepted it."

"And he didn't toss you straight into bed? I'm surprised he hasn't got you chained up somewhere so that no one else can look at you."

Aiden grabbed a flowerpot and started scrubbing a little too vigorously. He yelped as drops of cold water hit his face.

"He did something, didn't he? What? *What?* You have to tell me, Aiden."

"No, I don't."

"I'm your best friend! Of course you have to tell me. My intellectual curiosity needs satisfying."

Aiden shifted to grab another pot and winced visibly. Olly's eyes gleamed. "He spanked you, didn't he? Oh, my God, he did!" He was practically vibrating with excitement. "Did you enjoy it? What did he use? Did he ask you first?"

"Olly, it's private. Do I ask you what Joe does to you behind closed doors?"

Olly pouted then chewed on his lower lip. "No. But if you asked me I'd tell."

Aiden chuckled. "Well, you'll just have to use your imagination. But to answer one of your questions—no, he didn't fucking ask first."

Olly giggled, delighted. "Didn't think so."

Aiden decided it was high time to change the subject. "Why don't you tell me some more about the side of The Edge that I haven't really seen yet?"

Olly beamed. "Is that just idle curiosity, or are you a bit more specifically interested?"

Aiden scowled. "Heath's part of this scene. I want to understand what that means, Olly. I need to know what his expectations are."

He met Olly's eyes and saw only sympathy. "This is all new to you, isn't it? You've not been part of the BDSM scene before? You are so adorable."

"Am I going to have to dump a bucket of water over your annoying head, Olly?"

The target of his ire snorted. "No wonder Heath wants to take you over his knee." He shifted around and lay back, resting his head on Aiden's thigh. "Now I'm comfortable, I shall begin."

Aiden groaned. "Just the facts, Olly. Jesus!"

"Fine. Joe and Heath met when they were both members of a very exclusive BDSM club in London. I don't know all the details, but Joe took Heath under his wing and trained him. Joe believes that to be a good Dominant, you need to experience everything you might expect your sub to go through. You can probably imagine that it takes a huge amount of trust. Heath was only twenty-one and still finishing his studies. Joe had already qualified and was building a highly respected practice as a psychologist. This was about six years ago now. Back then, The Edge was just a straightforward corporate events company, albeit with a reputation for tough courses. Joe was consulting and running some business psychology classes as part of the programme—the company was owned by a friend of his father's.

When the opportunity arose to buy the business, Joe took it on and invited Heath to join him as a full partner. Heath's dad put up the money for him."

"His dad? The judge?"

"Hey! Don't interrupt my flow! Yes—the judge. Heath and Joe both saw the potential of running training courses for current and prospective Doms who took the lifestyle sufficiently seriously."

Aiden absently stroked Olly's soft hair. "So what do these courses consist of, exactly?"

"Lectures on communication, psychology, anatomy, first aid… Anything you can think of that might come in useful. There are also more practical sessions—how to use certain tools of the trade, rope work, electro-torture. Very occasionally they run courses where the subs are brought along too. They even do beginner's sessions for complete novices. When you think about it, it's reassuring that men who have so much control over others care enough to learn the right skills."

Olly's voice got serious. "You need to talk to Heath. Set boundaries. Let him know your limits. He'll listen, Aiden, I promise."

"What about you and Joe? How long have you been together?"

"About six months now." Olly looked dreamy. "I love him so much."

"But you are his submissive, right?"

"That's right." Olly rolled on to his stomach and propped his chin in his hands. "I belong to him. But he does nothing unless I consent to it, Aiden. I learnt the hard way that domination is about control, not force."

"But you don't wear his collar."

"Yes, I do." Olly reached beneath his shirt and pulled out a fine silver chain fastened with a tiny, delicate padlock.

"Oh... I thought..."

"You were imagining leather and buckles?"

"I suppose I was."

Olly grinned mischievously. "Well, that wouldn't suit me. You, however... I could see Heath requiring something a lot more obvious."

Aiden didn't answer. The pot he started scrubbing suddenly demanded all his concentration. He prayed that Olly wouldn't notice his tenting trousers or the obvious flush he could feel on his face.

Olly giggled. "Like I said. Adorable."

* * * *

After a quick shower and change, Heath sought out Joe in the dining room, where he was eating with the five members of the weekend course. Heath found himself examining their faces and their body language for any sign that they might be there under false pretences.

Joe caught onto his mood immediately and made his excuses, following Heath to the privacy of his office.

Heath made them both mugs of coffee, handed one to Joe, who was lounging in a chair, then focused on not spilling his own as he paced up and down.

"How did it go this morning?"

Joe tapped long fingers on the arm of his chair. "You mean, did I detect any potential assassins in the group?"

Heath stopped pacing for a moment, but only to give him a hard look. "Yes, I suppose I do."

"They all seem like good guys, Heath. Craig, Bryn and Simon are experienced Doms with long-term partners. They are friends and came up together. Ethan is more of a beginner, thinking about taking the next step into a more committed arrangement. The club he belongs to recommended the course to him, and he seems genuinely keen to learn. Even has a photo of the boy he has his eye on. That leaves our chap with the goatee, John Taylor. He is asking a lot of questions, but I think that's nerves more than anything. He's come out of a relationship that didn't turn out well, and he's here because he doesn't want to get burnt again. He also booked in a long time ago, more than eight months, so I don't think he's a likely candidate."

Heath was still pacing. Joe sighed, stood up and took the mug of coffee from Heath's hand. "Be still."

The words snapped cleanly across the room. Heath turned and locked eyes with his friend, knowing instantly that he needed to focus.

Heath sighed and allowed himself to accept that he wasn't thinking clearly. It had been a long time since he'd been in this position. He normally felt so controlled. Aiden had, in a few short weeks, managed to scatter his self-discipline to the winds, and that was something that had to be remedied. He wanted to move, to pace, to throw things, and his back ached with tension as he fought to keep still.

"He needs you to be strong, Heath. Close your eyes."

Heath glared daggers at his friend, but obeyed. He bent slightly to grasp the back of a chair and planted his feet a little apart for balance. His breathing was too fast and he tried to slow it. He gripped the chair like his life depended on it. He flinched as Joe rested a hand on his shoulder.

"Do I need to tie you down?"

He shook his head just a fraction.

"Answer me, please." Joe's voice was calm but authoritative.

"No. That won't be necessary."

"You like Aiden to be centred and calm, don't you? How can you expect it of him if you are so scattered yourself?"

Heath rolled his eyes behind closed lids and twisted his head to follow the sound of Joe's movements around the room.

"A few years ago, I might have taken a whip to you," Joe said conversationally.

Heath kept his eyes shut, but a smile flickered across his lips. "You're not training me now, Joe. Don't even think about it."

"Then take control of your body's responses. You need to be strong for Aiden."

Heath felt a brush of air against his face. The chair was moved away and he was left stranded in darkness, fighting to maintain his balance and his composure. Having a psychologist as a best friend could be a pain in the arse. Gradually he relaxed, blanking his mind, clearing his thoughts of everything but the need to be still. The tension in his muscles dissipated. He drifted, calm and at peace.

"Open your eyes."

His first sight was the glittering tip of a letter opener about a millimetre from his eye. Then it moved away and Joe was smiling at him.

"Better?"

"Yes, you bastard. Though if you'd skewered my eyeball, I would not have been pleased."

"It's been a long time since you needed that."
"Mm. Aiden has a lot to answer for."
Joe chuckled. "And I'm sure he will."

Chapter Sixteen

Heath felt as though his entire body was itching. Being in the tiny security office with Aiden sitting in front of him—so close, so tempting—was torture. He didn't know how much longer he was going to be able to hold off. He needed to claim this beautiful man with every fibre of his being. For the moment he had to satisfy himself with a view of the back of Aiden's head as he bent diligently over a computer. His hair looked so soft, and the perfect length to wind his fingers into and tug. He had a slim neck beneath the hair, and strong shoulders that were relaxed rather than hunched. That neck needed kissing, then collaring. As soon as humanly possible.

Aiden's slender fingers flew over the keyboard and code flashed across the screen.

"You standing there looming over me is not going to get this done any quicker, you know."

He had a soft, gentle voice. His tone was teasing, and an involuntary shiver ran the length of Heath's spine.

"I don't loom." Heath glared as Aiden raised one pretty eyebrow at that. "Can you fix it?" His voice sounded rough and gravelly, and more than a little impatient.

"There's some corrupt code to rewrite. It's not difficult, but it will take me about half an hour. Is it possible that anyone could have hacked the system?"

Heath thought about it for a moment. "It's possible, I suppose. The system just runs the cameras. We've had a couple of instances of bored yobs from the mainland coming over here—there was a bit of vandalism, the odd broken window, nothing serious. There's nothing of much value here worth stealing."

Except you. The thought came unbidden into Heath's head and he gripped the back of Aiden's chair tightly, continuing, "The insurance company insisted we install them, but we wouldn't be actively checking to see if they had been compromised."

"I can't be absolutely sure, but it looks like there was a gap in the feeds for about half an hour in the early hours of yesterday morning. Two cameras on the east shore. But whoever put everything back online forgot to adjust the time settings, and that's thrown the loops out."

Heath didn't say anything. He didn't want Aiden to know how worried he was. The east shore was the easiest place to land a boat without being seen, and that meant anyone could be on the island. It was big enough that a couple of people wouldn't be noticed, and there were plenty of wooded areas to hide out in.

"Fuck! I suppose you look at this one a lot?" Aiden was stabbing a finger at the monitor that now showed a perfectly clear image of his bed. The chair swivelled, and Aiden fixed Heath with a belligerent stare. He was flushed with anger, and Heath thought he looked particularly gorgeous. He couldn't stop the smirk that twisted the corners of his lips.

"Yes, I do. Have you always slept naked?" He straddled Aiden's legs, trapping him in the chair. Aiden's eyes were huge, his bottom lip trembling just a little. Heath leant forward and caught it between his teeth before stealing a breathtaking kiss. Aiden tasted sweet and minty, and his lips were soft—perfect for bruising. Heath grabbed a handful of dark hair and tugged Aiden's head back so that he could thrust his tongue deeper.

For a while there was no resistance, but then, gradually, Aiden started to fight back. He squirmed and twisted, but he grabbed Heath's arms and pulled him closer. Heath drew away with a short laugh, maintaining his grip on Aiden's hair.

"Do you object to me seeing you naked?"

"I'd like the choice!" Aiden jerked his head, but Heath just held on tighter.

"That wasn't the question. Not that I really need an answer. Your body is mine, to do with as I see fit." He leaned in for another kiss, but this time he was teasingly gentle. He glanced down to Aiden's lap and grinned. "Something tells me that your objections are just for show." He brushed his fingers across the black-clad bulge with a chuckle. "Hmm. Very nice."

Aiden glared at him and whimpered.

"Feeling a little frustrated?" Heath touched again, tracing the outline of Aiden's cock with featherlight fingers.

"Bastard! Stop...please." The words were only whispered. Heath knew that it would only take a couple more touches to push Aiden over the edge, and he didn't have permission to come. It was very tempting to make him do just that. But denial was just as much fun.

"Please what?"

Aiden bit down hard on his already swollen lower lip. "Please…Sir!"

Heath took a step back and smiled. "Finish fixing the computer, then you can get cleaned up. I want to see you in my rooms—one hour. Don't be late." He moved to the door and placed his hand deliberately on the handle. "And Aiden…"

Aiden's green eyes glittered.

"You won't need any clothes."

He stared down the protest he could see forming on Aiden's pretty lips, then, with one last evil smile, he closed the door gently behind him.

Chapter Seventeen

Aiden had to blank out all thoughts of Heath in order to get the computer system fixed. That, he could manage. He enjoyed the challenge of correcting the code and seeing his work yield results. It was harder to deal with his aching, rigid cock. Every mental image he created in an attempt to deflate the problem morphed into an erotic daydream. In the end, he got an icy cold can from the fridge in the staff lounge and sat with it resting against his groin as he worked.

Forty-five minutes later, he had run all the security cameras in a loop a couple of times and everything seemed fine. He rested his head back against the chair and sighed. Now he had nothing to distract him and an appointment to keep. He was tempted to not show up, but the desire to please Heath was too strong to resist. He put the now warm can on the desk and spluttered into laughter. Irn-Bru — it had been a bit of an unfortunate choice, though the 'iron' in question was now a little more malleable.

He headed back to his room, took a quick shower then shaved carefully. He towel-dried his hair into tousled disarray and shrugged at the mirror. It would have to do. His lower lip was still a bit swollen and his cheekbones were highlighted by a light flush of colour. "What the hell do I do now?" he muttered at his own reflection. "Does he really expect me to show up naked?"

Of course he did. That was exactly the kind of challenge Heath would issue. A test of his obedience. With a wry grin, Aiden picked out tight black shorts, pulled on an old pair of jeans that had come in a parcel from his sister, and a plain grey T-shirt that clung nicely. He didn't bother with shoes. Heath might punish him, but there was no way Aiden was going to show up at his door stark bollock naked.

Theirs were the only two rooms reached by the staircase they shared. It was highly unlikely that anyone else would see him. It still felt terrifying to take the few short steps across the landing, and his hand was visibly shaking as he raised it to knock on Heath's door.

The bastard kept him waiting for a full two minutes, and he was just about to turn tail and make a run for it when the door finally opened. *Oh, holy crap!* Heath was wearing a loose black shirt over leather trousers that hugged nicely without being too tight. His shirtsleeves were rolled casually to his elbows, exposing slim arms dusted with dark hair. Aiden felt his dick swelling as he gradually lifted his gaze the length of Heath's body. By the time he had passed a lightly stubbled jaw and smirking lips to reach a pair of amused grey eyes, he was rock hard.

"So, you couldn't manage to obey one simple instruction. That's not a good start, Aiden." Heath turned and headed back inside his apartment.

Aiden stood still, frozen to the spot. He couldn't go back. He didn't know if he was allowed to go forward.

"What are you waiting for? A fucking engraved invitation?" Heath hadn't even looked back.

Aiden took one nervous step forwards, then another. He closed the door gently and took in his surroundings. His bare feet sank into the deep pile of a rug that sat over polished floorboards that glowed with age and warmth. The walls were simple, smooth plaster painted a delicate cream. As he stepped into the spacious lounge-diner, he gasped. Beautiful paintings like individual jewels adorned the walls. Even with his untrained eye, he could tell that they were of exceptional quality. He moved closer to a small landscape in a simple gilt frame. It depicted stormy skies over wild hills — all dark purple and grey. It was stunning and, to Aiden, reflected its owner's temperament perfectly.

He jumped as Heath gripped his shoulder. He'd lost himself in the picture and almost forgotten that he was not alone.

"Do you like it?" Heath's grip was light but firm.

"It's beautiful." Aiden turned and looked into grey eyes that mirrored that stormy sky.

"So are you."

He ducked his head, feeling unusually shy.

"Why didn't you do as I told you, Aiden?"

"I wasn't sure you really meant it."

"Don't lie to me. You knew I meant it. I don't say anything I don't mean."

Aiden responded defiantly, "Fine. I was scared, okay? Absolutely bloody terrified." He turned away. "I'll leave. I'm sorry I disappointed you."

Heath sank into an armchair, stretched out his long, leather-clad legs and crossed his ankles. "I don't believe I said anything about being disappointed. What makes you think that?"

Aiden didn't turn around. "I didn't do as you asked. I'm not submissive enough for you."

Heath gave a soft chuckle. "So you think that submission is the same as unquestioning obedience?"

"Isn't it?" Aiden whirled around, eyes flashing.

"No." Heath's spoke gently, without mockery. "I have no interest in a mindless automaton. Obedience is important, especially in public, but if you disagree with me you must feel free to say so. We are both adults. But if we agree that you are in the wrong, you will accept my punishment with grace. Is that acceptable?"

He sounded so fucking reasonable. Aiden found himself nodding in relief.

"Good. Then stop acting like a brat. Come here and redeem yourself, and maybe you will be forgiven." He pointed at a spot on the floor. "Stand here and present yourself properly, as you've been taught."

Aiden took a couple of paces, chewing on his bottom lip. He stood with his feet a pace apart, hands clasped behind his back, chin up. He knew that his erection would be clearly evident. His dick seemed to be fighting to escape the confines of his clothing, twitching and leaking uncontrollably.

"Good. Take off your clothes."

Aiden lost control of his fingers as buttons and zips became tortuous tests of his dexterity, but eventually, clothing discarded, he resumed his original position and issued a challenge to Heath with his eyes. His young body was firm and lean. His rock-hard cock curved proudly upward, the plump head glistening.

"Kneel."

Heath stayed exactly where he was as Aiden sank awkwardly to his knees, hands still clasped behind his back. Aiden focused on a point on the floor somewhere between his own bare knees and Heath's booted feet. He was so turned on it hurt, but he was also on the verge of tears.

He was vaguely aware of Heath standing and towering over him.

"I don't know how you have managed to get this far without a Master to take care of you, Aiden, but if you are willing, I'd like to take on that responsibility."

Aiden felt curiously light, as if a huge weight had been lifted from his shoulders. He hadn't realised just how desperate he'd been for Heath to say those words. He still didn't really know why, but it felt so right and so very good. A tear rolled down his cheek and plopped to the floor.

"Yes, please...Sir."

A finger tilted his chin up, then Heath was kissing away his tears.

"A visit to the bedroom is long overdue. You have no idea how fucking hard it's been to keep my hands off you."

Then he was being pulled up and dragged towards the bedroom. At the foot of the bed, Heath drew him into a deep but gentle kiss. Aiden looped his hands around the taller man's neck and revelled in the sensation of hands stroking his back and squeezing his arse. He rose onto his toes, scraping his iron dick across the front of Heath's leather trousers. Heath circled his entrance with a teasing finger, touching lightly. Heath pulled his head back by the hair and stared down into his eyes. "You are severely testing my self-control, Aiden. Are you humping my leg, or is that my imagination?"

"*Your* self-control? Fuck, Heath, I'm the one standing here naked!" He rubbed himself up and down shamelessly. Then he was flying through the air to land on the bed with a bounce. Heath let him settle, then knelt across him and pinned his wrists to the bed before enclosing Aiden's cock in the warm wet heat of his mouth.

Aiden gasped, "Fuck!"

Heath knelt up and grinned at him. "Remember, you don't have permission to come." Then he got back to torturing him.

Aiden bucked his hips and yanked frantically against Heath's grip, but it was hopeless. He sobbed his frustration, knowing that it would be seconds before his body betrayed him. Then the suction was gone. Heath flicked his tongue across the tip of Aiden's cock and looked at him quizzically. "Problem?"

"You bastard!"

"That's 'you bastard, Sir'." He swirled one finger around the top of Aiden's slick cock, then left it to bounce back and forth.

Aiden discovered he was making sounds that wouldn't normally come from a human being. "Please! Sir! I need—"

"You need to learn a little patience, boy. I decide when and if you get relief."

Heath sat against the pillows and Aiden found himself pulled into his lap so that his back rested against Heath's chest. Heath encircled his waist firmly, holding him in place. He used his free hand to touch and tease. Stroking softly, squeezing Aiden's balls gently, the touches never enough to push him over the edge.

"I wonder how long I can keep doing this? Shall we find out?"

Heath was still fully dressed. Aiden could feel the hard ridge of his cock pressing into the base of his spine, but it was difficult to focus. He wanted to scream and cry from frustration as Heath brought him to the brink over and over again. Each time he tried to pull his knees up defensively, Heath just shoved them down again. Heath played with his balls, rolling and squeezing them gently. Then he stroked the hard length of Aiden's cock with a single finger and flicked the gleaming end before circling it lightly. He was so painfully aware of being naked while Heath was still fully dressed. He felt vulnerable and exposed, but the solid strength of Heath's arm around him kept him safe. He knew deep in his gut that Heath wouldn't hurt him.

Aiden's thighs trembled as Heath pushed his knees apart, spreading him wide, trapping Aiden in a position where Heath could reach the sensitive skin around his entrance. Heath collected moisture from the tip of Aiden's cock, then made lazy circles around his hole, spreading the wetness. Aiden jerked at every touch, wriggling and squirming but unable to escape.

Behind him, Heath chuckled and Aiden felt the vibration along the length of his spine. The tip of one finger slipped inside him as Heath sucked on his neck, no doubt raising a mark that would be visible for days. Aiden sobbed. The combination of sensations was just too much. Heath probed a little deeper. Heath tightened his hold, pinning Aiden's arms in place, then scraped Aiden's collarbone with his teeth.

"You fucking bastard! Please...please, Sir..." He couldn't even articulate what he needed. Then suddenly Heath twisted him onto his front, his rock-hard cock pressed painfully beneath him. Heath pulled his hands roughly behind his back and secured them with something soft but immoveable. Two pillows were shoved beneath his hips and Heath gently pushed his thighs wide apart. He could feel the air on his hole, caressing, tormenting.

Aiden twisted his head to the side, to be met with the sight of Heath's clothes landing in a heap next to the bed. *He must be naked too. Finally!* But he couldn't see anything. The unfairness of it made him want to cry. The bed sank a little under Heath's weight, then he could feel Heath's knees pushing him wider. The muscles in his arse clenched hard, but Heath's hands were on him, squeezing, kneading, separating his trembling cheeks. He heard a squirt of liquid, then Heath's slick finger slid into him smoothly. More liquid dribbled into his crack and Heath rubbed it in a soothing circular motion around his hole before teasing the sensitive skin of his perineum.

"You're so beautifully hot and tight." Heath's voice was low and sultry. "Too perfect."

The motion stopped and Aiden moaned as Heath withdrew his finger.

"Are you a virgin, Aiden?" Heath's voice sounded a little incredulous, as though the thought had only just crossed his mind.

"Yes! But not for much fucking longer, I hope!" He squirmed and forced his arse upwards.

"Brat!" Heath reinserted his finger and added another in a scissoring dance that had Aiden biting the bed covers. "I don't want to hurt you. Need to prepare you properly."

Aiden tried to impale himself deeper, but Heath withdrew.

"No! Please..." He sobbed out his need. "Don't stop!" The burn of a quicker penetration silenced him. Heath crooked his fingers and fire shot through Aiden's belly. He came hard and fast, grinding himself into the sheets. "Oh, fuck!" It was part scream, part yelp as he realised that he had come without his cock being touched, and without permission. Heath continued to stroke and stretch his channel for a while and when his fingers left him, Aiden felt hollow.

The rip of foil told him he wouldn't have to wait long. Heath grunted, then the end of something warm and blunt pressed against him before sinking past the ring of protective muscle guarding his entrance. Heath's cock felt massive as it inched into his passage. It hurt. Fuck, it hurt! But slowly the pain gave way to pleasure and Aiden felt his body relax to accept the invader. He pulled hard on the bindings around his wrists. "Move, goddamn it! Fuck me like you mean it!"

A slap seared his arse. "You're forgetting who's in charge here." Then Heath speared him, deep and hard. Aiden screamed his pleasure, bucking his hips violently enough to make his back ache. Heath was pistoning in and out, gripping his hips hard enough to bruise. Just as he thought he would be torn apart, Heath yelled his release and heat filled Aiden's passage.

For a few moments, Heath's weight rested on him before Heath rolled away with a sigh. There was a creak as he left the bed, returning with something wet and warm that he applied lightly to Aiden's arse and thighs. Heath released his hands and rolled him onto his back. Aiden was barely able to draw breath before Heath was thoroughly kissing him.

"Go and take a shower." Heath gently shoved him off the side of the bed and Aiden turned to look back at Heath's body for the first time.

"Holy fuck!" Aiden knew his jaw had dropped and slammed his mouth shut so hard his teeth rattled. Heath was reclining against the pillows, one knee raised, his ample cock curled softly into one thigh. His abs were sharply cut, his body lean and taut. He was absolutely bloody gorgeous. He was also smirking.

"When you've finished drooling, go and take a shower."

Aiden started, suddenly aware of the sticky mess drying on his stomach. He blushed furiously and fled to the sanctuary of the bathroom. He showered quickly, smiling inside at the ache in his body.

He wondered what would happen now. Would Heath banish him back to his own room, or make him sleep on the floor? He'd read all kind of things about the behaviour of Dominant men, but so far Heath hadn't conformed to any of the stereotypes. He was bloody bossy and Aiden couldn't imagine him putting up with any lip, but he hadn't pressured Aiden into doing anything he didn't want to do.

He slipped out of the bathroom with a towel still wrapped around his waist. Heath thrust a stack of bed linen into his hands.

"Change the sheets while I shower. And lose the fucking towel." Heath whipped the soft towelling off as he passed, looking back with a leer. Aiden's instinct to cover himself was foiled by the pile of linen he was carrying. Heath paused in the door to the bathroom and watched him. Aiden swiftly stripped the bed, terribly conscious of Heath's eyes on his arse as he bent to smooth the fresh cotton and tuck the corners. He took his frustration out on a couple of hapless pillows, pounding them into submission and stuffing them hard into their cases. It was only when he moved to the opposite side of the bed that he realised Heath had gone.

Swearing under his breath, he caught sight of the large picture above the bed and gasped. It was the most erotic image he'd ever seen. He could almost feel the chains stretching his arms over his head and the ache in his knees. It was his imagination at work—the image wasn't that obvious—but the adoration in the kneeling boy's green eyes seemed to glow. He was very beautiful.

"That could be you." Heath's voice sounded close behind him. Aiden hadn't noticed his approach. Heath pulled him back into a tight embrace. "Would you like that?" To Aiden, the question sounded just a little nervous.

"Is that how you want me, Heath? On my knees in chains? I don't know if I can do that."

"You didn't answer my question." Heath sucked on his neck and grasped his cock firmly.

"Fuck!"

"Oh, definitely. But not until you've answered the question, and only when I say so."

Heath stroked his cock a little more firmly and Aiden's mind went blank. He struggled in Heath's embrace, only to be pinned more tightly.

"Yes! Okay, yes. I would like it."

"Better. And to answer your question, yes. I will have you on your knees in chains, but only because you want it too."

Heath let him go and climbed into bed. Aiden hesitated, not sure what to do.

"What are you waiting for?" Heath patted the bed next to him.

"I wasn't sure if you would want me to stay." Aiden felt suddenly shy.

"Get in here, you idiot. I want you where I can keep an eye on you. You'll move in here from now on."

Aiden bridled at Heath's presumption. "What if I want to stay in my own room?"

"Not an option." Heath's eyes darkened and Aiden swallowed hard. He climbed nervously into bed to be gathered into Heath's arms. He couldn't help himself—he nuzzled into one shoulder and slung an arm around Heath's waist, holding on tight. It felt so good, so safe. He couldn't think of a single good reason to argue his case any further as Heath's warmth soaked into his body. His eyelids drooped and he slipped, unresisting, into his dreams.

Chapter Eighteen

Heath opened his eyes slowly. There was a warm weight on his chest and strands of soft, dark hair tickling his cheek. He could feel hot hardness pressing into his thigh, and he grinned. Aiden's dreams had clearly been stimulating.

Aiden sighed and stirred. His eyes flickered open and Heath watched, amused, as realisation dawned on Aiden's pretty face.

"Good morning." He stroked Aiden's hair gently and the tension in his face disappeared. "How are you feeling?"

Aiden rolled onto his back and grimaced. "I think I pulled every muscle in my body, but otherwise not too bad."

"Are you sore?"

"No." Aiden's cheeks coloured. "Why? Are you going to tie me up and fuck me again?"

"You sound like you want me to."

Aiden didn't reply and Heath laughed. "Much as I would like to get creative with you, I have to work and so do you." He sat up and rolled out the slight crick in his neck. He was achingly hard just thinking about all the things he intended to do to Aiden, but they really would have to wait.

Aiden gave him a cocky grin and yanked the sheet back to expose Heath's impressive erection. Seconds later, soft, warm lips were wrapped around his cock.

"Fuck!" Heath couldn't stop the exclamation as Aiden proved that despite his inexperience, he was bloody talented at what he was doing. The sucking and licking stopped and Aiden gazed up at him.

"I thought you said we didn't have time?"

"You little…" Heath grabbed a handful of hair and pulled Aiden back down where he belonged. He held his head firmly, but not so tightly that he couldn't pull away if he wanted to. Heath moaned his appreciation as Aiden opened his throat to him, then grazed his length lightly with his teeth before sucking hard. It didn't take long. Heath felt his orgasm building, his balls tightening and pulling up against his body.

"Coming!" He gave Aiden a chance to pull away but the sucking continued, and when he spilled into Aiden's welcoming mouth, it still didn't stop until he was completely clean.

Aiden looked way too smug.

"You and I are going to have a long talk about rules tonight, and the consequences of disobedience."

"Yes, Sir." Aiden's eyes sparkled.

"Go to the top dresser drawer and bring me back what's inside." Heath watched as Aiden walked across the room. He was incorrigible, wiggling his arse provocatively as he went. He didn't look quite so amused when he turned back with the contents of the drawer in his hand. He handed the items over to Heath with a scowl.

"Go and use the bathroom. Don't bother to dress yet."

"You're not really going to make me wear that, are you, Sir?" Aiden's voice shook just a little.

Heath looked at Aiden's pretty cock, swaying and hard.

"Definitely."

Fifteen minutes later, showered and shaved, Aiden was standing naked in front of him, legs spread, hands clasped behind his neck. He was blushing furiously. Considering what a beautiful body he had, Heath was surprised by how uncomfortable he seemed, but then, being naked when you were trying to face down someone who was clothed was kind of difficult.

Heath took his time measuring and adjusting the leather in his hands until he was satisfied. Keeping it where Aiden could see what was going on, he applied a generous coating of lube to a large, bulbous plug.

"Bend over."

He pushed gently until the plug was deeply seated. "Okay. Straighten up."

Aiden's expression was half scowl, half shock. Next came a leather belt, fastened around his slim waist. The rest of the harness dangled in front of him. Heath slid the metal cock ring into place, adjusted the leather plate that would ensure the plug stayed where it was meant to, then did up the buckle at the back. It all looked nice and snug. Aiden was still semi-hard and not looking impressed. Heath kept his face impassive as he snapped a small padlock through the buckle, locking everything in place.

"Perfect. You can dress. I'll see you here tonight at eight. If you get here before me, you will wait on your knees. Naked."

"That's twelve hours…Sir."

"You can tell the time. Good. You won't be late, then."

"But…"

"Aiden, I'm not known for my patience and you are trying mine severely. If you don't do as you're told immediately, you'll spend your lunch break over my knee." He kept his tone mild. Aiden looked like he wanted to cry or maybe hit something. Instead, he scooped his clothes up and dressed. He would have to change into his uniform in his own room, and no doubt inspect the contraption he was trapped in.

Heath took a step forward and kissed him softly, making sure that his thigh brushed across Aiden's groin.

"Have a good day, beautiful."

Aiden treated him to a prize-winning scowl and headed for the door, muttering under his breath about cruel, domineering Masters.

Heath chuckled to himself. Aiden might be a natural submissive beneath all that angst, but he was going to be a challenge. His stomach did a few flip-flops at the thought. Aiden was perfect—and all his. He felt a wave of possessiveness wash over him. There was no way he was going to let anything happen to his beautiful lover, and he would not tolerate any suggestion that he might leave. He abhorred the idea of using Aiden as bait, and a hint of anxiety probed persistently at his brain. He hated being out of control of any situation and he knew that Joe would be feeling the same. He wanted something to happen—the waiting was shredding his nerves. He needed to be rid of distractions and focus on the future—a future with Aiden.

Chapter Nineteen

Aiden pushed a wheelbarrow across the vegetable garden and tried to ignore the tremors going through his body as the plug in his arse was jostled with every step. Just thinking about what he was wearing beneath his company uniform was enough to keep him hard, and it wasn't comfortable. He had stared at the harness in the mirror while he'd changed clothes. The leather was pliable—it didn't rub, even where it disappeared between the cheeks of his arse. The ring circling the base of his cock was snug, but not painful. It made his erection jut obscenely forwards but it didn't hurt. The plug inside him made him feel stretched and full, sending sparks to his groin every time he moved enough that it rubbed against his prostate. It was a very tangible reminder of what he had given Heath—control over his body.

He loaded the barrow with the vegetables he had harvested earlier, then sat on the grass with a bottle of water and unzipped his fleece. It had only been four hours since Heath had locked him into the harness, but it felt like a lifetime. He ached to come, craved a hand or mouth around his sensitive cock. Fuck, he couldn't get Heath's handsome, smirking face out of his mind. He rubbed his neck, imagining what it would feel like with a collar around it.

"Bloody hell!" He needed to think about something that didn't turn him on. Even the sodding vegetables in the barrow were phallic. Jesus, he couldn't even look at a bloody courgette without imagining it fashioned from rubber and shoved up his arse. He splashed water over his face and took a long drink. Perhaps he should find Heath and ask him to take the harness off. No. That would be exactly what Heath wanted. He wouldn't give him the satisfaction.

He waved goodbye to Jacob and headed off to deliver his barrowload to the kitchen.

The rumbling sounds coming from his stomach sent him towards the dining room for some lunch. Olly was already parked at their usual table with a plate of salad and a glass of juice. Aiden fetched a plate for himself and sat down, laughing at Olly's pout.

"What's the matter? And why are you eating salad? You never eat salad."

"Joe says I'm not allowed any sugar today. No treats at all. No coffee, either."

"Olly, every time you have sugar or caffeine you end up bouncing off the walls."

"I wasn't even bad," he wailed miserably. "In fact I was really, really good this morning."

There was a lot of innuendo in that sentence. "I don't want to know!" Aiden laughed at the sly look that crossed Olly's pretty face.

"Joe gave me a riding lesson."

Aiden forked up some salad. "Oh? I didn't realise there were horses here."

Olly looked smug. "There aren't. I wasn't riding a horse. Though a crop was involved." He looked a little dreamy as Aiden choked on a piece of cucumber.

"And what about you? I know you didn't spend last night in your own room."

Aiden felt a blush stain his cheeks.

Olly toasted him with a glass of juice. "Well it's about time! I was beginning to think the two of you were never going to work out that A goes into B." He looked thoughtful. "Or C."

Aiden didn't know where to put himself. Olly looked like an angel, but he had the devil's own tongue. He made a brave attempt to change the subject. "I'm helping Georgia out again this afternoon."

"Rather you than me." Olly rolled his eyes. "Georgia's scary and there's a really big group in this week. I think they're investment bankers or something like that." He unfolded a small piece of paper and smoothed it onto the table. "Joe wants to meet me on the beach later, so I'm going to take a book over there and wait for him."

Aiden glanced at the printed note which just had the words 'East Beach, 3pm' written on it.

"Well, think of Georgia screaming at me to haul my arse over the scramble nets while you're enjoying your little romantic interlude."

Olly grinned and tossed his curls. "That's the benefit of not being a criminal mastermind."

"I'm not a..." Aiden caught Olly's smirk and laughed.

"You are so easy to wind up! I'll see you for dinner?"

"Sure. I don't have kitchen duty tonight so can we eat early — say six?"

"If you've been let off tonight, that means Heath has other plans for you. He should sell tickets, he'd make a fortune!"

"Olly, I suggest you leave now before I tell Joe that you ate three desserts."

Olly's blue eyes widened. "You wouldn't. Would you?"

Aiden just quirked an eyebrow and Olly ran for the door, taking his book but leaving his lunch tray and the note behind. Aiden crumpled the paper and stuck it in his pocket, then gathered up their dishes and returned them to the kitchen.

Georgia had thirty over-enthusiastic bankers queuing for the assault course, and for once some of her team were around to help. She still had Aiden doing all the demonstrations, and all the scrambling, climbing and jumping played havoc with his composure as the plug inside him drove deeper. He ended up having to demonstrate everything three times, and by four o' clock he was a sweating, jumpy wreck, cursing Heath's name under his breath. When Georgia finally dismissed him, he headed straight for the main house and a shower.

He was crossing the main hall when Joe emerged from his study with a frown on his face.

"Aiden, have you seen Olly? He seems to have done a disappearing act—has he been with you?"

"No, Sir." Aiden was on his best behaviour—Joe had the kind of presence that demanded it. "He went to meet you on the East Beach."

"What do you mean, he went to meet me?"

"He had a note from you, Sir..." Aiden's voice trailed off and he felt the blood draining from his face. He scrabbled in his pocket and pulled out the screwed up piece of paper that Olly had shown him.

Joe took one look and cursed. "I didn't send this. Go and get Heath—he's in the library."

Five minutes later they were all convened in Heath's office. Aiden looked out of the window, his thoughts swirling frantically around in his head. Heath got on the phone and organised a search party. "You know, it could be one of the staff playing a practical joke." Heath sounded as if he was trying to comfort Joe, but they all knew that he was clutching at straws. Joe's face was a mask—cold and emotionless.

"If anyone lays a finger on him—"

"They won't. Olly's not their target."

Aiden turned and looked at them both. "You're right. Olly isn't the target. I am. But what if they think he's me? They don't know what I look like." He felt sick to the core that something might happen to Olly because of him. Gentle, playful Olly, who didn't deserve to be scared or hurt.

The phone rang and Joe snatched up the receiver before the second ring sounded.

"Yes. You're sure? Bring it here." He slammed the receiver down and glared. "Freddie was already out on the beach when Georgia called, so he searched straight away. There was no sign of Olly but he found a paperback book under a bush with a note inside. The small rowing boat is missing from the boathouse. He's bringing the note back here."

Aiden knew that Freddie was one of Georgia's outdoor team. He ran survival skills courses and was based out at the beach. It was only four thirty—Olly could only have been gone for a maximum of two hours. There was every chance he was still okay.

They waited in uncomfortable silence for Freddie to make the two-mile journey back to the house. He arrived with Georgia and two of the other instructors.

One of them thrust the note into Heath's hand. Joe looked at Heath with an icy gaze.

"There's a grid reference and a time—midday tomorrow. It just says 'bring the boy to exchange'—that's it, nothing else."

Joe snarled, "The middle of the day—what the hell are they up to?"

Aiden sat at the computer and did some rapid typing. "The grid reference is on a small private airfield on the mainland. Just outside of the town." He swung the screen around so that they could see.

Georgia stared at the map. "Clever. Flights during the day attract less scrutiny. In a small plane or helicopter they could be well away in less than an hour. File a fake flight plan, fly low... Untraceable."

"Assuming whoever took Olly rowed ashore, they could still have been on the road for two hours. They could be anywhere." Heath placed a careful hand on Joe's shoulder. "I'm going to ring Becket."

Aiden couldn't make eye contact with anyone. "At least they definitely know he's not me. They won't hurt him." The words he didn't say pierced his brain—'because it's me they want to hurt'. He felt so helpless.

Joe took the phone from Heath. "Get Aiden out of here, Heath. He looks like he's going to faint. I'll deal with Becket." Joe started issuing instructions to the others, making sure the course members were catered for and that everything at The Edge would seem completely normal. Georgia and her staff went back to their duties with promises to help. Aiden allowed himself to be steered to the door, then up the stairs to Heath's apartment.

The calm of Heath's lounge was pervasive. Aiden allowed some of the tension in his shoulders to dissipate, but he still couldn't look directly at his lover. Heath cupped his face with one hand and kissed him softly. The touch was so tender, so understanding, and Aiden leaned into him, resting his head on Heath's strong shoulder. His body started to shake and Heath held him tightly, stroking his back until the tremors subsided.

"I have to go and help Joe. I want you to stay here. Try to relax."

Heath brushed Aiden's ear with his lips and cupped his arse, massaging the end of the plug Aiden had all but forgotten. His cock jerked and he moaned pitifully. "Please get me out of this thing, Heath."

"No."

"Do you want me to get down on my knees and beg? Is that it?" Aiden knew he should have controlled his spiky tone, but it was too late.

"That's better. That's the brat I fell in love with. Feisty. Disrespectful. Needing to be punished." Heath released him and headed for the door. "When I get back I want you ready for me, Aiden. There's nothing you can do to help Olly tonight."

The door was already closing by the time Aiden realised what he had heard. Heath loved him. Warmth suffused his body and his stiff cock twitched with need. He only hoped that he would get the chance to let Heath know that he loved him too.

Chapter Twenty

Agent Becket must have crossed the causeway at light speed, or he had been closer than anyone had thought, because by the time Heath got back to his study Becket was already there. Joe was holding in his emotions as well he could. Becket was speaking in low, clipped tones. Heath looked at the two of them — remarkably alike in some ways, so different in others. Both blonds, though Becket's hair was lighter. Becket's eyes were an icy, pale blue while Joe's were also light, but clearer. Joe was taller by a couple of inches, but both men exuded power. Heath wondered briefly whether Becket was gay. He could easily be into the scene — he had that kind of aura about him. But now was not the time to be wondering about the guy's sexual proclivities.

Becket gave him a hard look. "Good, Heath, you're here. I need to speak to Aiden alone. Can you fetch him, please?"

Heath wasn't happy, but Joe eventually persuaded him that the fewer people knew about Becket's plans, the safer Aiden would be. If that meant the two of them had to be kept in the dark, then that was the way it had to be. Heath returned to the flat, waited while Aiden threw on some clothes, then reluctantly left him sitting with Becket. He and Joe decided on a run and made themselves scarce.

Two hours later, Heath pushed open the door to his apartment and walked into the glow of lamplight and the sound of classical music. Aiden appeared in the bedroom door and Heath held his breath. Apart from the black leather harness, Aiden was naked, all pale skin and lithe muscle. His cock jutted from its restraining ring proudly, the head glistening. He met Heath's gaze boldly, took a couple of steps forward and dropped gracefully to his knees.

Heath took deep, calming breaths. He couldn't take his eyes away from the vision in front of him. Such perfection.

"Becket will give you to them tomorrow, won't he?" Heath could hardly control his emotions.

Aiden lowered his dark head. "That's part of the plan, yes."

"I'm glad there's a plan. But you're not going to tell me anything else, are you?"

"I can't."

"Can't or won't?" Heath challenged. "I'm sorry, Aiden, that wasn't fair. It's your life on the line."

Aiden sighed. "I wish it didn't have to be this way. It's hard, but trust me — it's for the best that you don't know."

Heath pursed his lips but knew when to give in. "So… I want tonight to be special. Do you think you are ready to submit to me properly? Completely?"

Aiden nodded once. "Yes, Sir."

There was such certainty and trust in those words that Heath felt his chest tighten.

"Come here." He took a small key from his pocket and used it to release the padlock on Aiden's harness. "Go to the bathroom. Clean yourself, inside and out. Shave your face and your groin. Call me when you are done so I can check you've done a good job."

Heath fixed his calm gaze on Aiden's face and waited for a retort that didn't come. Aiden just chewed on his lower lip for a moment, then headed for the bathroom.

"Leave the door open."

Heath raided the fridge and made himself a sandwich. He ate it slowly, drank a glass of juice and waited patiently for Aiden to call him. He couldn't wait to see what he would look like shaved smooth, or to investigate just how sensitive that bare skin would be. He slipped a hand into his trousers and adjusted his aching cock. He wondered if Aiden had any concept of how difficult it was for Heath to restrain his own needs. Well, that was part of being the dominant partner. He was being gifted with immeasurable trust—self-control was a very small price to pay.

"I'm done, Sir."

Aiden's soft voice broke him out of his reverie half an hour later. Heath looked up to see him standing in the bathroom door, looking deliciously flushed and very nervous. There was a small towel around his hips, doing nothing to hide a very obvious erection.

Heath got to his feet with a feral grin and pointed at the floor in front of him. "Come and stand here. Leave the towel in the bathroom."

Aiden did as he'd been told, standing still and steady with his hands clasped behind his back. Heath stalked around him, examining every inch of smooth, freshly shaved skin. His boy looked absolutely perfect.

For a moment he stood behind Aiden, breathing lightly on his neck, not touching.

"Have you any idea how hard it is to shave down there?" Aiden flushed at his own words.

"The result is worth it." Heath grazed a fingertip across the delicate skin above Aiden's dick. "But as you found it so challenging, next time I'll do it for you."

That had Aiden's rock-hard cock straining and twitching. "Oh, God!"

"Now, on your knees. Spread your legs. Keep your hands behind your back."

As Aiden complied, Heath slipped into the bedroom and came back with a flat, square box. He sat on the chair in front of Aiden and lifted the lid. Nestled inside on a bed of grey tissue was a circle of polished steel. He lifted it from the box and triggered the concealed hinge so that the circlet opened.

"Once this is around your neck, you belong to me. I may change it for a leather one or something less visible for certain occasions, but nobody removes it but me."

Aiden was looking up at him, eyes glistening with unshed tears.

"You really want me to wear your collar, Heath?" The words were just whispers.

Heath stroked his hair. "I love you, Aiden. I want everyone to know that you are mine. No one else gets to touch you. But this can't be just about what I want."

"I want it too. More than anything. If you can put up with me?"

Aiden's green eyes sparkled and Heath gave a low chuckle. He slipped the metal around Aiden's neck and snapped the collar closed. It rested at the base of Aiden's throat and was roughly a centimetre deep.

There was no mistaking what it was—it didn't look anything like jewellery. It wasn't delicate like the chain Olly wore for Joe. It was seamless, glinting dully in the light.

"You look stunning." Heath ran his fingers around Aiden's neck, admiring the collar's fit. If he had his way, Aiden would spend a lot of time wearing nothing else. Well, apart from some matching cuffs, perhaps. A dreamy smile crossed his face.

"Thank you, Sir."

The sound of Aiden's voice brought Heath back to reality. He sat on the edge of the chair and crooked a finger. "The list of your misdemeanours is so long I could justifiably spend the entire night spanking you, but we'll settle for a dozen. That should warm you up nicely before I fuck you until you scream."

Aiden got to his feet looking more than a little anxious.

"Over my lap. Now."

Heath shifted until he was happy that Aiden wouldn't fall. His arse was tilted nice and high, his cock and balls dangling between Heath's thighs. He used one arm to balance him, then brought his hand down hard. Aiden squirmed and moaned, and one cheek became suffused with a pink glow.

"Mm. Pretty." Heath spanked him hard, getting into a rhythm, not holding back. By the time he had finished, Aiden was sobbing quietly. His entire arse was hot to the touch and his rigid cock was dripping pre-cum like a faucet, betraying his arousal. Heath stroked his arse, soothing the soreness. "You'll feel this for a while." He helped Aiden stand and brushed the tears from his face before grasping his wrist firmly and tugging him towards the bedroom.

"On the bed, on your back." He stripped off his clothes without ceremony, grabbed a bottle of lube and a foil strip of condoms, then straddled Aiden's body. He was careful to prepare him thoroughly, knowing that this was still only his second time, but Aiden thrust against his fingers shamelessly, fucking himself as hard as he could manage. Wearing the plug all day had kept him stretched, but to Heath he still felt like a virgin.

"Please, Sir... Please! No more teasing..."

"Perhaps I should tie you down to stop you squirming? Or maybe put you in chastity?" Heath scissored his fingers inside Aiden's hot, silky channel and laughed at the expression of utter horror that passed across his face.

"No! Please, Sir! You can't!"

"Oh, believe me, I can." Heath withdrew his fingers and squeezed the base of Aiden's cock. "Convince me that I shouldn't lock you into a cosy cock cage and then have my way with you." He began to punish Aiden's nipples with his teeth and tongue until they hardened and Aiden was gasping.

"Because I love you!"

Heath stilled and looked into Aiden's eyes, seeing nothing but adoration.

Typically stoic, he simply said, "Good enough. I'll let you off this time." He sheathed himself in well-lubed latex and hoisted Aiden's legs over his shoulders. "Keep your eyes open. I'm going to make you scream, my love." He thrust hard, then went completely still, reaching for Aiden's iron cock. Aiden gasped and tried to impale himself even farther. Then Heath pulled out almost completely before slamming home his claim over and over again. It took every ounce of willpower to hold himself back, but when

Aiden screamed and shot all over his stomach and chest, Heath let go. After another punishing penetration, the world went red and a line of fire shot through his body.

He collapsed onto his back next to Aiden, dealt with the condom, then shifted onto his side so he could check on his lover. Aiden was flushed, his eyes gleaming. His body was splattered with globules of creamy liquid. Heath swirled a finger through one small pool, then held it to Aiden's lips. Aiden sucked it greedily and continued to suckle on Heath's finger until he pulled it away.

"Go and get cleaned up, sweetheart. There are bottles of water in the fridge."

Heath sat up in bed and waited for him to return. Aiden came back with two bottles and clambered into bed. The cool water was very welcome. Heath's senses felt blurry and he knew he had to rest. Aiden too must be exhausted.

"I know it's hard, love, but we have to sleep. Tomorrow will be tough on everyone."

"I'm so afraid for Olly. This is all my fault."

"Olly is a lot tougher than he looks, and stop blaming yourself, Aiden. You're as much a victim in all this as anyone."

"I would have gone tomorrow regardless of what Agent Becket decided. You know that?"

"And what if I had told you not to?" Heath stroked Aiden's hair and marvelled at how soft it was.

"I don't believe you would ever order me to do something that made it impossible for me to obey you. I trust you."

Heath kissed him softly before crawling to the end of the bed. From beneath the covers he pulled out a heavy, padded manacle fixed by a length of chain to the end of the bed. He snapped it around Aiden's ankle then crawled back up the bed, pulling the covers over them both.

Aiden glared at him. "What the hell?"

Heath smiled serenely. "You'll be chained to my bed every night from now on. Get used to it." He pressed himself close to Aiden's warm back and wrapped an arm around him. Within moments, the indignant rigidity in Aiden's muscles relaxed. Heath closed his eyes and absorbed the feeling of Aiden's pulse as it slowed towards sleep. He prayed silently that Aiden would have the time to become comfortable with his new role, because Heath could no longer imagine life without him.

Chapter Twenty-One

Aiden woke to several different sensations, all of which contributed to a sense of erotic euphoria. He could feel the heavy cuff around his ankle chaining him to Heath's bed. He could also feel Heath's rubber-clad and heavily slicked cock pushing persistently into his arse. Heath was slowly jacking his cock, which was more awake than the rest of his body and responding enthusiastically.

"Heath?"

Heath stilled. "Were you expecting someone else to have his hand around your cock?"

That woke him up. "No, Sir! Sorry, I was still half—aagh!"

The penetration was swift and unexpected. Heath had one long leg across his thighs so he couldn't part his legs to make access easier. For a while, Heath lay wrapped around him and in him, unmoving, then he began to torment Aiden's nipples, pinching and twisting each in turn until he moaned. He'd always been really sensitive there, and Heath seemed to know exactly how hard to pinch for the maximum effect.

"Hands and knees."

Heath moved with him, never leaving Aiden's body. The chain around his ankle restricted his movement, but there was enough slack for him to get into a comfortable position. Heath gripped his hips and Aiden wanted to scream 'Move!' at him, but didn't dare. When Heath did begin to move, the strokes were deep but gentle, brushing lightly against his prostate. His body begin to heat and there a tingle beginning at the base of his skull.

Heath increased his speed slowly but steadily. It wasn't enough. "For fuck's sake, Heath—I could die today. I want to still be feeling you if I do."

That got him a hard slap across his arse. "I seem to recall collaring you just last night. You understand the concept?" Heath punctuated his words with harder thrusts. "Obedience. Respect. Submission."

"Yes, Sir, I understand, and if I survive today I know you'll punish me thoroughly. But please…"

"Beg for it."

"Fuck me harder, you sadistic sod!"

"Brat."

The pounding that followed sent Aiden to heaven, and for a few moments he was able to forget the day ahead. Heath reached around and grasped his cock. It took only two sharp tugs and he was spilling all over the sheets. Heath slammed into him with one last punishing thrust, and warmth flooded his channel. Other than a satisfied grunt, Heath made little noise.

Aiden collapsed in a sweaty heap while Heath visited the bathroom. On his return, he unlocked Aiden's ankle chain, then climbed back into bed next to him.

"I hope that left enough of an impression to satisfy you."

"You certainly rose to the challenge, Sir."

"Oh, you really are asking for it, aren't you? I am going to enjoy giving you a lesson in respect tonight."

Aiden couldn't think of a thing to say. He was so afraid that Heath might never get the chance to teach him that lesson. A shiver shook his slim frame. Heath pulled him in to a warm hug and kissed him softly, brushing a few strands of dark hair away from his face.

"Don't be frightened, love."

"I'm trying."

He snuggled closer to Heath's hard body, trying to absorb some of his strength and composure.

"When do you have to leave?" Heath's voice was gruff.

"We have some time, Sir."

Aiden closed his eyes and breathed in Heath's masculine scent, trying to fix it in his memory. Wrapped in Heath's strong arms, he wanted the moment to last forever. He touched the metal around his neck and gave a small, wry smile. The last few weeks had been such a revelation, and it had all happened so fast. He'd always known that he was submissive, but admitting it had been hard. Olly had been the one to make him see the truth, and that it was nothing to be ashamed of. Heath made him feel secure and cherished as well as horny as hell. Resisting him was fun, though Aiden knew that he would always submit eventually. Heath certainly seemed to relish the fight. God, how he loved that stern expression and the feel of Heath's hard palm against his bare arse. He snuggled a little closer and sighed softly.

"Whatever happens today, Heath, know that I love you."

"I love you too, brat. You don't regret your decision last night? Choices under pressure aren't always wise, but I just couldn't wait."

Heath brushed Aiden's neck with a kiss, just above the collar.

"I knew exactly what I was doing, Heath. It wasn't a choice I made lightly. I think I fell in love with you from the first moment we met. I want to be yours and I want everyone else to know it."

"That's good, because you're mine and I'm a little possessive."

Aiden snorted. "A little?"

Heath chuckled. "You have some leeway today, Aiden, but tonight you are going to pay for this attitude. I'll leave that to your imagination — it will be a nice distraction for you today. Now, I'm afraid we have to get up. I need to take that tracker off your ankle."

"I wish you were coming with me."

"I do too, love, but I can't. Becket won't allow it. I don't work for the government like you do. I know Becket's planning something dangerous. The Secret Service doesn't usually respond to blackmail or make exchanges. I just hope it's not anything that risks Olly's safety."

"Please don't ask me, Heath. I hate keeping anything from you, but they made me sign the Official Secrets Act. I can't tell you anything."

"I know. I'm sorry."

Aiden swung his legs out of bed and leant back to stroke Heath's hair away from his eyes. He stood up and wiggled his arse provocatively. "Just so you don't forget..."

Heath growled, a sound that made Aiden tingle in all the right places. "Get dressed, or you'll be leaving with a plug up your arse."

Chapter Twenty-Two

They could have cut the tension in the car with a knife. Heath drove and Joe sat in the passenger seat with his hands clasped tightly in his lap. Agent Becket had left believing that he had persuaded them to stay on the island, but he had been in a losing battle from the get-go.

After Becket and Aiden had left, Joe had turned to Heath and summed his position up succinctly. "If he thinks I'm staying here when Olly's in danger, he's deranged." His mouth had been set in a thin line, his eyes chips of ice.

Heath had shrugged nonchalantly and smiled with obviously false sincerity. "Becket's stubborn, Joe. Easier just to pretend to give him what he wants."

Joe had still looked pissed off. "That bastard threatened me with his gun."

"If it was his boyfriend on either side of this equation, he'd understand. As it is, he's just doing his job."

"His boyfriend? Do you know something I don't, Heath?"

Heath had grinned. "He told me. You owe me a tenner. I think when this is over, Agent Becket may be back for one of our more specialised courses."

Some of the tension in the room had dissipated, and now they were travelling to the airfield, not far behind the plain white van carrying Aiden and Becket.

"However this turns out, Joe, it changes nothing between us. Our friendship is too important," Heath said seriously.

"How the hell did we get ourselves into this, Heath? I feel so out of control. If anything happens to Olly... I just don't know what I'll do. And what about you? It didn't go unnoticed that Aiden was wearing your collar this morning."

"We're both lost causes, aren't we? We're supposed to be in charge whilst our sweet, submissive boyfriends do as they're told. In fact, Olly has you wound around his little finger and Aiden is proving to be a professional brat." Heath grinned. "He looks bloody good in that collar, though."

Joe grinned at his friend's obvious pleasure. "He does. Despite everything, he was positively glowing this morning. I'm glad for you, Heath, I really am. Finding someone you could be with long term was overdue. You need him as much as he needs you."

"Which makes today that much harder."

They were driving alongside the high perimeter fence of the airport. "We're here. There's a waiting room with a small balcony. Plane spotters use it, apparently."

He parked the car and the pair of them went into the small reception area. The attendant behind the counter was short and stocky, with tattoos peeking from the neck of his white shirt. He didn't look comfortable in a tie and Heath knew instantly that he must be one of Becket's men.

"We were told to expect you. Becket left a message — he said, and I quote, 'Keep out of the fucking way or else'."

The agent nodded them through to the observation area, which was up a short flight of stairs. Comfortable seats filled a small room with a coffee machine in one corner. A large window opened out onto a balcony with a sweeping view of the airfield.

A young woman in the airport uniform, neat hair and little makeup slipped into the room and asked if they would like coffee. They refused the offer and she left after giving them a candid, appraising stare.

"Another of Becket's team?"

"Or maybe she just fancied a piece of you." Joe grinned at Heath's wounded expression. "Becket has this whole place sewn up, doesn't he? The man's good, I'll give him that. He had the brains to realise that there was nothing he could do or say to stop us coming along."

"I hate not knowing his plans. There's so much that could go wrong." Heath had started to pace anxiously, but then a small truck appeared from a hangar, pulling a small plane behind it. There was only a single runway, but the truck manoeuvred the plane to the far end.

Heath and Joe moved out to the balcony and watched. Heath gripped the rail so hard that Joe placed a hand on his shoulder, reassuring him. "We need to stay calm. Our boys are going to need us when this is all over."

"You're right, of course." Heath took a shuddering breath and forced his fingers to unlock.

"I usually am."

Heath rolled his eyes, then stared hard at a figure strolling across the apron, dressed in a pilot's dark trousers and white shirt, gold tabs on his lapels catching the light.

"Hey! Isn't that—?"

"John Taylor. From the course."

The two men looked at each other. "Maybe Becket didn't tell us quite everything?" Joe growled angrily.

For a moment the man seemed to stare directly at them, though by now he was little more than a speck in the distance. Then he began going through pre-flight checks on his aircraft. The tow truck returned to the hangar and for ten minutes or so there was little activity.

Suddenly Joe stiffened. A car drove out of the hangar towards the aircraft, a blond head clearly visible in the rear window.

"Olly."

Heath put an arm around his shoulders. "It looks like him. I wish I had a pair of binoculars."

The car slowed, then stopped behind the aircraft. They could see three figures walk around to the front of the plane. Olly's blond head was clearly visible, and two larger men flanked him, one on each side. One of them had a grip on his arm.

"That ape has his hands on my boyfriend." If looks could kill, the guy in the distance would have been a puddle of goo on the tarmac.

"He's alive, Joe, that's the main thing, and it doesn't look like he's been hurt." Heath attempted to be the voice of reason, but he knew how he would feel if it was Aiden they were looking at in the distance.

They almost missed the two figures that emerged on foot from the hangar and began a long, steady walk across the tarmac. Heath froze. It felt as if every muscle in his body had gone into stasis. He couldn't see Aiden's face, just the back of his dark head. He was wearing a thin, light-grey T-shirt and black jeans. The dull glint of silver around his neck confirmed that it was him, but Heath would have known his walk anywhere.

"He must be cold." Heath couldn't remember the last time he'd cried, but now he couldn't stop the well of tears. A hot trail trickled down his cheek, contrasting with the chill he felt deep in his soul.

"If this doesn't end well, Joe, I'm going to hunt Becket down and rip his spine out. Slowly."

Joe's eyes narrowed to slivers of ice. "Not if I get to him first."

Chapter Twenty-Three

Aiden kept his back straight and walked steadily across the tarmac. Becket was half a pace behind, a cold presence at his shoulder. The air was chilly and he shivered, wondering again why Becket had insisted that he leave his fleece behind in their car. The man had told him to remain calm and obey orders. *Easy for him to say.*

The only things that gave him any comfort were the feel of the metal collar around his neck and the memory of the kiss that Heath had given him before they'd left. Deep, passionate but so tender. It tied his stomach in knots and pierced his heart to think of it.

As they approached the waiting plane, Olly's face came into focus. Aiden automatically scanned his friend's body for any sign of damage, but other than a highly pissed-off scowl he looked okay. Aiden gave him an encouraging smile and attempted to look nonchalant. They were still about thirty feet away when the man standing to Olly's left held up a hand and gestured for them to stop.

"Take his shirt off. I want to know he's not wired."

Becket nodded. "Do it, Aiden."

Aiden stripped off his shirt and turned in a slow circle, then pulled it back on.

Olly's second guard threw something onto the tarmac in front of them.

"Put those on him."

Becket scooped up the handcuffs in front of his feet and snapped them around Aiden's wrists.

"He can walk forward now."

Becket's voice was strong and clear. "Oliver moves too."

Olly got a gentle push and took faltering steps forwards. In twenty paces, he and Aiden came face to face.

"Don't do it, Aiden. They'll kill you."

"I have to, Olly. Are you okay?"

"I'm fine." His voice was shaking, belying his words.

Aiden fixed his eyes on his destination and started walking again. He couldn't take the pain in Olly's eyes any longer.

He heard Olly begin to run towards Becket and glanced back. As Aiden turned, something hit him like a hammer, propelling him forwards. Pain bloomed across his back and he was vaguely aware of wetness against his skin. He pitched forwards onto his face, unable to raise his arms to protect himself. He felt nothing. The world went black as he hit the ground.

All hell let loose. Olly screamed and raced back towards Aiden's prone figure, ignoring Becket's calls for him to get the hell down. Becket pulled a revolver from a holster around his ankle and began to fire at the two men racing towards the plane. Engine noise filled the air, and the plane was already taxiing towards the runway as the two men launched themselves through its open door.

Aiden's T-shirt was soaked with horrifyingly bright red blood, and he was far too still. Olly was just about to look for a pulse when Becket pulled him roughly away.

"Run to the hangar or I'll fucking shoot you myself."

"I'm a nurse, Becket — let me help him!"

"You can help by getting the hell out of here! There's nothing you can do for him, Olly, now go!"

Olly stumbled away, looking back over and over as Becket bent over his friend's body. Tears streamed down his face, making it difficult to see, and he scrubbed them roughly away. Heath tore past him, running full tilt in the other direction, his face chalk white.

An ambulance screamed across the runway and two paramedics leapt out. Olly stopped, unable to do anything but watch as they ripped Aiden's shirt off and worked on him. All too soon they moved away, shaking their heads. Olly sank to his knees as his friend was lifted on to a gurney and covered with a sheet. He looked up in horror as the small plane carrying Aiden's killers swooped low over their heads.

Wait. This isn't right. Neither of the men who had been holding him had lifted a gun — not that he had seen. Aiden had been hit in the back. The shot had come from somewhere else. Olly's head buzzed with confusion. He couldn't seem to get up. Then a pair of strong, familiar arms wrapped around him and he turned into Joe's embrace.

"Sweetheart, we need to get you out of here. Are you hurt?"

Olly shook his head numbly, unable to find any words. He didn't understand how Joe could be there, but he was and that was all that mattered. Joe heaved him to his feet and his brain remembered that he could walk. One foot in front of the other took them to the small building housing the airport's waiting room.

Safely installed in a chair with his hands wrapped around a paper cup of coffee, Olly stared at Joe with tears in his eyes.

"He's dead, Joe. Aiden's dead. There was so much blood." Drops of coffee spilt over the rim of the cup as his hands shook with grief and anger. "Why did he come? I'm not worth his life."

Joe knelt on the floor in front of him, took the cup from his hands and replaced it with his own warm grip.

"We don't know he's dead, love."

"He is! I saw it!"

"You saw him shot. I pray that doesn't mean he's gone, but I hope the people who wanted him dead saw it and believe it too. I suspect that's exactly what Agent Becket wanted everyone to think."

Slowly, Olly's anguished sobs calmed. He knew that Joe would never lie to him, so it had to be true — there had to be a chance that Aiden had survived. Joe sat in the next chair and pulled him around into his lap, kissing his neck and face until he managed a faint giggle.

"So tell me, Oliver, what the hell did you think you were doing getting into a boat with another man?"

Olly nuzzled into his neck. "I went to meet you on the beach — you're always sending me little notes, so I had no idea it wasn't real. I was reading, waiting for you, when that guy with the goatee appeared — John? From the course. You know? It didn't even cross my mind that he should have left the island. He was friendly. He sat next to me—asked about my book. Then I felt a little sting in my arm and that was it. I don't remember anything else until I woke up locked in some kind of shed. It was filthy and there were spiders. Ugh!"

Joe chuckled and stroked his hair.

"I must have been out a while. I was looking for something to use as a weapon when those two men I was with today dragged me out and brought me here. The light hurt my eyes. John was there too. He wouldn't let them hurt me—said I had to be in one piece for the exchange. I didn't get what he was talking about until I saw Aiden walking towards me across the runway." He squirmed a little in Joe's lap. "You really are pleased to have me back, aren't you?"

"If you don't stop wiggling around, we are going to be caught in a compromising situation."

Olly immediately squirmed around a bit more. "My God, you feel so hard! I'd love to unzip you and get my hands on that big, thick—"

"Oliver! Behave."

Olly pouted. "Won't. Behaving's no fun, and I need to be distracted."

"When I get you home I'm going to bend you over the spanking bench and decorate that squirmy little arse with some pretty stripes. Then I'm going to find a nice heavy cock ring to lock you in before I fuck you while you're still tied to the bench. If you are really, really good, I might just let you come. But probably not."

Olly went quiet, then started extricating himself from Joe's arms. "I really need the bathroom." He ran for the door.

Chapter Twenty-Four

The instant Aiden had hit the ground, Heath and Joe had torn down the stairs and out through an emergency exit onto the tarmac. No one had tried to stop them. It was a good job, because Heath would probably have killed anyone who tried to get between him and Aiden.

He had heard the crack of the gunshot, seen the bloom of red across Aiden's back, and his heart and brain had frozen. He hadn't been able to accept what had happened. His legs had carried him outside without any consideration for his own safety. He had been vaguely aware of Olly running in the other direction, then he'd been on his knees on the tarmac as an ambulance crew had loaded Aiden onto a stretcher with grim faces.

He had never felt such complete and utter despair. His eyes met Becket's and made every accusation they could.

"Get in the fucking ambulance, Heath." Becket was not exactly oozing sympathy.

Blindly, Heath climbed in, desperate to take a last look at Aiden's face. The doors shut behind him and Becket gave him a sympathetic glance as he pulled the sheet away from Aiden's body. "Sorry, Heath. It was essential that this looked real."

Pale but very much alive, Aiden smiled up at him and Heath nearly punched Becket's lights out. He was absolutely fucking furious and jubilant with relief at the same time. He put his head in his hands and took a ragged breath. "Thank God."

As the ambulance drove away, Heath winced at the huge bruise that was developing across Aiden's back and shoulders. He could clearly see the spot where the false bullet had hit him and exploded in a shower of synthetic blood. When he had been watching from a distance, it had looked absolutely real.

Aiden had horrible grazes on his face and one arm, where he had fallen with his hands restrained. The handcuff bracelets were still around his slim wrists as the paramedics had no key, but they had managed to cut the connecting chain.

Aiden held Heath's hand, gripping him tightly, as Becket explained.

"Officially, Aiden is dead. It's the only way we could guarantee his safety in the future. We couldn't tell you in case you gave the game away. The shooting had to look real and I knew you and Joe wouldn't be able to stay away."

"It felt fucking real!" Aiden grumbled.

"A fake bullet from that distance was always going to sting a little."

"Sting? I blacked out, you fucker!"

"At least that way you didn't feel it when you hit the deck."

Heath chuckled at Becket's utter lack of sympathy and the look of furious indignation on Aiden's pretty face.

"Hey! Whose side are you on? You're as bad as he is."

"Jesus, Anders, you've got your hands full with this one." Becket and Heath exchanged looks.

"I know. He has some way to go… Plenty of training still required."

Aiden slumped back in defeat. "I give up! You two are as bad as each other. What about my family? What does this all mean?"

"There will be a small, discreet cremation and some suitably sympathetic press work. Your sister and your parents will be told the bare minimum—just that you are in witness protection."

"My parents will probably breathe a sigh of relief."

"You'll join the agency as planned under a new name."

"Aiden is my middle name—I've never used my first name, so can I keep it?"

"Perhaps. I'll look into it."

"You'll take my surname." Heath said the words with some satisfaction and smiled as a flush stole across Aiden's cheeks.

Becket looked very pleased with himself. "I also have a proposal for some changes at The Edge. You can continue to run your courses—just not solely for the general public. I'd like to set up some regular training for government staff."

"You mean spies?" Aiden asked.

"Undercover agents, military personnel…" Becket grinned. "The Edge is perfect for our needs and nobody would suspect that a small 'technical' unit would operate from the same place. That means that you could be based there too, Aiden. The staff would know you. I doubt anyone would talk but they'd have to sign the Official Secrets Act anyway."

"You had this planned out from the start, didn't you? Even down to taking Olly? John Taylor is one of yours too," Heath realised.

"Yes. He is piloting our friends back to their boss, where they will confirm Aiden's unfortunate demise and no doubt take the credit. John is a very effective agent and has been deep undercover for some time. In a few weeks' time he will disappear, and several arrests will be made. It had to seem like they were getting away."

"But we checked into his background. He'd booked onto our course long before all this happened." Heath wanted an explanation for the last piece of the puzzle.

"The real John Taylor won a rather nice holiday and took himself off to the Caribbean. Our staff offered to cancel his booking at The Edge for him."

Aiden rolled his eyes. "You are a cunning bastard, aren't you? What about the other courses at The Edge?"

"Nothing has to change there. A certain high-powered judge has a lot of influential friends, a surprising number of whom seemed to be aware of your services and endorse them."

Heath noticed that Aiden was looking very pale. "This is a huge amount to take in, love. You need to rest. It can all wait until tomorrow."

"You'll have to lie low for a couple of weeks. Take your time. If you have any questions, Heath has my number."

The first part of the journey home was made in the ambulance, which headed towards the hospital. Under the cover of a tunnel, they swapped their transport for a transit van with signage from a local plumbing company. Aiden sat in the back and Heath could tell he was fighting down nausea as he was jogged mercilessly around. Heath held his hand the whole way, keeping a careful eye on his green-tinged skin.

They crossed the causeway in lashing rain, reminding Heath of the first time he had brought Aiden to the island all those weeks ago. So much had changed in such a short time.

Upstairs in the comfort of his apartment, Heath settled Aiden into a chair and went to find some keys to get rid of the metal bracelets around his wrists.

"This should do the job."

The cuffs fell away and Aiden massaged the sore indentations with a groan.

"Thanks." He met Heath's eyes nervously. "I'm sorry about all this, Heath. You didn't ask for any of it. You must think I'm the biggest pain in the arse."

Heath stretched, relieving some of the tension in his body and revealing a few inches of toned abdomen. He looked down at Aiden with a grin. "Caught you staring again, didn't I?" He stripped off his shirt and stood there, hands on hips.

"You are a pain in the arse. You're a brat. But you're my brat and it's my job to turn you into the obedient, compliant submissive I know you want to be. Becket's orders are that you stay indoors for the next two weeks, so that gives me plenty of time to start moulding you." He could feel Aiden's gaze fixed on his bare chest. He pointed to a spot on the floor at his feet. "Strip and kneel."

Aiden slowly undressed and knelt with barely a wince. Heath looked down on him and couldn't stop his smile. Bruised and battered, Aiden was still gorgeous. His cock looked hard and needy. "You'll remain naked in my presence while you're in this apartment unless I give you something to wear. Understand?"

"Yes, Sir." Aiden's voice was soft.

"You may use the bathroom, then go and lie on the bed."

Heath watched him go, then headed for the bedroom. When Aiden joined him, Heath made sure he had enough pillows to cushion his bruised back, then spread Aiden's legs wide. After crawling between them, he didn't hesitate before taking Aiden's cock into his mouth. Some powerful suction and tormenting nibbles later and Aiden was a whimpering wreck, shaking with need. Heath gave a final lick, then withdrew and slicked a couple of fingers with lube. He thrust into Aiden's channel without warning, then bent to mouth his balls, rolling each in turn around his tongue.

"Fuck! Heath, please… I need to come!"

Heath concentrated on fucking him hard with his fingers and met his eyes. "Your control needs some work, but just for today…" He sucked him again, and Aiden's arse lifted from the bed. His back arched and he shot in warm, creamy streams down Heath's throat.

"Welcome home, my love. Sleep now."

"But don't you want me to…"

"I said sleep. I give the orders, remember?"

Heath smiled at the taste of Aiden in his mouth and the warmth of his firm body as he snuggled closer.

"Take this while you can. I'll not be so lenient in future."

Aiden didn't answer. He was already fast asleep.

Chapter Twenty-Five

Two weeks later, all his bruises and grazes fading, Aiden knelt at the foot of Heath's bed with his arms pulled taut above his head by a chain running from a hook in the ceiling. He was naked apart from thick leather cuffs buckled around his ankles. He looked as if he were modelling for the picture on the wall behind him, and kept his eyes lowered. He'd been there long enough that his arms were starting to ache, but not so long that he had lost any feeling. Heath was always very careful with his timings. He knew exactly when pain turned into something more harmful. It wasn't the first time Aiden had been in this position over the last two weeks, and he suspected it wouldn't be the last. Heath would chain him and leave him there until he attained stillness and calm.

Aiden knew better than to raise his head when Heath's booted feet came into view. Heath unhooked the chains and Aiden lowered his arms slowly. He admired the snug fit of leather around the section of Heath's legs that he could see and continued to breathe slowly.

"Stand."

He rose gracefully to his feet and stood with his hands clasped behind his back. Heath snapped a tight leather cock ring around the base of Aiden's dick, then looped two more rings around his balls, separating them. Then he began to flick Aiden's nipples into arousal. Aiden groaned, knowing what was coming next. Heath tightened the screw clamps just to the point of pain, then linked them with a chain. He used the chain to lead Aiden around to the side of the bed.

"Hands and knees."

Aiden climbed onto the bed and assumed the correct position. His cock throbbed and the dangling nipple chain was causing him all sorts of interesting problems. He heard Heath circle the bed and couldn't resist looking up.

Heath gave an evil smile at his mistake. He pulled the chain between the clamps up and placed it between Aiden's lips. Because his head was up, it pulled much harder than it would have done if his head had been submissively lowered.

"Drop the chain and you get six strokes of the cane. Keep your head up."

Aiden glared. He hated the cane. It hurt like a bastard. He could deal with the floggers and paddles, but the cane put lines of fire across his arse that he would feel for a week.

"For that look, you don't get to come tonight."

Aiden really wanted to curse, but was forced to keep quiet because of the chain between his teeth. He was so hard he could feel the leather around his cock and balls digging into his flesh. That made him even harder.

Heath was behind him again, then suddenly the cold slick of lube was being massaged into his bound cock and balls. The sensation of Heath's hand and the cool, smooth lubrication were torment. Every puff of air seemed to be magnified into a teasing, licking breeze. He expected the lube to be applied to his arse next, but Heath trailed his tongue along Aiden's crack and circled his hole lightly. Without warning, Heath plunged his tongue through the tight ring of muscle and tasted him. Aiden screamed and dropped the chain.

"Fuck, fuck, fuck!"

Aiden tried to push back to get more of Heath's tongue inside him, but instead Heath moved away.

"Oh, dear. You must really like that cane."

"Fuck you! You don't play fair!"

Heath slammed two lubed fingers into him and he couldn't speak any more as Heath twisted and prodded at the sensitive bundle of nerves inside him. Then Heath's cock replaced them. The bulbous head came first, then the hard length of him, pushing deep and fast. Heath gripped his hips and he had to fight to stay in position.

Heath's stamina was remarkable. He hammered away for what seemed like forever before shooting hard and fast with a satisfied moan. Aiden loved everything about the way Heath took him. The weight of his body, the calluses on his hands as they grasped him, the feeling of absolute fullness as he was breached by that beautiful cock. He loved that Heath didn't hesitate to take what he wanted, but never failed to show his love in a myriad of tiny, revealing ways.

Aiden knew that Heath let him get away with murder. There were days when he achieved a level of submission that had him flying in a space all his own. But if Heath had punished him for every smart remark or disobedient action, he knew that he would spend ninety per cent of his time either in chains or unable to sit down.

"Can you think of one good reason why I should relent and let you come?"

Aiden thought about it. "You love me?" He cocked his head on one side and made puppy eyes.

"Another reason."

Aiden sighed. "No, Sir." He ached with need, but there was no way he was going to admit it.

Heath kissed him and removed the nipple clamps, sending fire straight to his groin.

"Holy fuck! That hurts!"

Heath smirked. "I know."

Aiden moaned pitifully.

"Olly and Joe have invited us to dinner in the private dining room. I intend to show you off. If you behave, I'll fuck you again later."

Aiden rolled his eyes. "You'll fuck me again anyway."

"True. But if you want any chance of getting off this week..."

"This *week*? You are an utter bastard, you know that?"

"But you love me."

Aiden took in the handsome face and spectacular body lying next to him and melted. "More than anything."

"So get cleaned up and then get back here."

When Aiden returned, Heath had chosen clothes for him. A pair of soft leather trousers and a slim chain that ran from his cock ring to his collar. Nothing else.

"You have to be fucking joking." He bridled at the thought of sitting down to dinner semi-naked.

"Get dressed, Aiden." Heath used a tone that allowed no dissent.

"This isn't dressed," Aiden muttered, but did as he was told.

He followed Heath down the stairs, dreading that they would come across another member of staff, but his luck held. He walked into the dining room and gasped. The table was laid with all the best silver and crystal. Candles flickered everywhere and fresh flowers scented the air. Joe, looking handsome in a crisp white shirt and dark tie, was pouring wine into the glasses. Olly was kneeling silently in the corner. He was wearing leather chaps and his slender cock was bound tightly in a criss-cross web of leather thongs. Aiden gaped at the sight and just caught the sly wink that Olly gave him when Joe turned away.

"Oliver looks beautiful, Joe." Heath picked up a glass and toasted him.

Joe smiled proudly. "He has been behaving exceptionally well these last two weeks, though that wink he just gave Aiden has earned him a few stripes tonight. Aiden is stunning."

Aiden felt a blush steal across his face. He sank to his knees at Heath's side and bowed his head. It felt like the right thing to do. As Heath and Joe chatted above him, he felt serene and safe.

Joe served the food from a heated trolley and he and Heath took their seats.

"You may join us, boys. No rules tonight." Heath touched Aiden's bare shoulder lightly and brought him to the table. When they were all comfortable, Heath raised his glass. "A toast." They all lifted their crystal goblets. "To the future. To love."

As Aiden echoed the toast with a smile, he caught the expression on Heath's face. Love, pure and simple. They had so much to look forward to now.

As he sipped the mellow wine in his glass, the straps around his cock and balls got just a little bit tighter, and so did Heath's hold on his heart.

About the Author

Lucinda lives in a small village in the English countryside, surrounded by rolling hills, cows and sheep. She started writing to fill time between jobs and is now firmly and unashamedly addicted.

She loves the English weather, especially the rain, and adores a thunderstorm. She loves good food, warm company and a crackling fire. She's fascinated by the psychology of relationships, especially between men, and her stories contain some subtle (and not so subtle) leanings towards BDSM.

L.M. Somerton loves to hear from readers. You can find her contact information, website details and author profile page at http://www.totallybound.com.

Totally Bound Publishing